KENT WYATT

Seeing Beyond
A Special Heroes Book

By Kent Wyatt

Published by Forget Me Not Romances, a division of Winged Publications
Copyright © 2018 by Kent Wyatt

All rights reserved. No part of this publication may be resold, reproduced, stored in a retrieval system, or transmitted in any form or by any means, electronic, mechanical, recording, or otherwise, without the prior written permission of the author. Piracy is illegal. Thank you for respecting the hard work of this author.

This is a work of fiction. All characters, names, dialogue, incidents, and places either are the product of the author's imagination or are used fictitiously. Any resemblance to actual events, locales, or people, living or dead, is entirely coincidental.

Unless noted, scripture quotations are from the Holy Bible, King James Version.

If cited as NLT:
Scripture quotations marked (NLT) are taken from the Holy Bible, New Living Translation, copyright ©1996, 2004, 2015 by Tyndale House Foundation. Used by permission of Tyndale House Publishers, Inc., Carol Stream, Illinois 60188. All rights reserved.

If cited as ESV:
Scripture quotations are from the ESV® Bible (The Holy Bible, English Standard Version®), copyright © 2001 by Crossway, a publishing ministry of Good News Publishers. Used by permission. All rights reserved. May not copy or download more than 500 consecutive verses of the ESV Bible or more than one half of any book of the ESV Bible.

Book Cover: Cover design by Rebekah and Kent Wyatt, eye and background art by DesignBetiBup, water photo by Kwinn Wyatt, boat photo by Diana Aishe on Unsplash, silhouette couple by CanStock, couple in boat and photo modification art by Kent Wyatt, author photo by Rebekah Wyatt.

Winged Publications
PO Box 8047
Surprise, AZ 85374

ISBN-13: 978-1-0881-6318-4

Dedication

To my Father God first and foremost, forever the Author of all things. Men are always searching for the treasure. Some are blessed to find You. Thank you, Jesus, for getting us back together.

Also, my beloved wife, Rebekah, my biggest fan, always behind me, hands to my back, ever pushing upward. None of this would be possible without you. Your research and editing form these words as much as my imagination. Without you guiding the romance in these pages, we would soon be in the swamps of superficiality, sinking in the quicksand of male ego.

And to my son, Kwinn, who foots the bill so often. A man after God's heart. You have sacrificed so much for your family and a life lived for The Lord. May He reward you greatly. Our talks are some of the highlights of my life. Thanks for keeping me going.

To my son, Korwin, thanks for kicking around story ideas with me and sending me little snippets of information. I love your tender heart for your family and others. I cherish our electronic chats.

To my daughter, Kasi, always kind to children and God's creatures. I adore that you have a taste for words and imagination. I wish I could, once again, visit your zoo of stuffed animals or buy a plastic apple from your bedroom store.

Special Heroes

This story includes characters with special needs, particularly Fragile X syndrome and Williams Syndrome. I have tried to render the conditions accurately based on my research. However, only someone walking in that skin can truly know the challenges and the triumphs they experience. Any errors in portrayal of these fascinating people is due to my limited viewpoint, and I ask forgiveness. While each syndrome has its own unique traits, people with special needs are as varied as the individuals that they are. We know from Psalms 139:13-14 that God guides the forming of every person. He makes no mistakes. Any fault is in our limited, flawed perspective.

This story is a tribute to the Special Heroes that Rebekah and I have had the privilege to know. We appreciate your contribution to our world. How much we would miss without you.

HERO JON THOMPSON
WHOSE SHINING FACE REFLECTS
THE LOVE OF CHRIST
THIS IS FOR YOU

You can learn more about Fragile X at the following link:
https://fragilex.org/learn/

For further information about Williams Syndrome go to:
https://williams-syndrome.org/

For now we see through a glass, darkly, but then face to face. Now I know in part, but then shall I know even as also I am known. 1 Corinthians 13:12 (KJV)

... And ye shall know the truth, and the truth shall make you free. John 8:32 (KJV)

Chapter 1

"Tee, it happen'n again." Janie's thick lisp formed a worried whisper in the quiet produced by the crowd's anticipation.

Talisa's attention snapped from the sky to her sister. Watching for the spectacle about to begin in the Oklahoma night above her, she hadn't noticed what was taking place two lawn chairs away. Janie's hand rested on Teddy's shoulder as she stared at his face with a wide-eyed expression that betrayed the condition her genetic disorder produced—childlike simplicity wrapped in her adult body.

Talisa leaned around her sister and scrutinized Teddy's expression. The first rocketing firework exploded over Lake Gallant, making her shoulders jerk. The display reflected in Teddy's deep brown eyes, but they gave no indication that the deafening eruption of color or the exclamation from the other celebrators registered in the brain of Theodore Baskins. Talisa watched the unblinking stare for a moment, captivated as always by the thought that those eyes were seeing beyond the perspective in which she was bound. "Teddy, what do you see?"

Movement in her periphery let Talisa know her friend Kaylee had also abandoned watching the fireworks and pivoted in her chair to be a part of the drama closer at hand. "Is that it? Is it happening?"

Teddy spoke without changing his gaze. "I'm leaving." His brow furrowed. He whipped a backhanded strike toward his shoulder like he was trying to get someone off him. "Don't touch me."

His slap knocked Janie's hand away. She drew back. A wounded expression flickered across her eyes then she relaxed, and her face turned sympathetic again. The anger wasn't really Teddy's and it wasn't for her.

Falling forward, the young man caught himself with his forearms on his thighs. For a moment he sat bent over. Talisa could tell the vision had ended.

Kaylee stood and moved in a wide arc toward Teddy like she was approaching a creature she feared she might startle. "Is that really it? What's he seeing? You said he didn't see things that often, but that's twice this evening. Do you think it's something big like a plane crash or school shooting? Maybe someone is using the fireworks to mask the gunshots."

As if on cue, the sky blossomed again, punctuating her statement with a thundering report that made them all flinch.

Talisa shook off the urge to check herself for bullet holes and glared at her friend. "Don't do that." She left her own chair and moved toward Teddy. "I don't know what's going on. Give me a minute." She frowned back at her friend. "It's 9:30 at night on Memorial Day weekend. How could it be a school…? Let me talk to him a sec." Talisa placed her hand on Teddy's back. "Tell me what you saw. Does someone need help?"

Teddy looked up at her. His broad forehead, small wide-set eyes that turned downward at the outside corners and the slight hook to his nose gave him a manly, elfin appearance.

"I don't know. A hand was on my shoulder. I didn't see them, and all I had time to think was that I was mad and wanted to leave."

"Mad, but not afraid?"

"Yeah, I think so."

Kaylee leaned in like she was yelling into a cave. "Teddy, it's Kaylee. Can you hear me?"

A burst of beauty in the heavens lit up Teddy's confused expression along with the hillside overlooking the marina. The crowd in the parking lot below gave an exclamation of wonder as Teddy blinked his eyes and twitched at the detonation.

Kaylee had positioned herself in front of Teddy, inspecting him. At his reaction, she called as if he was far away. "What are you seeing, Teddy? Do you hear anything like maybe explosions or gunshots?"

Teddy smiled at the embers raining from the sky and nodded.

Talisa gave the woman's enthusiasm a wave off. "It's over. He's not seeing anything now. Let me talk to him."

Kaylee straightened, looking disappointed. "Really? That's it?"

Talisa took over the questioning. "Could you tell who you were, you know, the person whose eyes you were seeing through?"

Teddy looked to the side like he was thinking, but his head was already shaking. "It didn't feel like anyone I know. But it was really quick."

"What did you see around you?"

"I was in a room. I didn't recognize anything, so I don't think it was anywhere I've been before. I wasn't paying attention to what was around me except the door because I wanted to get to it and leave. It seemed like everything was real nice, like fancy furniture and things. I tried to go to the door and someone put their hand on my shoulder, and it made me mad, so I knocked their hand away. That's all I saw." Teddy reached over and rubbed Janie's hand. "Sorry. Did it hurt?"

Janie grabbed his hand in both of hers and smiled as she shook her head, causing her straight blond hair to swish around her slender form.

Talisa frowned. "And you didn't see who touched you?"

Teddy moved his own wavy, perpetually unkempt, brown hair back and forth. "Sorry, Ms. Tee. That's all there was."

Teddy was doing the best he could. Talisa smiled despite her frustration. Figuring out Teddy's visions was never easy, but this one gave her nowhere to start. Two times in the last few hours—Kaylee was right. It wasn't like the others. Though they varied in length, it was always one vision, one event, and it was over. And the visions were always about someone in trouble. What Teddy was describing sounded more like a disagreement, nothing warranting divine intervention.

God, what are You trying to show us? Talisa had to believe it was God. Nothing else made sense. She didn't care what some of the small-minded individuals in Gilead County said about "The Enigma," as they called Teddy, thanks to her using the word to describe his gift. Those people didn't understand Teddy and his gentle naïve nature any better than they understood her use of the word that day. They wanted to make Teddy part of the area legends, like the lake monster some claimed to see or the old man at the prison who supposedly had a hidden treasure.

It saddened her when Teddy told her how his family had to leave the last place they lived because people didn't like them. And it wasn't about the visions. They didn't start until he moved to Gilead County. How could humans be so cruel?

Weariness wound its way around Talisa. As a singer belted out a rousing song paying homage to patriotism and lost loved ones, a finale of fireworks lit the air and betrayed Talisa's countenance.

Kaylee came to her side. "Hey, you okay?"

"Just tired."

"Go on up to your house. You've worn yourself out with this whole thing. I'll walk Janie up in a little while and make sure Teddy gets off okay."

"I told his dad he could sleep in the guest room. I don't want him driving at night."

"Okay, I'll make sure they get up there. Go rest. This has all been too much, too soon. Luke helped your dad organize this event almost as long as you did, plus he's also the sheriff. He'll make sure nothing goes wrong."

Luke. She was almost ready to concede until Kaylee said the name. She hoped her face didn't betray her feelings.

Too late. Kaylee was scrutinizing her. "You know it's been a long time since we were in high school. Don't you think it's time you let it go?"

Talisa pulled herself erect. "You didn't spend your junior year being called *frog legs.*"

"I think he meant it as a compliment. You're the best swimmer I've ever seen, next to…Luke."

"I'm sure it *was* his idea of a compliment. That just proves what an idiot he is. And when I told him I didn't like it," Talisa gestured with her hand, "in front of everyone, he made a fool out of me."

Kaylee started giggling. "You have to admit what he said was funny." Her voice deepened as she mimicked Luke's accent. "You ever take a good look at a set of frog legs? You put a frog in a skirt and some high heels, and no sir, they don't even need pantyhose." Kaylee giggled for a second until she saw Talisa's face. She brought her eyebrows together in a fierce scowl. "It was awful of him to say that. Next time I see him, I'm going to tell him so." Kaylee's eyes strayed to a tall figure in a sheriff's uniform who stood at the edge of the parking lot, surveying the crowd. "Probably not tonight, though, since he's busy."

Talisa glared at the woman. "Our friendship has survived a lot. Not the least of which has been the last few minutes.

But if you say anything to him about any of this..." Talisa wasn't good at threats. "I'll want back all those CDs I loaned you in high school. Got it? Besides, there's more to it, but let's drop it, okay?"

Kaylee forced a smile as her head bobbed in silent acquiescence.

Talisa needed a subject change. "I'm the owner of the marina now. I can't just leave. Besides, I think the VFW planned a tribute to Daddy. What would it look like if—" When she said, "Daddy," the words stuck in her throat until she finally had to stop and turn away.

Kaylee wrapped her up in a hug.

Another set of arms encircled her, and she heard Janie's voice. "It okay, Tee. I'm here wiff you. Rememba, Daddy's with Jesus." They held her for a moment. Talisa squeezed her eyes shut, determined to make it through the night without crying.

Keeping her arm around Janie while Kaylee patted her shoulder, Talisa stood to face the music. When it ended, the military speaker the event committee had brought in from Fort Sill came to the platform near the docks. He spoke of remembering loved ones who were no longer with them while the crowd threw flowers into the lake. Janie drew a handful of petals from her pocket and threw them to the night breeze.

The presenter talked of the sacrifice made by EMS, Fire, and Law Enforcement. Along with the rural inhabitants, half the town of Havilah was packed onto the marina grounds for the presentation. A man with a spotlight pivoted it to members of each profession represented in the crowd as the speaker called out their names and also spoke of those who had lost their lives in service to the community. The light fell on Luke who stood at respectful attention. After he spoke of Luke's service, the man honored Luke's father who was killed in the opening days of the Second Gulf War. Then the speaker began to name other brave men and women who had fallen for their country.

Gazing at Luke, Talisa remembered what a crush she had on him as they grew up, starting on the playground her first day of kindergarten. The stocky second grader helping her up when she fell in front of him. Luke dashing away to play again, her running after him by instinct, skinned knee forgotten. Heat warmed her cheeks. It still embarrassed her to think what a little Luke tagalong she'd been through elementary school.

When Luke's father never came home from the war, Talisa's daddy stepped in to fill the gap in Luke's life. She squeezed her eyes at the memory of how she thought it was a dream come true when she and Luke were thrown together even more. *What a minion you were, Talisa. You made such a hero out of him.* If that's all he had been, it would have been okay. A little girl needs a hero. But as she got older, it was her other feelings that made it hurt like a hole through her middle when he left.

The memories flooded Talisa's eyes and almost spilled over when she heard her name over the loudspeaker, and the spotlight transfixed her like a butterfly on a pin. She threw on a smile. Talisa hoped she was far enough up the hill for her eyes not to glisten too brightly.

The presenter on stage extolled the former Navy SEAL who began this Gilead County, Oklahoma Memorial Day Tribute fifteen years earlier. How it began at the State Park and moved to the current location when her father bought the marina. A man who had lived his life in service to others in uniform and at home. The orator told of her father's sacrifices to care for her mother as she was dying of cancer during the previous two years. A man who was the true example of devotion to family, friends, community and country—her father, Michael Hollenbeck.

The parking lot lifted like a wave on the ocean as in unison, the participants stood to their feet and applauded the man whom she still cherished, even though he had struck a devastating blow to her heart.

Chapter 2

Talisa finished the ceremony in a daze. She almost fell apart when they ended with bagpipes playing "Amazing Grace" as they launched a single blazing blue rocket that traced its way high into the dark sky, dimming until it disappeared as if it had joined the stars. But her sleep-deprived mind had shut down. She took the praise for the event, the condolences, and the anecdotes about her father with grace, but little made it to her memory. When the last of the well-wishers made their way down the hill to the parking lot, Talisa stood, empty.

Kaylee gave her a last hug and admonished her to get some sleep.

Sleep. Talisa didn't want to admit that sleep had become a tangled, ugly thing, troubled by dreams of drowning. She watched her friend walk to where Teddy visited with the last group on the hill while Janie stood behind him, holding his hand. Kaylee whispered something to Janie, who turned and peered at Talisa. In a moment, her sister extracted Teddy from the conversation and the pair headed her direction.

Luke was getting everyone out in record time this year.

The parking lot was almost empty and everything that couldn't wait until tomorrow had already been packed up. Talisa's sleepy eyes meandered over the scene. They fell on Luke near the grandstand, talking to one of the last volunteers. As the man left, Luke made a similar scan of the grounds. His gaze wandered up the hill and locked with hers. She didn't break the contact. His expression reminded her of the look he had on the day he walked away. The familiar broken sadness filled her.

It was high school again, Luke was cute and confident, and Talisa daydreamed of being married to him. His esteem was everything to her. *Couldn't you see why your teasing hurt? You were all I had. The other girls talked about the romantic things boys said to them. Maybe they were exaggerations, but no other boy even asked me out.* She continued her stare down with Luke. *They were afraid of you—you and Daddy. Good old "Frog Legs" would always belong to Luke. And I wanted to. I thought we were meant for each other. That's why I wanted to be more to you than just convenient.*

God, I know I shouldn't have been flirting with other guys. I was a stupid school girl. I needed someone to take my dreams seriously and tell me my hazel eyes were pretty without it being a joke. She wanted Luke to fight for her, to win her. *But when that kid swung on him and Luke put him on the ground so fast...forgive me, God. I knew it was my fault. Luke didn't hurt the kid like he could have, but the humiliation was worse. How would I know Luke would act that way when I told him to leave the kid alone?*

Luke was still gazing up the hill at her. He could have been Luke the high schooler, who looked stunned when she stood between him and the boy on the ground. Luke looking like he had never seen her before. It could have been him walking away, never coming over again, never calling. *You didn't even try.* It was the same Luke who graduated, joined the Marines and left without a word. Even her parents were shocked. She hadn't known if she would ever see him again. When he returned home after his enlistment, she was away at school. But then came her mother's diagnosis.

She remembered the day she came home from college, the hope in her parent's eyes when they invited Luke over to visit. It was like her mother didn't even care about her own life. All she would talk about with Talisa was Luke this and Luke that. How much help he had been. What a good sheriff he was making. Talisa did appreciate the things Luke had done for her folks. But it had been awkward. Still, Talisa had cherished the moments with her Mama. They all had time to prepare to face the grief. Her mother's face vanished from her mind. It was only her father and then—. Nothing could have prepared her for... *Why, Daddy?*

Her memories fled from the pain. She turned from Luke's eyes.

Now all she had left was Janie. And Janie was there, taking her hand, bringing her back to the present. "Come on. It time fo' bed." Her sister turned her, and they walked up the hill toward home.

A quick look over her shoulder showed Talisa that Luke was still watching. She faced forward. *Don't look back, Talisa.*

***

Luke watched Talisa walk away. She had locked eyes with him so long and hard that he was about to march up the hill and straighten things out between them. Then she turned away.

He had hoped to talk to her during the week of preparations for the night's event. He had prayed for some time when Janie and Teddy would have their own jobs, and Talisa would be alone. But she had communicated with him mainly through texts and other people. The few times they were together, she was all business.

Where had it gone wrong? When they were kids, they were inseparable. He always liked having her around, even when the other boys wanted to ditch her. Several of his classmates got their noses rubbed in the dirt when they teased him about his "Talisa True Love." In truth, he always let the hecklers off easy because he didn't mind that much.

She encouraged his ideas, defended his statements, told him how good he was at everything. She was his confidence. His folks didn't give him much support. Talisa had made him what he was just by believing in him.

He never imagined being with anyone else. Everything was so natural, so comfortable with her. God seemed to have put them together right from the start. They were meant to be. Everyone else thought so too, even Talisa, or so he had let himself believe. She was the queen, and he was her court jester because he loved to make her laugh with his teasing.

But every year she became smarter and more beautiful. Luke didn't measure up. His jokes stopped being funny to her. The more he kidded her, the more she drew away and flirted with other guys. As hard as it was when his dad died, it was harder when he lost Talisa. He was just the school jock and class clown, and she wanted something more.

He never thought he would come home from the military. He thought he would die there like his dad. But God carried him through that dark time. Whenever he was about to give up, God always stepped in. He could feel that he wasn't going through it alone.

He had grown so much in his faith, in his understanding of things. He came home hopeful. But Talisa had been through so much, it wouldn't be right for him to push her.

***

Walking up the hill, Talisa reflected on what a surreal evening it had been. Her mind replayed the events. She had almost forgotten about Teddy's vision. What was it all about? There were so many questions about Teddy's gift for which she didn't have answers. *God, why do You let him see so many things and You didn't let him see my own...?* She chastised herself. *Like somehow the gift belongs to you?* But that didn't settle it. The question that God wasn't answering was still standing between her and the One in charge of everything.

A cool breeze touched her. She inhaled the fragrant scents of early summer. Talisa had heard they were supposed to get some wind. The movement of the trees drew her attention to the dark hillside across the thin cove that separated her property from Sawyer's. Her neighbor's lights had been on when the tribute started. She'd hoped Sawyer would take her up on her offer to come over and join the festivities, so she would have a chance to talk to him again. He must have turned off his lights to watch the fireworks from his deck instead.

Right next door all this time. Why didn't her father tell her the house had changed hands? If she had not met Sawyer in town, who knew how long it would have taken her to discover she had such an impressive new neighbor. *Maybe Sawyer can help with some of the answers.* She longed for a chance to find out.

The breeze had turned steady with an occasional gust that helped push them up the hill to the home her father had built overlooking the marina. When Talisa opened the door, the curtains in the living room fluttered upward as the breeze rushed in the open window and pushed past them to get out the door. Talisa trudged in. She hoped Teddy and Janie were as ready for bed as she was.

"No! They are not fo'you." The sound of Janie's laughing voice made Talisa turn. Her sister had brought a leftover container of cracker and cheese morsels from the celebration. She held it out of Teddy's reach. "I made these fancy fo' the guests. I want to take 'em to Sunday schoo'. There's a plate in the fwige for you."

Teddy hustled toward the offer.

Talisa caught Janie's attention as she started after him. "I'm exhausted, so can you guys get ready for bed soon?"

Janie nodded, but her sympathetic eyes darted toward the sound of the refrigerator opening. "You 'ike my cooking?"

There was a muffled, mouthful response. Janie's face lit up as she headed toward the kitchen.

Talisa envied Janie and Teddy. Janie had her tough times as a teen, but she survived. Now she seemed to share Teddy's happy nature. At the smallest kind gesture or wonder of nature, their contagious smiles burst forth, so that their cheeks had no choice but to mold around in sunny dimples.

Talisa warmed at the thought. She had worried the loss of their parents would have more of an effect on her sister. Janie had even done surprisingly well with all the visitors despite being naturally shy of strangers. It was because she had Teddy. Their genetic syndromes balanced each other. For Teddy, no one was a stranger as long as they returned his happy greeting. He gave a smile to get a smile. Nothing satisfied him more. Talisa could hear his infectious laugh from the kitchen.

Pastor Cooper was wise to make him a greeter at the church. Talisa remembered when the new addition met her family at the church door. Teddy's outgoing friendliness enchanted them all. But when he looked at Janie, his smile pushed through her introverted nature, and she smiled back. Teddy touched an inward part of her no one else had. Talisa warmed, recalling how her Daddy had taken on Teddy like a son.

Daddy. Talisa's pleasant thoughts were snatched away. It was the ultimate injustice. The good memories pulled out the bad, like a perfect fly-cast that became fouled in a nest of old line and hooks.

The doorbell rang.

Talisa tipped her head back and closed her eyes. *Now*

what, Lord? She started for the entrance.

Teddy came racing out of the kitchen yelling. "I'll get it." He tripped over his own feet and stumbled forward, grabbing the lampstand beside the door. The lightweight piece of furniture did nothing to stop him. Teddy, table, and lamp hit the floor. The porcelain base of the light cracked in several pieces on the ceramic tile.

Janie let out a scream from the kitchen door. Talisa huffed in disbelief.

Someone opened the door and tapped on it as they did. Pastor Cooper peeked in, and the wind from the window ruffled his hair. "Is everything okay?" He looked at Teddy on the floor beside the table and lamp and raised his eyebrows. "Are you redecorating in here? Give me something breakable and I'll help."

Talisa chuckled and shook her head in surrender. "Thanks. We've decided to go with Contemporary Disaster, so just grab anything."

Janie ran to Teddy and pulled him up and away from the wreckage, checking him for injuries.

Talisa bent and gathered broken pieces of lamp and threw them in a nearby trashcan.

The pastor balanced a stack of food containers on one hand and used the other to pull the storm door closed behind him to stop the cross breeze. He held up the containers. "Maddie rounded these up from the snack table and said they belonged to you. She sent me in with them." He handed the items to Talisa. "She's out in the car. We won't stay." He grinned at Teddy. "You know, Mr. Baskins, this looks a lot like that table in the church foyer last month. Is there something you have against this particular...Teddy?"

Teddy pressed his lips together until they were white. Janie grasped his arm, her eyebrows furrowed as she stared at him. His hands lifted and pushed at the air as if in a struggle.

Talisa moved closer. "What are you seeing?"

The young man continued to struggle, thrashing his arms and almost throwing Janie off.

She wrapped her arms around him and pressed her cheek into his back. "It be okay. It be okay."

Teddy bucked like he was in a fight for his life. His beet-red cheeks bulged. Stark desperation shown in his eyes. He arched his back and squirmed. Giving a violent shove, he thrust his head forward. His mouth came open and he sucked his lungs full as if to yell.

Through the open window came a scream, a warbling, piercing womanly cry of sheer panic. It sounded like it had yet to reach its peak when it stopped.

Janie jumped back with a gasp. Teddy extended both of his hands and blew out a huge breath. He blinked and looked at Janie. "That wasn't me."

Janie gave a quick shake of her head, her eyes spyglass wide.

Everyone stared at the window where the curtains danced in the wind. Pastor Cooper rushed to look out, grabbing the waving fabric to clear his view. "I don't see anything." He crossed to the entrance and pushed open the storm door, grabbing it with two hands to fight the gust. The wind rushed in, snatching at everything. It emptied a napkin holder, sending the papers fluttering like a flock of birds. The group poured out the door, following the flow of air.

Talisa was the last out and the pastor let her have the storm door as he hurried to check the area. The wind grabbed it out of her hand, ripped out the screws holding the hydraulic closer, and banged the door against the side of the house. Everyone spun toward the sound. Talisa stood there, transfixed by the stares of the others.

Teddy yelled, "You scared me, Ms. Tee."

"Ross, what's going on? What's all the screaming?" Maddie stood by the open car door, calling to her husband.

"We're not sure, honey."

Teddy stood near the corner of the house, pointing. His

voice rose, and the wind carried it out into the night. "It sounded like it came from over that way." Teddy's gesture took in the waters of Lake Gallant at the bottom of the hill where the shoreline cut in forming the cove. Light from the moon coming up over the turbulent lake flashed off Sawyer's ski boat that bobbed under a covered slip on the other side of the water. Sawyer's house was dark. He must have gone to bed.

Pastor Cooper hurried in the direction Teddy pointed and disappeared around the corner of the house.

"Ross?" Maddie raised her arm as if she might reach across the driveway and yard and pull her husband back from his folly.

Talisa's eyes followed Pastor Cooper then glanced at his wife's face, which was full of questions. "Sorry, Maddie. We had a little accident inside. Nobody's hurt, but that last scream came from outside, and we're not sure what's going on." Talisa stepped away from the house. "Did you see anything out—"

Slam! The door blew shut behind her. She jumped. Janie screamed. Maddie gasped, raising her hand to her throat, and Teddy yelled, "You sure keep scaring me, Ms. Tee."

Pastor Cooper appeared around the corner, his eyes searching for the source of the trouble. "What happened?"

Talisa let out her breath. "The door." She motioned toward the offending piece of hardware.

The pastor raised his eyebrows and gave a little shake of his head. "It looks like they're all cleared out down at the marina. I think Maddie and I were the last ones to leave besides Luke. His SUV is gone, and I'm sure he wouldn't leave until he knew everyone was out of there. I didn't see anything around your house. It sounded like it came from farther away. Do you know your neighbors over there?" He pointed toward Sawyer's. "Maybe we should go check on them."

Talisa glanced up at the gentle hill behind her house that

led to the plateau on top of the cliff overlooking the cove. It then sloped down to the backyard of Sawyer's property. She envisioned the entire group marching over the windswept hill, descending on Sawyer, gnarly trees bending in the background. All they would need were torches to complete the scene. "I think that might worry him. He lives by himself. There shouldn't be any females over there."

Talisa imagined her handsome neighbor alone in his bed, listening to all the racket they were making. He might think the scream came from their house. Had he already called 911 about "that crazy bunch" next door? It wasn't the kind of attention she wanted from the psychiatrist. "Maybe it was someone on a boat."

Pastor Cooper approached Talisa, so he could speak over the wind which seemed to be increasing by the minute. "Regardless of where it came from, it sounded pretty serious. Especially with the way Teddy was acting. I don't think it was a coincidence. I'm going to call and report it."

The scream had pushed Teddy's vision further back in Talisa's mind. She recalled the scene of the young man opening his mouth just before the awful cry. The timing had been perfect.

Teddy was pacing back and forth and peering around the corner like something might jump out at him. Janie stood nearby watching him, the wind whipping her long hair like a gothic movie. She hoped the vision and the scream weren't related. It was too close to home and she was so tired. The excited rush of blood in her veins was slowing. She remembered his other visions and how long she had spent helping determine what they meant and who needed help. It was the last thing she wanted at the moment. "Okay. I'll get these two inside and calmed down."

Pastor Cooper followed her gaze. "Good luck. I'm going to drive around a little bit, then get Maddie home. I'll drive by your neighbor's house and check."

"Oh Pastor, please don't bother him tonight. I mean...he

might have to get up in the morning."

The pastor's face was serious. "I'll just park out front, take down license plates, and sneak up and look in his windows."

What? Wait, he's joking.

Pastor Cooper winked. "Relax. I'll just cruise the area and see if anyone's moving around and then head home. I *do* have to get up in the morning." He regarded Talisa in a fatherly way. "I'm going to ask Luke to stop by and check on you after he investigates the scream. I hope you can sleep in in the morning. You look beat."

Luke? "Don't you think Luke's tired too, since he was here all evening helping supervise the celebration? He's probably halfway home by now. He'll send a deputy, won't he?"

A smirk formed on the pastor's face as he took out his cell phone, pivoted and walked toward his car. "Oh, I'm sure he'll want to look into this personally. I'll wait in the driveway until you're inside. Be sure to lock up, and don't open the door until Luke gets here."

Talisa sent her frown after him. "Okay." She put on a smile as she waved goodbye to Maddie.

Luke. By communicating through the volunteers, she had managed to limit her conversation with Luke during all the preparations for the night's event. Now there would be no getting away from him.

Teddy was still out in the yard pacing and massaging his throat. He saw her and yelled. "I think that scream had something to do with what I saw. It felt like I couldn't breathe. Something bad happened, I know it."

Talisa waved her hand back and forth and shook her head, trying to get Teddy to stop sharing his narrative with their neighbors.

He saw her and waved back, laughing. "You don't have to wave at me, Ms. Tee. I'm not leaving. Remember you said I could stay the night." The exchange didn't break his stride.

"It sounded like a woman. It was really squeaky." His loud voice rose an octave.

Talisa thrust both hands out in front of her, moving them across each other like an umpire calling safe. She pressed her lips together, willing Teddy's to do the same.

He didn't notice as he surveyed the darkness. "I sure hope the person is okay. That was the worst thing I ever felt."

"Teddy!" Her clipped whisper flew away on the wind.

Janie hurried back to Talisa and took hold of her arm. "What you think, Tee? Who you think it was?"

Talisa started to answer, but Teddy called out again, and Talisa whirled back toward him not bothering to disguise her frustration.

"It was like I was choking." He stood in the driveway, clutching his chest. Casting his voice above the blustering air whipping around the side of the house, he hollered. "I couldn't breathe. Then–"

Talisa shrieked. "Teddy!"

The young man spun in her direction, crouched with his hands out, palms down like he was bracing for an earthquake.

Talisa motioned for him and returned her voice to a harsh hiss. "Come here. And be quiet." He bounded across the drive to her. His astonished expression fixed on Talisa as she snapped at him. "It's getting late. If you don't stop yelling, *I'm* going to choke you."

Teddy's neck collapsed into his shoulders as his mouth displayed clenched teeth. "Sorry Ms. Tee, but the wind's really loud."

"Not as loud as you." Talisa herded them back to the house and grabbed the storm door. Again, the wind took it. Slam! Teddy and Janie stiffened as Talisa sucked in a breath and closed her eyes, fists clenched. Breaking the pose, she took Janie by the wrist, moved her toward the door and pushed Teddy in ahead of them. They were just inside when the gusting wind shifted again and banged the door shut.

Talisa stumbled into the living room and collapsed into an armchair.

Janie and Teddy crept to the couch across from where Talisa sat. She stretched her legs out and let her head fall back onto the chair. Staring at the ceiling, she took deep, deliberate breaths for a few seconds. Blowing out a puff of air, she considered the pair seated in front of her. They shared a look of attentive trepidation.

"You two are going to kill me, drive me out of my mind if I'm not there already. Since the day you met, you have been in the middle of every calamity that a town this size can produce. And no place this small should have so many calamities. Sometimes I think the two of you conjure them up when your wild imaginations get together."

Janie was quick to the defense. "Yeah, but, Tee, we wealy heard it, and you did too. And the Coopers."

"That's the trouble." Talisa raised her hands in surrender. "It's always real." She lowered her arms and studied the pair. "I think I'd like it better if you were making up lies."

Janie and Teddy glanced at each other in astonishment.

"I didn't mean that." Talisa slowly shook her head. "It's not your fault. You've helped people with this gift, and I'm proud of you." She deflated into the cushions. "I just want a normal life some days." She grinned at them.

Teddy snickered while Janie beamed.

Talisa focused on Teddy. "You think the scream was about what you saw?"

A wrinkled brow chased away Teddy's grin. He avoided her gaze and pressed his lips together.

Talisa sat up. "What's wrong?"

"I'm scared, Ms. Tee." When he looked at her, his lips trembled. "That was the worst thing that I ever felt."

Janie shot across the couch like a magnet to metal. She wrapped him in her arms before the first tears fell.

Teddy clung to her and wailed. "I'm afraid something real bad happened."

Janie stroked him and rocked him like a toddler. "He scared, Tee."

Talisa strode to the door and locked it. Snatching napkins from the floor, she went to where the curtain was conducting a symphony with the wind. She pulled down the glass and latched it. Moving to the large windows overlooking the marina, she scanned the terrain for any activity. Down the hill toward the lake, the sign proclaiming "Shelter of Cyprus Sailing Club" flapped next to the entrance to the empty parking lot. She continued her visual search to the docks. A light shone in one of the sailboats.

It was new to the marina. She had been so busy preparing for the Memorial Day events, she must have overlooked it. The large craft rolled with the water that heaved like the chest of a reclining giant. Rhythmic swaying of the tall mast interspersed with quick jerks when a gust batted it. *Who would be on one of the boats at this hour in an Oklahoma windstorm? Maybe I should call Mack and have him check.* No, Mack was reliable and a talented handyman, but if a disturbance was going on she didn't want the older man walking into something. She heaved out a sigh.

Better wait for Luke.

Chapter 3

When Talisa opened the inside door, Luke stood on her doorstep holding the wind-battered storm door. The door shuddered and bowed with the force of the gale, but his powerful hand didn't move. With his other hand, he fiddled with the closer. "You ought to get this fixed. It would come in handy on a night like this."

Talisa clenched her teeth. "Thanks for the tip." She glared at him a moment. "Come in out of the wind." Stepping back, she sent Janie skittering to get out of the way, and then Teddy had to move to avoid Janie. The duo settled into place behind Talisa in the entryway.

"Okay, detectives, the mystery's solved." As Luke stepped in, he grabbed his holster and hoisted up his equipment belt. His six-foot frame still carried his military fitness. The grin under his thick rugged nose gave him a good-natured, attractive appearance. Not the most handsome face, not like Sawyer's.

Talisa gazed into the eyes that had always carried Luke's countenance, laughing brown eyes that seemed to play sport with all the secrets of life.

"I'm glad it was nothing worse," Luke grinned and glanced over her shoulder toward Janie and Teddy. "Stand down, detectives."

Talisa looked away. *Same old Luke.*

"It was one of the doc's people."

"People?" Talisa frowned. "You mean a patient? One of Sawyer's patients?"

Luke tipped his head back at her use of the first name. "I know what you're thinking. It wasn't one of the ones that he sees out at the prison. They don't let them out. This was a woman from his office in town."

"A woman…from his office?" The question popped into Talisa's head. *Was she pretty?* That was ridiculous. She would not be asking that. Instead, she said, "What did she look like…in case I see her around?"

Luke raised his eyebrows. "She was gone by the time I got there." His face registered another thought. "But, I suspect she looked like most women that come to a man's house late at night, uninvited."

Talisa narrowed her eyes at him. "But it was a patient?"

Luke gave one slow, precise nod.

"What was she doing at his house?"

He paused before answering. "I'm going to tell you this because you live next door, and I don't want you worrying, but I don't want it going any further." He glanced at Teddy and Janie. "Okay, detectives, this is confidential information, and I need your word that you won't tell anyone about it."

Talisa cocked her head. "You know these two don't gossip."

"I know, but I want to make sure they don't say something without thinking. Can I count on you guys?"

Janie spoke first. "Pwomise."

"Yes, sir," Teddy said.

Luke appeared thoughtful as if considering what to say. "The lady has a little problem and misunderstood her and the Doc's relationship. She showed up at his house, and when the doc told her to leave, she made a scene and started yelling. That's what you heard."

Teddy wrinkled his forehead. "It wasn't yelling. It was a scream."

"Well, like I said, she has some problems, so she might have been doing some screaming. Anyway, she left. Doc said she lit out on foot. A comment she made led the doc to think she parked her car down the road somewhere. He said he made it clear to her that she was not to come to his home again. He doesn't think there will be any more trouble."

Teddy shifted back and forth on his feet and shook his head. Luke saw it. "You think there's more, Teddy?"

"It felt like more." Teddy muttered with his head bowed. "It felt like I was dying."

Luke's expression was pensive. "The doc didn't make it sound like it was anything like that. Is it possible you're getting this wrong?"

Talisa dipped her head and glared at Luke. "When does Teddy get things wrong?"

Luke shrugged, "Well, everything wasn't quite right on the Weavers' boy."

She let out a breath to show her exasperation. "Being in a dark well is similar to being buried underground. Teddy told what he was seeing."

"I know it wasn't Teddy's fault. It's just that the good people of Gilead County can get a little nuts sometimes. I don't want to spend another day and a half searching for shallow graves in the woods when we should have been looking in the abandoned yard next door."

"He was found, wasn't he?"

"Yes, he was." Luke approached Teddy and squeezed his arm. "All because of my best detectives." He gave Janie's chin a gentle flip with his finger.

Turning back to Talisa, he said, "But I get into enough trouble on my own."

Talisa raised one eyebrow. "I can't argue with that."

He smirked back. It was the face Talisa had grown up with, the face that used to elicit memories of laughter and fun. Regret crept into her feelings. He had become part of their family after his dad didn't come home from the war. While his mother worked, Luke stayed at their house. Talisa's father taught them to swim like the SEALs had taught him. The lake had been their playground.

With Luke standing tall in front of her, they could have been standing on their dock again, all dripping wet on the day that her father had "drown-proofed" them. She and Luke each taking their turn at having their ankles and wrists fastened together with rubber bands, arms behind their backs, bobbing to the surface, treading water with no hands, swimming like dolphins. Luke had even been able to kick and roll himself back onto the dock at the end.

She relived the feel of his strong arms reaching down and snatching her out of the water when her turn was over, his hug of congratulations. Eye to eye, Luke expressed how impressed he was with her. The way he made her feel, the approval those eyes imparted linked her to him. Everything had changed. Her body might have been drown-proofed, but her heart was in way over its head.

The smirk vanished from Luke's face as she looked at him. She had to admire the way he had stepped in to help with Janie and Teddy. "Thanks for coming back to check this out. I know you must be tired."

Luke grinned. "Hey, when the Enigma calls, I come running." He shifted toward Teddy. "What do you think? Do we need some kind of signal in the sky?"

Teddy's mouth was ear-to-ear teeth. "Yeah, we need one."

Talisa sighed. It didn't matter how natural it felt to have Luke back in their lives, she wasn't going to let him hurt her again. She couldn't take anymore. He was the same happy-go-lucky jokester he had always been. She was twenty-four years old, not some teenager. She needed someone to understand the pain, someone who could help her work through the depression before it took her like it took her father.

Luke's face became serious as he turned back to Talisa. "All I'm saying is before we go accusing the doc of anything, let's make sure we know what we have."

Accusing Sawyer? Talisa wasn't accusing anybody. Where did he get that idea? "I didn't mean that. I'm sure he wouldn't—"

Luke regarded her. "Well now, I don't know what the doc would and wouldn't do. You apparently know him much better than I do."

Talisa averted her eyes and fumed. She knew she was blushing. How could one person be so irritating? "No. Not really. I only met him a few times."

A slight grin played with the dimples on Luke's cheeks. "Well, sure you've met him. After all, you *are* neighbors. I can see how he would make quite an impression on…someone."

Talisa raised her head, sticking out her chin. "Yes, he is my neighbor, and I also met him in town before I knew he was my neighbor…at a book signing at the library."

"Book signing?"

"Yes, he's written a book about his experiences treating the criminally insane and how it relates to our own inner healing."

"Whose inner healing?" Luke's grin won the game, lifting his dimples up in triumph.

She wanted to ask Luke how many books he had written. "Everyone's inner healing. You know what I mean."

"Absolutely. Whenever I feel like I need inner healing, spending a day with a serial killer perks my inners right up."

"Do you always have to be so difficult? What I'm getting at is he seemed… honest, professional. I just mean that…maybe something happened to this woman after she left his house." Talisa glanced around the room, feeling Luke examining her. She hated his ability to make her feel like he knew what she was thinking. When he turned his grin toward Teddy, she lowered her shoulders in relief.

"Okay, detective, tell me everything you saw."

Teddy jumped in with eagerness. "We were getting ready for the celebration. Janie and I was putting out the snacks. That's when the first time happened."

Janie nodded. "I yelled fo' Tee, but by the time she woke up, she missed it."

Talisa scrunched up her face. "I just laid my head down on the table a minute. I…haven't been sleeping well lately."

Luke focused on Talisa again. The grin was gone. His face seemed almost concerned. She didn't know which was worse. *Please, Lord, make him stop looking at me.* Luke gave her a gentle smile, then turned back to Teddy who was into the story again.

"I was holding Janie's hand 'cause Ms. Tee said we could hold hands, but we're not supposed to hug each other when we're alone because she wants us to be pla-bonic or something like—"

"Teddy," Talisa jumped in, "Luke doesn't need to know all that. Just tell what you saw."

"Pla-bonic?" Luke's grin was back on Talisa like a prison spotlight on an escapee. "Is that anything like bubonic? I know exactly what you mean. Humans have been *plagued* with that hugging problem for centuries."

"Platonic," Talisa tried to move the attention back to Teddy. "Just tell your story."

"Like I said, I was holding Janie's hand and then, I started feeling funny. It felt like someone else was holding me and I felt weird. It was like I wanted the person to like me, but I didn't know if I could trust them. I knew it wasn't Janie." Teddy shared a glance with Janie. "It was mainly a feeling, then it was gone. Then during the fireworks, all the sudden, I was in a room and I felt mad. I wanted to leave and started to walk away. Then someone put their hand on my shoulder, and I knocked it off because I was going to leave. Then that was gone, too."

Janie reached forward to insert herself into the narrative, "Then at the house, Teddy got weal bad."

Luke was one of the few people to whom Janie would express herself. Talisa encouraged her. "Tell Luke what you mean when you say 'Teddy got real bad.'"

"He started jerk'n, an' fight'n an' acting like he can't bweath."

Teddy took over again. "I never felt anything like that in my life. It was like someone was killing me. Then we heard that scream. After that, I was scared." His face held regret. "Maybe I could have helped the person if I had tried to see more."

Janie put her arm around him. "That scweam was scawy." She emphasized each word then faced Luke. "We never had it happen so close we could hear someone scweam."

Teddy still hung his head. Talisa said, "You didn't do anything wrong. It unnerved all of us. It takes a while to recover from something like that. I know you would have helped this person if you could. Think of all those people you helped before. No one else could have done that."

Teddy looked at each person with the beginnings of a smile. Then he looked down again and shook his head. "I don't do nuthin. God just lets me see things. All I do is tell people what He shows me."

Luke put his hand on Teddy's back. "That's the best thing any of us can say, Teddy. You did good." He squeezed him around the shoulders. "You said you couldn't breathe? Did it feel like someone was strangling you?"

"It happened so fast, I don't know. I just felt like someone was gonna kill me. Everything was all dark and blurry looking. I couldn't see anyone's face. It was like a shadow was over me, and I was holding my breath because I knew I'd die if I didn't."

"And you couldn't see who was holding you?"

"I was so scared I was gonna die. I guess that was all the person felt. They just couldn't think of anything else."

Janie's eye's opened wide at the memory. "Then he acted like he was gonna scweam, but someone else did it first."

Teddy's face acknowledged the statement. "I shoved hard and found air, so I took a big breath and opened my mouth to scream 'cause I wanted loose. But the scream didn't come from me."

Talisa pointed. "It came right in that window. Like it came from over toward Sawyer's house."

Luke nodded. "Which we've determined already. But this sounds different than what the doc described."

"You didn't hear the scream. It was awful." Talisa shook off a shiver at the thought. "Could someone have been outside waiting for her? Maybe that's when she screamed."

Luke brought his eyebrows together. "If that happened, the doc should have heard it. He said she was yelling at him. After he let me walk through his house, I looked around outside. I didn't see anything unusual." Luke rubbed the back of his neck. "Now that I hear Teddy's story, things aren't making sense. The only thing I can do is try to find this woman." He stopped and examined Talisa's face then leaned toward her. "I've got a deputy driving around the area. I'll have him hang around in the neighborhood tonight."

Sawyer's story and Teddy's statement mingled in Talisa's mind.

Luke softened his voice. "Maybe she hyperventilated or had a panic attack or something and couldn't breathe. That could have been what Teddy was feeling. When I find her, I can ask her."

Talisa turned to Teddy. "What do you feel right now?"

Teddy's eyes stared out into the room. His voice sounded defeated when he said, "Nuthin. I don't feel nuthin."

***

Luke crawled back into his Tahoe and sat for a minute. *Well, this night sure turned south on me.*

He should have known anything involving Teddy would be complicated. He'd seen the gift work too many times to disregard it. But it was always like that, puzzling until they figured it out, and then it all made sense. If it was a gift from God, it would be just like Him. Like prophesy in the Bible, no one knew what it meant until it happened. *Lord, it sure would be nice if You would spell things out a little better. Why is everything such a mystery?* Luke stared at the side of Talisa's house and listened to the mysterious silence.

That was something else he wished he could have an answer to. Talisa was there, just beyond the wall, but she seemed to be getting further away all the time. Sometimes, he thought he saw something in her eyes, but then it vanished. *If I'm fooling myself, Lord, please let me know. I can see she's hurting. She needs something like You did for me. The way she talked about Doc Kincade—she must think he's it. And maybe he is. God, I don't need anything but You. I learned that lesson. But if You're telling me no on Talisa, I'm begging You to take this ache out of me. Let us both know.*

Nothing he could do but wait. He shifted the Tahoe into gear. The doc had told him the woman who came to his house was Phebe Agnew. If she was involved, who knew what might be going on? Talisa was right, the doc had seemed professional. He had no reason to doubt his story…until he talked to Teddy. He needed to try and get some sleep. If his deputy didn't find Phebe during the night, he would have to start the search tomorrow. Maybe that was one mystery he could solve.

Chapter 4

Talisa stared at the bedroom ceiling as it came into focus. Sunshine warmed the room. There was a sound, the droning of an engine. *Why did I sleep so late? Oh, yeah. That scream.* She couldn't even remember what time she got to bed.

She pushed to a seated position and surveyed the room. It still felt out of place to be there. She had justified the irreverent move to her parents' bedroom with two rationales. One—as the new owner, she needed to keep a better eye on the marina, and the room's windows faced the lake. Two—Janie needed more space, and her sister said she didn't feel right sleeping in her mommy and daddy's room. But Talisa couldn't lie to herself. The real reason was that every time Talisa looked at *their* door from the other end of the hall, she expected she might see her mother or father coming out of it. It made the pain's bite even worse, like a familiar pet turning on her.

She couldn't let the depression keep sending her back inside, door closed, huddled on her bed. So, she had given Janie her bedroom. That way Talisa couldn't change her mind. She had moved down the hall into her parents' room. Now she had nowhere to run and hide. The memories were right there, all around her, and she would face them. *Just like you taught me, Daddy.* Talisa's thoughts attacked her. How could she win, when he couldn't?

Needing a distraction to rid herself of the dark feelings, she rose and wandered to the side window. The engine noise was coming from up the hill. When she pressed in close to the window, she could see up to the rim of the plateau on top of the cliff. It was the only area on the property that received good sun. She had been up there with her shovel trying to work the rocky terrain into a garden without much success.

Something appeared above the edge then disappear again. It happened several times, and she realized it was a man's head. The wavy blond hair could only belong to Sawyer. He was riding his tractor in her garden.

What is he doing? Talisa mentally nudged herself. *Well, go find out. This is your chance to see him again without making some obvious excuse.*

Hurrying into the bathroom, she washed her face, brushed her teeth, and fixed her long, thick brown hair. She started to grab her gardening pants but stopped. Throwing them on the floor of the closet, she put on a pretty dress instead, and then spritzed some perfume. Talisa was bringing the mascara brush to her eye when she confronted herself in the mirror.

What are you doing, Talisa? She put the brush away. Her reflection stared back at her. Was she the type of woman who showed up at a man's house in the middle of the night uninvited. *Don't look desperate. He deals with kooks all the time.* She stood and headed for the door, then stopped. Should she change the dress? *You're already wearing it. Now you're just being silly.*

When she walked over the rise, she remembered how close to perfect a man could get in the looks department. Sawyer was commanding and manly on his shiny new

Kubota. *What is he doing?* Her garden. The rocky, disobedient earth that had defied her spading fork and shovel was tamed and tilled. Sawyer navigated his tractor down a row of churned soil, the heavy-duty rototiller he pulled pulverizing it even finer. When he spied her, he pulled the machine at a right angle to where she stood, even with his seat and engaged the brake. Fresh dirt fell from the teeth on the front bucket, and the earthy aroma smelled good enough to eat. He throttled down the engine and shut the tractor off. The instant silence made her uncomfortable as Sawyer looked her over.

"I hope you don't mind." He launched his tanned frame from the machine and landed on the ground in front of her, brushing dust from his hands. "I wanted to do something to make up for last night. What a drama. I'm sorry you had to be a part of it."

Talisa smiled, shook her head, and tried to think of what to say. When she was slow to respond, Sawyer continued. "Anyway, I noticed you over here working on this, and I've been meaning to help. I decided it would be a good way to get to know you."

Talisa recovered. "You didn't have to do that."

"Already done."

She considered the dark dirt. A small trailer was piled with white sacks on the other side of the cultivated area.

Sawyer's head turned in the direction of her gaze. "I brought over some fertilizer I had out in the shed. If you don't mind, I'll leave it here until I get a chance to work it in. The stuff's kind of potent, so don't touch it until I get it watered down."

Without thinking, Talisa said, "I was going to go organic." Then she added. "But it was so thoughtful. The old ground might need some fertilizer. This garden has been a dream of mine. It's the only flat spot around here that gets any sun, but the ground was so hard I could barely dent it. It was sweet of you to think of me. I'm sorry to put you to the trouble."

"Least I could do. Organic it will be then. I know it's late in the season, but don't plant anything yet. I'll have Pete's Peat bring up a load of soil mix in a few days. I'll tell him to make it organic. When I work that in, you'll be all set."

"Sawyer, I can't let you do that. None of this is necessary."

"No argument. You have to let me do it right. My reputation is on the line. It's not often that my work follows me home. I won't feel right until I make it up to you."

"Honestly, there's nothing to make up. Last night wasn't your fault. When you deal with the type of people you do, I'm sure issues pop up from time to time. Are you okay?"

"Certainly. You're right. In my business you get used to issues. But my patients are for me to deal with, not my neighbors." Sawyer took a step closer and gave her a perfect white smile under his perfect blue eyes. "Especially not you. Besides, a girl should have her dreams come true once in a while."

Talisa smiled and returned his gaze.

"Morning." The call came from the direction of Sawyer's house. Luke was halfway up the hill. He waved at them, looking as calm as ever. "I'm glad I caught you two." The climb hadn't even affected his breathing. He looked over the scene, taking in the new garden, the tractor, Sawyer and finally Talisa. "You look nice."

Talisa gave an imperceptible groan. "Thanks." She crossed her hands in front of herself.

"So, you got your garden. Be careful not to get that dress dirty."

She wrapped her gaze around Luke's throat. "I'm not gardening."

"Well of course not. Looks like the doc's doing the gardening. What was I thinking? You must be getting ready to go into town. Someplace special?"

Talisa smiled hard at Luke. *I don't care what you were*

thinking, she wanted to say. Instead, she told him, "Nothing special. This is just something...I grabbed out of the closet."

"Hmm," Luke said nodding. "Nice grab. Never seems to work that way for me. I guess some people are better grabbers." With eyes still on Talisa, he said, "Sure was nice of you to help her out, Doc. I know the garden's something she's been wanting."

"Are you here again about what happened last night, Sheriff?" Sawyer asked.

Talisa seized the topic like a life preserver. "Oh, yes. Did you find the woman?"

"No. That's what I came to talk about. I did find her car. It was hidden in the trees down the road a ways on a trail that leads to the lake." Luke glanced at Sawyer. "Just like you thought, Doc. She must have walked to your place from there. A pretty good stroll, but the last time I saw Ms. Agnew, she looked to be in good shape. That or they need to train the city officers a little better on handcuffing a combative female." Luke's mouth turned up just enough to produce a dimple.

"I'm not surprised," Sawyer said. "She kept saying we could be alone, and no one would know she was there because she hid her car." He glanced at Talisa, then continued to speak to Luke. "She was uninvited and unwelcome. When I told her to leave she started screaming at me."

"I don't doubt what you're telling me, but no one's seen Ms. Agnew since last night."

Sawyer shrugged. "She probably thought she was going to be arrested and left town."

"Maybe, but then her car wouldn't still be hidden around the corner."

Sawyer appeared to be thinking.

Talisa asked Luke, "Do you think something happened to her?"

Sawyer interrupted. "I'm sure she'd been drinking. She

might have worried about getting a DUI on top of a disorderly charge. Maybe she decided to hitchhike or call for a ride."

"You could be right. She'll likely turn up in a day or two. Meanwhile, Doc, I was hoping you could help me with one more thing. You know how it is in this town. People get to talking and start making up stories. I don't want you to be in the middle of all that, and I don't want them saying I didn't do my job. Would you mind if I searched your house again?"

Sawyer eyed Luke without breaking his smile. "Of course I don't mind, Sheriff, but was there something you weren't satisfied with last night?"

"No, you were very cooperative. It's just that I want to be able to shut the gossips up before anything gets started, and I figured you wouldn't mind helping me out. That way I can tell people, 'Listen, the doc has nothing to hide. He let me look all through his house, and I didn't find any bodies there.' You know, put things to rest before they get started."

Sawyer started down the hill. "No bodies at my house, Sheriff. Come on down, and you can look all you want." He stopped and turned back to Talisa. "Sorry about this."

"That's fine. Thanks again."

"Coming, Sheriff?"

Luke glanced at Talisa. "Teddy's folks said he stayed the night at your place. I was hoping to talk to him again, if that's all right?"

Her answer was cool. "I didn't want him driving home in the dark. I called Teddy's parents and put him in the guest room."

"Perfect. I'll be around later." As Luke pivoted to follow Sawyer, he said loud enough for her to hear, "Don't bother changing on my account."

It was all Talisa could do to keep from hurling a fresh dirt clod at him. She spun away from the men and huffed out a breath that tousled her bangs. Then she marched back down toward her house.

Chapter 5

Talisa fumed until she reached the bottom of the hill. Mack was on the marina grounds, picking up limbs knocked down by the wind. He threw an armload onto a trailer attached to a four-wheeler. She headed his way.

"Good morning, Miss Talisa." The caretaker took off the fisherman's hat he wore and rubbed his bald head as he looked at her. "Sure look pretty today. You go'n someplace?"

She sighed and forced a smile. "No plans. Never hurts to be prepared."

Mack rubbed his head again and returned his hat to its place. "Mighty big blow last night. Knocked down a heap a' kindlin' for the firepit down by the dock. Unless you want it up there at your house."

"No thanks. Go ahead and take it. I just had a question."

"What is it, Miss?"

"I saw a new boat in the marina."

Mack's gaze traveled to the marina. "That's a feller I got set up in there day 'fore yesterday. Seems decent. College professor on some kind of a sabbath."

"I saw a light in the boat last night."

"Yes, Miss. He's paying an extra $100 to stay in the boat. Hope you don't mind. It was something your fath— I mean, it's something the marina has done in the past." Mack appeared interested in a small limb to his right and bent to pick it up.

"I remember." Talisa wanted to relieve the man's awkwardness. "It's okay. You can talk about my father."

He straightened again but continued to consider the stick in his hand. "I'm sorry. It's just that last time we talked... I don't like to see a lady cry like that."

She blinked her eyes and bent to collect a stick of her own. *God, help me.* She inspected it for its worthiness, then passed it off to Mack's tight, sinewy fingers. "I'm crying less."

He took the stick and threw it in the cart along with his own. "Known your dad most of my life. He helped get me in the army. Then after the war, he helped get the army out of me, if you know what I mean. I kinda did some drink'n. Sure wish I coulda helped him like he helped me. I knew it was bad with him when your mom passed, but I never thought he'd ever do something like that, especially with Miss Janie needing him so bad." Then he added, "But you're still here for her. Your dad'd be happy you keep'n the marina. I know this's kinda interrupted you own plans. Think you'll ever go back to school?"

"I'm not sure. I need to think things through."

"What was it you was study'n?"

"I wanted to get my degree in aquatic therapy."

"That's like helping people in the water, right?"

The memory of Talisa's dreams warmed her. "I had hoped to help kids that were having problems with speech and motor skills. They have some great programs using dolphins."

"They sure do some interesting things now-a-days." He chuckled. "I remember now. Luke...Sheriff Sanders was teasing you about that."

Her memories faded, and she stiffened, but Mack didn't seem to notice. His chuckle continued as he reminisced. "Didn't see how a dolphin could teach someone to speak when all they did was cackle." Mack moved his head back and forth as he mimicked Luke. "Might as well use a hen. It's cheaper, you don't get wet, and they supply breakfast." He was shaking his head again. "He's quite a character, isn't he?"

"That's one word."

Mack went on, insensitive to any offense. "Well, if anyone could do it, it'd be you, Miss. Always said you kids was born with gills. You take all the time you need to figure things. It's good havin' you here. I'm sure Luke's..." Mack scratched his beard and picked up another stick. "Well, everyone's glad. I appreciate you lettin' me stay on."

Talisa paused at Mack's slip. She was almost going to ask what he meant but let it go. "You belong here, Mack. I appreciate all your help."

Mack was silent for a moment as he arranged the sticks in the cart. "So, you want me to introduce you to your new tenant?"

"Yes, I'd like to meet him."

Mack led her down the hill to the long metal ramp that led to the floating dock. Talisa stopped halfway and stared at the cabin cruiser tied in the first slip.

The image came sudden, unexpected. The cabin of the boat shut up, her father's body lying inside, the exhaust fumes pouring in from the hose attached to the boat's engine. Talisa drifted to the ramp's handrail and leaned against it. She tried to push the thoughts away, but they forced their way in. What would he have felt?

The thoughts formed a physical pain. She dug her fingernails into her palms. Her father had never lied to her before, but the last thing he told her was he was going diving. If the autopsy had not confirmed he died from carbon monoxide, she never would have believed it was possible, not her father. Had he thought of her and Janie at all? Running from his own pain, just to throw it on them. Did he have any concept of what it was going to do to those he left behind?

"Miss Talisa, you okay?" Mack looked at her, concerned.

"I'm okay. Just give me a minute." *Please, God, I need something.*

Mack slipped his arm around her shoulder. She grasped his hand and laid her face against it. "I'm sorry."

"It's gonna be okay. Some things just don't make no sense, and there's no use trying to make sense out of 'em. Just gotta give 'em to the Lord and trust Him." He squeezed her tighter. "Shoot, most the time we think we got things figured out, but we just fooling ourselves anyway."

They were silent for a time until Mack said, "You want me to sell that boat?"

Talisa took a deep inhale. "No..." She glared at the craft then forced her eyes away. "I'll let you know." Talisa shook her head. "I don't want to let this do that to me. I have many good memories. I just need to concentrate on the good ones and get the others out of my head."

Mack gave her a last squeeze and then let go. "Come on. I'll introduce you. Take your mind off things. One foot in front of the other. That's what got me through."

Talisa nodded, wiped her eyes, and followed him. He led her around to the slip where the pristine sailboat was moored.

Mack slapped his palm on the deck a couple of times and called out, "Mr. Welch. I'd like you to meet the owner of the marina if you have time, sir."

A man's voice grunted inside the boat.

"Mr. Welch?" Mack tried again.

Another impatient sound and the boat rocked. A mat of unruly gray hair bounded up from the cabin, followed by a wide form. When the hair turned, it was attached to a full face with round ruddy cheeks and a bulbous nose. He had the lines and belly of a man in his fifties and eyes that conveyed impatient friendliness. The eyes gave recognition to Mack and analyzed Talisa. He gave a rapid wave of invitation. "Mr. Mack, come in and bring your lovely companion, but you must bear with me while I finish something."

They followed him into the cabin. Whiteboards surrounded them like savages encircling jungle intruders. Open books sprawled across the countertops and on the backs of the built-in couches reminding Talisa of wounded soldiers, left where they had fallen. A laptop computer was open on a table.

Talisa and Mack were looking at the hair again as the man faced the largest of the whiteboards at the far end. He held a marker which he moved back and forth between mathematical equations scribbled on the board. The man muttered below the intelligible range. The same type of equations stared at them from the other boards.

The man swung around and gazed in Talisa's direction. Just when she was starting to feel uncomfortable, he lunged at her across the small cabin space. She stumbled backward a couple of steps, but the man grabbed the whiteboard beside her and swung it to sit beside the one over which he had been pondering. His marker hovered over some figures for a few seconds and then went back to the other board.

"Ohhh," he growled. Circling the offending equation, he dropped onto the cushion beside him and, crossing his arms in disgusted resignation, glared at the board. After a moment, he gave a start and swiveled as if just remembering his guests.

He motioned rapidly. "Please, sit down."

Talisa lowered herself onto the edge of the nearest cushion, afraid if she leaned back, her hair would erase something important from the board behind her.

"Forgive me." The man gathered the boards and stacked

them in front of the larger board.

Mack still stood, glancing around at the indicators of intellectual industry. "This here is Talisa Hollenbeck. She's the owner of the marina. I thought you might like to meet her since you said you would be staying for a spell. Miss Talisa, if it's all right, I'll get back to my work and you can visit?"

Talisa smiled and nodded.

The man with the hair spoke up. "While I have you both here, I wanted to mention that I heard a scream last night. Later, the sheriff came around and asked me if I had seen anything. Is everything all right?"

Mack spoke up, "Yeah, I heard that too. I came out to the marina and checked everything. Saw you on your boat, Mr. Welch, and I could tell you was okay. Everything else looked fine. Sheriff stopped by my place too." Mack turned Talisa's way. "He told me he was gonna talk to you, Miss Talisa."

"I should have known you would be checking into it. I looked out at the marina, but you must have gone back in by that time. Since I didn't know what was going on, I let the sheriff handle it. He came by later and said it was nothing to worry about. An issue at one of the neighbors'. Thanks for keeping up on things. I should have called and let you know."

"No problem. Part of my job. Speaking of which, I'll get back to it." With a nod to the other man, Mack climbed out.

"Ruben Welch, Ms. Hollenbeck." The man extended his hand. "Thank you for letting me stay."

"Mack tells me that you will be living on your boat." Talisa shook his hand. "He said you were taking some kind of sabbath?"

The man chuckled. "Sabbatical is what I believe Mack heard me say. But then, what is a good sabbatical made of but the ordinary days between Sabbaths? I'm on leave from the University of Oklahoma. As you can see," he gestured around the room, "I teach there to support my research habit."

Talisa raised her eyebrows. "I suspect I should call you Doctor Welch then. We're honored. What made you choose our marina?"

"You mean besides your wonderful facilities and the natural charm of the lake?"

Talisa dropped her head for a moment and came up grinning. "Forgive my curiosity. We are certainly glad to have you, but Havilah is not known as a hot spot for scientific research."

"Oh, but it has a necessary ingredient—uninterrupted quiet."

Talisa's smile turned sheepish. "Unless the neighbors are screaming, or I come around interrupting you."

"An isolated incident, I'm sure." His eyes widened. "Oh, no." Welch grimaced. "Forgive me, Ms. Hollenbeck, I did not mean to imply that your visit was unwelcome."

Talisa joined him in a laugh.

He continued. "On the contrary, you have perfect timing. I needed the distraction from a particularly difficult problem I have been working on." Welch leaned forward with a serious expression. "And, in the spirit of full disclosure, there is one other reason that I chose Havilah, something with which you might be able to help me. I was hoping to meet a young man named Theodore Baskins. I believe he is sometimes known as 'The Enigma' if you prefer. I understand that you are well acquainted with him."

Talisa cringed inside. "Why do you want to talk to Teddy?"

"There are, what shall I call them...*reports*... surrounding Mr. Baskins. I believe it might relate to my research. I have heard that he has the ability to feel and see things outside of the scope of average human awareness."

"At least you make it sound scientific. But I am afraid Teddy is not interested in being studied for any paranormal research. Besides, I am sure his abilities have been greatly exaggerated."

"I promise you I am not some ESP hunter. I have done my share to expose such things. My research is in condensed matter physics. I am working with a professor at the University of Tulsa whose specialty is neuroscience. I am not here to exploit Mr. Baskins. I simply want to verify his ability and see if it might help us to understand extra sensory brain phenomenon. If Mr. Baskins' mind is able to span spatial dimensions and connect with other minds, it is possible something is happening on a quantum level."

"Let me guess. You got stonewalled by Teddy's parents, and now you're trying me?"

Dr. Welch's look was soft and understanding. "I am sure it has been trying for them."

"It has." Talisa crossed her arms. "What if I told you that I believe Teddy's abilities are a gift from God?"

"You would get no argument from me. I would just like to see how God does it. Sometimes He gives us a glimpse if we look hard enough. I'm a believer, Ms. Hollenbeck. I have to be careful, though, how I approach such subjects in my field. There is an overwhelming naturalistic bias in secular academia, but I am completely convinced of special creation and the power of God. That is why I am not as quick to dismiss Teddy's abilities as a hoax or superstition. I believe in a spiritual world, and I believe the spirit-brain connection is one of the most fascinating areas where we see the physical and spiritual world intersect. I am exploring if that might occur in that area of strange uncertainties we have called *quantum*. What is uncertain to us may be the area where God reaches in from the spiritual world and makes the infinite, subtle adjustments to our universe that lead to the flavor of our existence."

Talisa raised her eyebrows. "Sounds very profound, but I don't know much about physics."

"It is not necessary that you do. I can see you care a great deal for Mr. Baskins and know him well. It is my understanding that while Mr. Baskins is an adult, he has special needs. You sound like a reasonable woman. You could monitor all my interaction with him and only participate in activities with which you mutually feel comfortable."

Talisa stood. "Not interested."

The man's nod conveyed congenial disappointment. "I understand, and I will respect your decision. The only thing that I might leave you with is that I have done groundbreaking research in this area. The things I have learned might be of benefit to you sometime. The spin-off value of my study is a better understanding of what we sometimes label as developmental disabilities. Often, the unique way such individuals process information and observe the world can give them extraordinary abilities."

"You won't get any argument from me about that idea. Teddy is special. That's why I don't want him used for research, no matter how noble."

Dr. Welch appeared to be considering Talisa's statement, then continued. "Teddy is not the only person with such challenges, and many do not have someone like you as a support system. I think individuals like Teddy will ultimately profit from such studies. If you ever have questions or want to talk, the interaction might be beneficial to both of us. I will be here taking advantage of the other reason for my decision to come, providing I am still welcome."

"You can enjoy the peace and quiet. That's in the brochure. Teddy is not."

Talisa rose to leave. "Pleasant meeting you, Dr. Welch."

The man seemed to be wrestling with something in his mind. As Talisa turned to go, he said, "I am sorry to hear about your father. He was a good man."

Talisa whirled around to face him. "How did you know my father?"

"He donated some items to the Sam Nobel Museum on our campus. He didn't want his name associated with them, and I would not have betrayed that confidence to anyone else."

"I'm glad you did." Talisa's view became misty. "Any good memory of my daddy is a blessing. I always loved searching for lost artifacts with him. He did some deep-sea salvaging in his past. It was always a passion of his. He switched to fresh water diving here in the lake. I went with him whenever I could. We found relics from before the valley was flooded by the creation of the dam."

The hair bobbed up and down in acknowledgment. The face beneath it wore a melancholy smile. "While he was at the university, one of my colleagues at the museum learned that he was connected with Mr. Baskins. He knew I was interested in meeting Mr. Baskins, so he introduced me to your father."

Talisa sat down and studied the floor, then Welch. "He never told me about that. Why would he keep it a secret?"

The man frowned. "I'm sure he had his reasons. Just because he has passed does not mean you should stop trusting him."

"It's just that I had been away at college. When I came back, my dad seemed different. My mother had cancer and I thought it was because of that. But then when he—." Talisa's eyes teared up. "I felt like I didn't know him at all."

Taking a handkerchief from his pocket, Dr. Welch moved over to the bench near Talisa and handed it to her. "I'm so sorry. I hesitated to mention it because I thought you might see it as an attempt to manipulate your father's memory to sway you on the issue concerning Mr. Baskins, and I would never do that. But now I've dredged up something worse. Forgive me."

Talisa shook her head and took a moment to wipe her face. "It's okay. I still have things I need to work through."

"Of course. I experienced similar feelings when my wife died. I had spent too much time with my research and not enough with her. Regret consumed my days. Then it occurred to me that such regret lived only in my mind. My Helen was past all that. I also realized she would not be pleased with me living that way."

Talisa sniffed. "More profound wisdom. I'm glad I came to visit with you today, Dr. Welch."

"For the Lord gives wisdom. From His mouth come knowledge and understanding." The doctor's voice was quiet and solemn as he quoted the proverb. "Perhaps this meeting was His doing as well."

She regarded the wizened face and wild hair. "My father liked you, didn't he?"

Dr. Welch raised his eyebrows. "I like to think so. We had some good conversations. When you're ready, I would be happy to share what I remember of them. Perhaps help you reclaim some of what you lost."

"I would like that."

"When you're ready," he said. His eyes softened, and the edges of his mouth turned up.

Talisa stood and offered her hand. "Thank you. I'll let you get back to your work."

"It has been a pleasing diversion for me. I wish it had been more so for you."

Talisa lifted her shoulders, gave another sniff and smiled. "I'm not displeased."

Chapter 6

When the knock came later that afternoon, Talisa knew what she would find before she opened her door. Luke would be standing there with his stupid grin on his face. She wasn't disappointed.

He scrutinized her sweatpants and oversized shirt. Talisa looked at the ceiling, drew in a breath and asked, "Find any dead bodies?"

"None that would admit to it."

"Hi, Luke" Janie kneeled on the seat of the couch and waved.

Teddy stood up and smiled. "Hi, Sheriff Sanders."

"Mind if I come in?" Luke asked Talisa.

She moved back from the door.

He passed her, smiling at Teddy and Janie, but whispered out of the corner of his mouth, "Still look nice."

Before she could respond, he moved into the living room and greeted the other two. "How ya guys doing today? Get any sleep?"

"No," Janie giggled, "Cuz Teddy kept making animal noises from his bedwoom."

Teddy snorted out a laugh.

"Are you sure?" Luke asked Janie. "We had a bunch of animals escape from the circus. Maybe they came to your house."

Janies eyes flickered, then she smirked. "Uh uh. The only animal here is him." She made an exaggerated pointing gesture at Teddy.

Talisa was sure that Teddy's pig-like snicker had a purely unintentional resemblance to the barnyard creature.

"So, Detective Baskins," Luke addressed him. "I need your help on another case. Are you available to do your duty, to serve and protect?"

The remnants of Teddy's amusement dried up. "Sure, Luke. What case? What do I do?"

"Same as usual. You look mean and intimidating, and I'll do the rest. You be the bad cop, I'll be the good cop. You be the heavy, I'll be the easy. They don't stand a chance against *The Enigma*."

Teddy snorted again. "The Enigma." He repeated the word with as much sinister effect as one could accomplish while making swine sounds.

Janie appeared gleeful. "Sounds exciting. I wanna go."

"Of course. The Enigma can't go without his partner." Luke glanced up at Talisa with a hopeful puppy face. Janie and Teddy followed suit.

Her glare was only for Luke. "You have the nerve to ask me anything after how you embarrassed me up there?"

Luke shrugged. "Just making some observations. You don't have to be embarrassed in front of me."

"I wasn't..." Talisa thought through her options for finishing the sentence and didn't like any of them.

Luke addressed the kids again. "How old are you?" He pointed at Teddy.

"Twenty-two."

He directed his finger at Janie. "How old are you?"

"Twenty-one." She bounced with her knees on the couch

while using her index finger to make a motion like she was slam dunking a basketball.

Luke spoke to the air in the room. "Okay, now listen up. Even though you two are both of legal age, and even though this is the most fun a person can have at a sheriff's office, which happens to be an extremely safe environment. And not least of all, even though we have the chance to put away an especially bad man," he paused before continuing, "I would never consider letting you go without the express permission of the one and only person whose opinion matters." He glanced over his shoulder at Talisa. "Ms. Tee, our fate is in your hands."

Talisa's emotions were a turbulent storm, a mix of malice and mirth, cloud and sun. "You are such a manipulator. Why do I let you in this house?"

Luke displayed a crushed look, resting his chin beside his badge. Holding the position, he spoke into his chest, "Go get your purse. You know you want to come."

Talisa shook her head, a slight smile forming. "Wait in the car. I'll be out in a minute." Luke's head came up, and the kids cheered. She pointed her finger at Luke. "Don't call me Ms. Tee. You have not earned the right to call me that."

He bowed his head. "As you wish, Miss Hollenbeck."

As Luke and the kids went to the door, Talisa started back toward the bedroom. After she turned away from them, she allowed herself a broad smile.

Just as the door was closing, she heard Luke call out. "Might want to change again."

She stopped, face scrunched, fists clenched. *I'm going to kill him.*

Chapter 7

Wearing a conservative, dark blue pantsuit, Talisa stood on the observation side of a one-way mirror. Janie and a female sheriff's officer named Liz stood with her. The officer had been nice, but she still wondered if Luke had put her up to complimenting Talisa on her outfit.

On the other side of the mirror, Luke was interviewing an unpleasant-looking man. He was dirty, with greasy hair and a scraggly beard. He glared at Luke with a defiant scowl. Luke sat in a rolling chair, so he could move in and out on the man while the suspect's chair was stationary. The rest of the room was empty except for a partition in the corner.

Luke was talking. "This isn't about whether you caused the injuries to Mrs. Morgan or not. That part of the case has already been established."

Rodney sat back and crossed his arms over his chest. "Now see, I don't get how you come off telling me 'it's already been 'stablished' 'cause I didn't do this. You got the wrong man in here. I don't mind talking to you 'cause I got nothing to hide, but you need to quit saying it's already 'stablished 'cause it ain't stablished a tal. There ain't nobody can say I was there because no one was there 'cept...I mean I wasn't there." The man shifted his legs back under his chair and bounced his right foot. He brought one hand up and leaned his mouth against his fist.

"Listen," Luke said, "I feel bad about this whole thing. I don't think you're a bad guy. They're calling you a little old lady beater, but that's not fair. I think this just went down before you knew it. Surely you didn't want anything like this to happen. And I told my boss that we didn't have to bring in—" Luke looked away with a deep sigh. While his face was turned away from Rodney, he gave a quick wink toward the mirror.

Invisible to the men in the room, Talisa, Janie and Liz watched the interaction.

Luke turned back to Rodney. "I know you've heard of Teddy Baskins."

Rodney wrinkled his forehead and narrowed his eyes. "The Enigma." He grunted. "He's a freak or something."

"You know what he can do." Luke leaned in toward Rodney with a concerned look. "I don't like to use him, but sometimes my boss makes me."

"I thought you were the boss. Ain't you the sheriff?"

"Everybody has a boss. I want to keep this between you and me. When someone starts messing with a man's mind..." Luke lowered his head and moved it back and forth, then looked back at Rodney. "...it ain't right. You never know what can happen."

The words "you never know what can happen" were Teddy's cue. Talisa watched as he tiptoed out from behind the partition and crept up on Rodney.

In reaction to the words, Rodney dropped his hands to his lap, and his leg bounced faster. "Yeah," he said frowning at the floor.

Luke leaned in and touched Rodney's leg. The man looked up at him. "I didn't want it to be like this." Luke glanced over Rodney's shoulder and widened his eyes in a look of fear at the moment Teddy touched the man on the shoulder.

"Whoa!" Rodney leaped away from the touch and sent his chair clattering to the floor. Luke threw himself between them to keep anything from happening to Teddy, but he made it look like he was protecting Rodney. Teddy had the most menacing look on his face. Talisa rolled her eyes. What had they created? She smiled despite herself.

"Mr. Baskins," Luke was saying, "Rodney and I weren't finished yet. Could we have a few more minutes?" He had his hands on the man's shoulders and looked with desperation into the man's eyes. "We weren't finished, were we?"

"I ain't talkin' to him. You get him out of the room, and you and I can talk." Rodney demanded.

"Just ten more minutes," Luke pleaded with Teddy who moved to the door. He gave Rodney one last intense stare and then stepped out.

Luke picked up Rodney's chair and steered the man to the seat. Rodney plopped onto the chair, and his arms hung to his sides. Luke sat and pulled in close.

"You know what they say. Baskins only needs one touch. You know we know what happened. But, just as important to me is why it happened. I don't think you're a bad guy. I'm guessing you just got caught up in this thing, and before you knew it, it was out of control." Luke leaned even closer. "You didn't plan for this to happen, did you?"

Rodney hung his head. He looked like he might cry. "I never meant for it to happen at all."

Luke put his hand on the man's shoulder in a comforting gesture. "I knew you weren't like that, Rodney. You're not a bad guy. I want to turn this around for you as best I can. I can't promise anything, but it would mean a lot to Mrs. Morgan if she could get her things back. Where are those things now?"

"They're in a hole behind my house. I put a piece of plywood over it and then stacked hay bales on it like..." Rodney seemed to be nearing the limit of his ability to articulate. "...a haystack."

While Luke kept encouraging more information out of Rodney, Liz said, "I gotta go get a warrant to search for that hole. It will be a little hard for Rodney to say he didn't beat up that lady when we find all her things right where he said they would be. You guys can wait in Luke's office while he finishes up. Tell Teddy he did a good job as usual."

***

"So, did you feel anything when you touched Rodney?" Luke leaned across his desk toward Teddy.

Teddy shook his head.

Luke frowned in frustration. "If we could find a way to control this, make it happen when we need it." He sat for a moment in contemplation, then his grin returned. "But we still got a confession. Good job." He tousled Teddy's hair, leaving the young man looking elated. "Okay, ice cream time. You two go wait in the lobby. I need to talk to Miss Hollenbeck for a minute."

It caught Talisa by surprise. *What are you doing, Luke?* Her breathing increased as she watched the kids walk out.

When the door closed, Luke gazed across the desk at her. "Thanks for letting Teddy do this. It really works with some of these guys."

"I don't own Teddy. He likes to help. The reputation it gives him doesn't please me, but it's good Mrs. Morgan will get her things back. It's a relief to hear she's going to be okay."

Luke studied Talisa. "How are you doing?"

"Fine."

"That tells me nothing."

"Maybe it tells you that this isn't a good time to talk

about it. I don't need to come out of your office with red eyes, and I don't need to go out for ice cream that way either."

"Sorry. I hadn't thought about that. I worry about you." The concern in Luke's voice brushed gently against Talisa's heart.

"I'm making it through." She crossed her arms over her chest. What was it about this guy? Every time she thought she was over him, he would do something that made her think he cared. But not this time. Not going there again.

"I'd like to see more for you than 'making it through.'"

"I'm sorry my life isn't one long clown parade like yours."

Luke didn't react. After a moment, he said, "If you ever want to talk..." Luke's worried expression morphed into something she couldn't read. "I mean as a friend, I'm sure we can find the right place and time. We've known each other most of our lives. You don't have to do this alone."

Talisa moved her gaze to the wall, determined to hold back the emotion. *That's it, Luke, be careful. Don't let your pity for your old friend get you entangled again.* Once she had her composure, she leaned toward him. "You don't talk. You laugh and joke and make fun of people."

He leaned back in his chair and raised his eyebrows. "Only when they're funny."

She shook her head at him. "Well, sometimes *that's* not funny."

"You know it's been years. You could try forgiving me."

Oh, that's rich coming from the man that just walked away when I made a mistake. She avoided looking at him. "For what?"

"For whatever you're still hanging onto."

Talisa inspected the opposite corner of the room. "What could that be? I'm not hanging onto my dreams because you were right. They were crazy. And I'm not hanging onto my parents because they're gone." Talisa's eyes bored into Luke for a moment. "I'm not hanging onto anything anymore."

When she was finished, it was Luke that looked away. He slapped his hands on his legs. "Okay, well I wanted you to know that I'm concerned and I'm praying for you. Even if I can't help, I know God can." He gave her his friendly smile again.

Yeah, go ahead and grin. You almost had me. God, I don't know if he's doing this on purpose or not, but I need him to stop. While he's praying for me, would You please tell him to leave me alone. "If you're taking the kids for ice cream, we'd better get there before your next big case, Sheriff. I'll follow you."

***

Luke watched Talisa pull out of the parking lot behind him. *God, please help me. Watching her be torn up like this is killing me. I want to support her, but it always comes out like I'm still after her. Am I that transparent? I don't have any trouble fooling these criminals to get a confession, but I can't fool her. Maybe inside, I keep hoping there is still a chance.*

He could see Talisa in the rearview mirror. She was too far behind him for her to see anything but the sun's reflection off his rear window. Her face still captivated him. He imagined her smiling at him again like she used to. But he had to keep his mind on his driving, and he knew it wasn't right, looking at her that way when she didn't feel the same.

Lord, You're going to have to help me get rid of these feelings because it's obvious I can't do it myself. She wants nothing to do with me. She's putting up with me for Janie and Teddy's sake. I thought we could at least be friends, but that's not working. All I seem to be doing is harassing her. Maybe he should leave Havilah and Gilead County for good. He could get on with the State Police and move to Tulsa or somewhere on the other side of Oklahoma.

I feel like I need to help with Janie and Teddy, so I can't walk away. Besides, You've shown me that running away is not what You want me doing. But this is so hard, being around her. Why did all this have to happen, her folks, Teddy, Janie? God, You keep throwing us together. Is there something here I'm not seeing? You know, Lord, sometimes I don't understand You at all.

Chapter 8

On the drive home, Talisa tried hard to get Luke out of her mind. When she left the parking lot of the Arctic Summer Ice Cream House, she could see him in her rearview mirror, sitting in his Tahoe, watching her drive away.

Seeing him cut up with Janie and Teddy over ice cream always brought a smile even if she didn't feel like one. She had even laughed a little. That's when she had a flash of insight. *He's trying to get along with me for Teddy's and Janie's sake.* It was honorable. She was being selfish. Janie and Teddy needed him. She needed to let the past go and try to be friends. *Talisa, you're so stupid. That's all you want is to be friends. You don't want him fooling you, acting like there could be more. Isn't this the clarity you've been hoping for? Luke's fun. Why do you keep torturing yourself, trying to make something else out of it, getting your feelings hurt over a little teasing?*

When they arrived home, Talisa saw Sawyer walking up the hill from her house. By the time she climbed out of her car, he was striding in her direction with a large bouquet of flowers.

"Hello, neighbor," he called out. "I brought you something to tide you over until you can get started planting."

"Sawyer, you're doing too much. But they are beautiful."

"Hey, looks like someone has been out for ice cream." Sawyer eyed the cups in Janie and Teddy's hands.

"Luke took us," Janie informed him as she headed for the house.

Teddy smiled at Sawyer. "We can't tell you why."

Sawyer narrowed his eyes." "Ooo, mystery and intrigue is it?"

Teddy nodded.

Talisa let out a nervous laugh. "The sheriff had them helping around the office."

Sawyer's eyes darted from the house where Janie waited at the entrance, then back to Talisa. "Do you want me to take these in for you?"

"Sure." Talisa hurried to the door, fishing in her purse for her keys.

Sawyer talked as he followed along behind her. "Someone told me your father built this place himself."

Talisa took in a quiet breath. "With a little help from family and friends, but mainly it was him. My mother was always there, doing what she could, but she started needing more rest at that time."

"I heard about her disease. I'm sorry."

"Things happen in life." Talisa bent her head over her purse for a moment and pushed the items around inside to be sure she had her composure before she looked up. *Don't blow this, Talisa, by falling apart.* "That's the reason my dad bought the marina and built this place. It gave him a steady income and allowed him to be home with her, especially later when she needed him the most."

"He sounds like he was quite a man. I wish I could have

known him better. Maybe I could have helped. One thing for sure. It sounds like he loved your mother the way a man should."

Talisa had her keys out and was unlocking the door when he said it. He was so close behind her she could smell the scent of the bouquet mingled with his cologne. His voice was deep and sensitive. A tingle went through her.

"Tee!" Janie's voice was in her ear.

She jerked her head to face her sister and saw Sawyer backpedaling to make room.

Janie's brow scrunched. She whirled to face Sawyer. "You need ta go."

"Janie, that's rude."

Janie processed Talisa's words, "Oh." She addressed Sawyer again. "Thank you fo' the flowers. Goodbye."

"Janie!" Talisa took her sister by the shoulders and moved her out of the way. "Stop it. What's wrong with you?" Keeping one hand on Janie's arm, she said, "I am so sorry about this. She doesn't always understand social situations."

Sawyer shook his head and smiled, mouthing the words, "It's okay," while he studied Janie's face.

A sideways glace showed Talisa that her sister was rotating her head in frustration and staring at the sky.

"It's Teddy," Janie blurted.

"What?" Talisa peered at Teddy who stood behind Janie, watching with wide eyes.

"Someone needs Teddy's help." Janie took Teddy's hand and pulled him toward Talisa. "Tell her, Teddy."

Teddy took in a sharp breath, and his eyes looked into nothing. Then his face grimaced, and he clenched his stomach with his free hand. "Someone's hitting me." He rocked back and forth at his waist. "Owwww."

Janie petted his head. "It be okay."

Talisa moved in. "Who is it? Who's hitting you?"

Teddy seemed to be looking through her.

"Teddy, what do you see?"

"He's got a tattoo all over his neck, like a snake. My hair keeps getting in my face." Teddy's hair was unruly, but too short to fall into his eyes.

"Can you tell where he...where you are? What do you see around you? Are you inside or outside?"

"I see trees. I can feel water on my feet. Uff!" Teddy doubled over. "I never should have gone with him. If I can get away, I can run to Pony Park and get help."

Pony Park? Talisa ran the name through what she remembered of the area. Pinto Pony Park? "Teddy, is it Pinto Pony Park?"

"I don't know." Teddy squeezed his eyes shut and clenched his teeth.

Janie caressed his head. "Huwwy, Tee."

"Sawyer, call 911 and tell them it's an emergency, and the sheriff needs to call me right away."

Sawyer pulled out his cell phone and dialed, then stood watching the scene with the phone to his ear. In a moment, he was talking to someone.

Talisa's attention reverted to Teddy. "Do you see anything else?" The park brought back memories of summer fun. She and the gang going to– "Can you see a rope swing?"

Teddy seemed to force his eyes open. He nodded. "I skinned my knee when I was swinging. He was holding my leg, then he started to–" Teddy flailed his arms, pushing at an unseen attacker. Janie held on tight, tears in her eyes.

"Talisa," Sawyer was calling her. "They were able to transfer me. I have the sheriff on the line. I told him about Pinto Pony Park. He's heading that way, but he wants to talk to you."

"He's on your phone?"

Sawyer nodded.

Talisa held out her hand, but Sawyer pushed a button and said, "Sheriff, go ahead. Talisa can hear you."

Talisa moved closer to Sawyer and listened.

"Talisa, I have you on my handsfree. What's he seeing?"

"Listen, remember the old rope swing on Swope Creek? It's across that field from Pinto Pony, so it's not that far on foot."

"Okay, I know what you're talking about. That's right off Samson Giles Road. I'm closer to that than I am to the park."

Talisa could hear the revving engine of Luke's Tahoe in the background.

Then he came back on. "Does he have any idea what's going on?"

"It sounds like a man assaulting a woman. He said the guy had a tattoo like a snake all over his neck."

Luke gave a heavy exhale. "Not him again. I hope I can get there. The last little girl wouldn't testify in the end."

Teddy was crying out, "Please don't. Please stop it."

Janie lowered him to a sitting position on the concrete. She sat also with her arms around his head. "Tee, can he 'top? Can he 'top?"

"Yes, if he can stop it, tell him to stop. Luke knows where he's going."

Janie eased Teddy down until he was laying on the driveway. "You can 'top." She sat back and bit her knuckle.

Teddy inhaled, swelling his chest, and shuddered.

"Is okay, jus' bweave, jus' bweave." And Teddy did, heaving his chest up and down. Gradually his breathing slowed.

Talisa's eyes were on the pair, but her ear was on the sounds coming from Sawyer's phone. She heard Luke calling on his mobile radio and having backup meet him at the location. It seemed an eternity of engine noise, clunks, metallic groans, and Luke's hands slapping the wheel. Tires slid, and the vehicle was shifted into park.

"Okay, I'm here."

"Be careful." *Please keep him safe,* she prayed over and over in her mind.

The door opened and slammed. The sound of running and Luke's heavy breathing. Branches scratching across fabric. Then it all stopped except the breathing, creek sounds in the background. In the distance came a high-pitched shriek that grew into the sound of a woman screaming, pleading, begging for her life. Then running again. The screaming got louder.

Luke's voice came so loud into the microphone it made Talisa jump. "Get off her!"

A thud and a groan, the sound of something hitting the ground, the smacking of skin against skin. Rolling, scuffling.

Then someone was again pleading, "Get off me." This time it was a strange man's voice. "You're hurting me." The voice spat out curses.

"Get your hands behind your back." It was Luke. Then the sound of ratcheting metal. "Give me your other hand." Another thud. Perhaps from a knee. "Give me...your...other hand...now!" Luke gave a grunt of dynamic exertion.

"Uuuhhh." The other man moaned in pain, then they heard the second cuff go on.

"Stay there." Luke's voice held menace. "If you get up, I'm gonna hurt you." Then it softened. "It's okay. Are you injured?"

There was the rustle of something against Luke's uniform and whimpering close to the mic.

Luke spoke like he would to a frightened kitten. "It's okay. You're safe now. You're gonna be all right."

Chapter 9

"That was the most amazing thing I have ever seen." Sawyer watched Teddy who was lying on the couch, his head in Janie's lap. She stroked his hair and eyed Sawyer.

"How do you feel, son?"

"He not you son."

"Janie!" Talisa could not understand her sister's behavior. "She's very protective of him, isn't she?"

"I can hear you. I'm wight here."

"Janie! If you can't stop being rude, could you please go to your room."

Sawyer held up his hand. "It's okay. Today was very stressful. I can understand that she might see me as a threat because I was here when it happened."

"That may be, but there is no excuse for this behavior. Janie, please apologize to Mr. Kincade." Talisa knew her sister was not stupid. She knew how to behave.

Janie furrowed her brow and lowered her head. "Sowwy."

Sawyer gave her a gentle smile. "I'm sorry, too, Janie. I should not have talked about you like you weren't here. That was also rude. Forgive me."

Talisa tipped her head and caught Janie's eye.

Janie inhaled. "It okay."

"Do you mind if I ask Teddy a question?"

She glanced at Talisa's stern face. "You have to ask him."

"Teddy, may I ask you a question?"

Teddy sat up. "Okay."

"Does it still hurt where you got hit…where you felt the girl get hit?"

Teddy shook his head. "I kinda remember what it felt like, but it doesn't hurt now."

"Okay. Here's another question. When Talisa asked where you were, you described the area. Were you able to look around or were you just seeing what the girl was seeing?"

"Just seeing what she was seeing, I guess."

"You said that if you got away, you could run to Pony Park. Could you hear what the girl was thinking?"

"I don't know, I just knew it."

"Did you know about Pinto Pony Park or did she?"

"I don't know. No difference, I guess."

Talisa was amazed at Sawyer's insight, things she had not even thought about.

"So, when you were…when it was happening, did you know everything that she knew, or did you have to go looking for information?"

Teddy cocked his head and appeared to be thinking. He threw up his hands. "I don't know. It feels like I knew what she knew. I felt really smart then. I liked that part."

"Do you know it now?"

"No," Teddy said, hanging his head just a little. "Now, it's just me."

Janie stood up and rested her hand on Teddy's shoulder. Her eyes implored Talisa. "Please Tee, no mo questions. Teddy tired."

She was right. Teddy's shoulders sagged, and his eyelids

drooped. "Sawyer, maybe we should call it a day."

Sawyer didn't answer. He stared at Teddy, preoccupied, then shifted his gaze to Janie.

It was obvious Janie didn't like him. *What is her problem?* Sawyer's gentleness with Teddy impressed Talisa. How patient he had been with Janie's animosity. What was keeping her sister from seeing that he was trying to help? Here was someone who might be able to walk them through understanding it all. Maybe even help Talisa cope. She thought Janie had gotten past all of that.

Talisa noticed something more. There was something about Janie's face that she had never seen before. It was the lack of something. The way she looked at Sawyer didn't seem like the Janie she knew. There was an innocence that was missing.

Janie told Sawyer, "Tee talkin' to you."

Sawyer straightened up. "I'm sorry. I'm sure you're tired. I didn't mean to wear everyone out."

"Oh, please don't think that," Talisa reassured him. "It isn't you at all. I think it's been helpful to analyze all this. We've been a part of it for a while now, but I'm sure it seems strange from the outside. I can't imagine what you must think of our bizarre family."

"I think you have a very special family. There are connections here that I have never seen in all my practice. Not that I think of you as some clinical study. Anyone would envy your family, and they should. I also understand the significant risk of Teddy being exploited. So it's wise to be cautious. I hope I can earn the privilege of getting to know you all better. But right now, I should let you rest."

Talisa saw him to the door where he shifted and put his hand on her shoulder. "You live in a unique situation, Talisa. I'm sure it is as challenging as it is rewarding. I know these special people are in good hands, but be careful and don't burn out. If you ever need to talk, you know where to find me."

"I'll look forward to that."

She took her time closing the door, watching the handsome doctor walk away. Then Talisa returned to the living room to have a word with Janie. Teddy lay asleep on the couch. Janie had curled up in an armchair and appeared to be sleeping herself. She couldn't help but wonder if Janie's was a sleep of convenience.

She thought Janie had grown past all the sensitivities and anxieties that were a part of her syndrome. Why was it that now, when Talisa had the chance to form a relationship with a caring, understanding man, her sister was acting strangely? The scene played back in her mind. *This whole thing is strange. How could we not need therapy?* Maybe Sawyer was what they needed, an expert of the mind and emotions. Perhaps Janie was afraid of what was trapped inside of herself, and she knew Sawyer could bring it out.

Chapter 10

The man went by "Hiss." Luke had dealt with him many times before, and he was as repulsed as ever. But Luke played the game. He had Liz take care of the juvenile Hiss had attacked. The girl had been in a bad way when he pulled Hiss off her. Well, "pulled" might have been softening things a little, so he told the man he was sorry for having to get rough with him, assuring him that he was going to help him through the booking process as painlessly as possible. And he did, snapping the mugshot photos with lighthearted kindness.

"I still can't get over that snake tattoo," he told Hiss. "The neck's a tender spot. Most people can't endure pain like that. Gotta admire a fellow that can take it like a man. Did Tooley do that one on you?" Luke loved it when criminals got tattoos, the more unusual and prominent the better. Nothing identified a bad guy like a highly visible tattoo.

Hiss nodded. His scowl softened a little as Luke chatted with him.

"That's one thing I appreciate about you. I never have to worry about you whining like a little girl whenever we scrap a little. Most guys I get in here are like, 'Oh, you hurt me, Sheriff. I'm gonna sue you.'" Luke acted like all the bellyaching and threatening that Hiss had done on the ride to jail never happened. "But not you. Like I said, you take it like a man."

The snake painted crook stood a little taller. "I know you're just doing your job. Thanks for letting me talk to my mom. She'll get me bailed outta here."

"What are mamas for." Luke shrugged at Hiss. "I know you ain't scared of those guys back there," Luke motioned his head toward the thick metal door that separated the booking area from the main cell block of the jail, "but you probably got things to do."

Hiss raised a half smile in Luke's direction and licked his lips. "You know this charge ain't gonna stick. That little girl and me was just play'n. She's scared right now, thinkin' she's gonna be in trouble. She'll tell you later, Sheriff. It's all good. You're wasting your time doin' all this."

You keep on thinking that. Luke nodded in response to Hiss' statement. "You know how it is. We do our job and let it sort itself out. Like all this paperwork, just something we gotta get through." Luke acted like he was checking another mundane item off the form in his hand as he asked Hiss, "You remember the rights I read you out there at the river, about remaining silent and everything, right?"

"Yeah, I know those by heart."

Good, Luke thought. *Then your lawyer won't be able to say you didn't know what you were doing when you tell me what I need to hear.* Luke knew that one of the things that was not required in criminal procedure was for the girl to "press" charges. Maybe Luke could talk the county prosecutor into filing against Hiss even if the little lady backed out.

Luke gave Hiss an understanding look. "But I do know what you're saying. Girls that age get scared. If I'm getting you right, though, you're saying that she was the one that started getting rough? I'll bet that surprised you from somebody that young."

"Oh, yeah. You should have seen her."

Luke shook his head. "You know, no matter how long I do this job, something is always surprising me. I'm sure you never expected that out of a fifteen-year-old girl. Before long, it's not even going to be safe to be around a thirteen-year-old."

Hiss was all agreement. "You know it. Sometimes the younger ones are the nastiest."

Luke wrinkled his brow. "Boy, I can see how bad things can happen to a guy. I'm sure, after this, you've probably decided to stay away from girls as young as this one."

"You got that right. But, you'll see. She ain't gonna press charges. It'll be just like last time."

Luke nodded as he went through the booking checklist. In his mind, he had another checklist, one with all the possible reasons that Hiss' lawyer might use in court to get him out of any of the many charges Luke intended slap on the criminal. By the time Hiss' mama got him out, Luke intended to have as many things checked off as possible. On his mental list, he crossed out the excuse that Hiss might not have known how young the girl was when he was enticing her to go to a secluded spot with him. He had just let the criminal wipe that one out with his own words.

Luke's smile broadened knowing the digital recorder on his belt had lots of storage space. He let his grin rest on the tattooed man in front of him. "You know, Hiss. I don't care if I do have to arrest you once in a while. I like you. You're easy to talk to."

Hiss shrugged. "Yeah, you, too."

"Come on. We can talk while we're getting your fingerprints. We don't want to keep your mama waiting when she gets here."

***

It was taking Luke a long time to finish the report. Every time Teddy was involved in a case, it became more complicated. Always begin with the end in mind, and in law enforcement, the end was in court in front of a lawyer asking questions. *How did you know this crime was occurring, Sheriff? What led you to the river that day, Sheriff?* Luke wanted to type, "An act of God." Instead, he had to spend pages establishing Teddy as a "reliable" informant. *This officer has been involved in numerous situations in the past in which Mr. Baskins has given reliable information concerning crimes in progress. On this date and that date, Mr. Baskins informed me of such and such, which led me here and there, where I discovered one thing or another, and responded in the following manner, and this occurred.*

It didn't matter that the judge had heard it all before, he was forbidden by the rules of evidence from ruling based on personal information. He could only act on the evidence that was presented to him in this specific case. And Luke had to present it every time. Much of the narrative on past incidents he could cut and paste from earlier reports, but he always had to tweak it to fit each specific case.

Also, it didn't matter that everyone in Gilead County knew about "The Enigma." He had to write his report for any higher court that might review the case, courts full of skeptics that had never seen the miracle that was Teddy's gift.

And people wonder why I spend so much time in the office.

But he had another problem. His mind kept wandering. *Talisa Hollenbeck.* He kept telling himself, *That ship has sailed.* But for Luke, she was always sitting there on the horizon, beautifully trimmed sails and sleek lines with a precious cargo of hopes and dreams that he longed to share. He remembered her, full of faith and compassion, ready to take it to the world. Now, she seemed battered and broken, and it broke his heart.

He had fought his own spiritual battle when he joined the Marines. Talisa was so much a part of his life that when she wanted to leave him behind, his world shattered. It shook his confidence in himself as a man and made him wonder if God was angry with him.

The Marines provided a method to run away, get lost in the discipline and routine. He practiced his faith, having Bible studies with the other soldiers and attending services when he could. He laughed and joked with his buddies, same old Luke on the outside. But he never told anyone how often he hoped that God would just let him be killed on the next mission. When he came to the end of himself, he realized the lesson God was trying to teach him.

Lord, please, I don't ever again want to let anything be greater in my life than You. I felt like Janie and Teddy needed my help, but maybe I should have stayed out of it. Maybe I'm just making excuses to be around Talisa.

He was finding it hard to be honest with himself. He thought he could laugh it off, just keep things light between them. That wasn't working. Talisa didn't want anything to do with his teasing anymore. But ribbing her was what Luke always went back to, back to where things felt right.

When it came to her psychiatrist neighbor, joking was what he could do to keep his control. Surely, Talisa could see through the guy. Or maybe he was reading too much into the situation. The more Luke was around Sawyer, the more he didn't trust him. The whole thing with the Agnew woman grew more suspicious all the time. Luke was beginning to wonder if Sawyer had done something to her. But then he had to ask himself if he was just jealous. The doc was a respected psychiatrist who frequently worked with law enforcement. Maybe Luke's suspicions were his imagination wanting the poor guy to be a criminal, so he would have an excuse for coming between him and Talisa. It was getting harder to keep his job and his feelings separate, and that

wasn't good.
Please, God, I can't see my way through this. I need Your wisdom.

Chapter 11

Talisa left Teddy and Janie to nap and walked outside. The evening was drifting in on a warm breeze. The summer sun sagged over the lake but still had over an hour to go before it painted the water and sky. Several ducks bobbed on the slow rippling surface out past the marina as Talisa headed down the hill. A large spoonbill jumped with an impressive splash. It was the kind of evening that would have found her and her father sitting on the dock, lines in the water, watching the sunset.

He's gone. We'll never do that again.

The ache started in her stomach and pulled down on her shoulders. Talisa drew her arms into her body and squeezed, trying to force the pain away. *Lord, please help me. I don't want to lose another day.* She couldn't touch it. It was deep inside, out of reach. She wanted to run back to her room and hide. *It's Janie's room now,* she countered. But she couldn't muster the strength to fight. *Daddy, where are you? I can't do this without you.* He couldn't be gone. It wasn't real. She didn't even get to say goodbye as she had with her mother.

There must have been some sign that she missed.

Something in his eyes that day when he left. The image of her father floated in her mind, but it was fuzzy and indistinct. A horrible realization shoved everything else out of the way. She couldn't remember his face. How could she not remember him? There was no way she could forget, no way. Why didn't she go with him? It would never have happened if she hadn't been so tired from helping at the church. *God, how could You let this happen when I had just been at the church? How could You? Why don't You just take me, too? I don't want to live anymore.*

Talisa had said it. The thing she had sworn would never come to her mind. *God, I'm sorry. Please don't let this happen to me. I don't want to think that way. Please.*

The odor of something delicious cooking on a grill touched her nose. Under the canopy that covered the patio overlooking the docks, an unruly mat of hair was bent over something on a barbecue. Desperate, Talisa headed that way.

His back was to her, and the hair nodded approval of what he was turning with a metal spatula. He returned the cover and turned to the prep table. Talisa scraped her shoes on the concrete walkway to announce her approach.

The hair rose from looking at the table and allowed the eyes to see her, which alerted the smile on Welch's face. "Miss Hollenbeck. You are just in time. I told the Lord I would put on an extra steak, but He would have to bring someone to dine with me. I couldn't think of a more pleasant companion than you this fine evening." His smile collapsed. "You look upset. What is wrong?"

"Noth—," Talisa started to lie, but she couldn't manage it. Her head sank, and her body shuddered as she attempted to hold back a sob.

Dr. Welch hurried to her and, encircling her shoulder with a thick arm, he led her to a table and eased her onto a seat. "Can you tell me what is wrong?"

Talisa shook her head, clenching her teeth behind her lips to hold it in. Her body shook again.

"You are grieving. But, if you will forgive my saying so, you are doing it poorly. It isn't healthy to hold this in. I've been in your place. The only answer is to cry. You must let it out and let grief run its course. There is no one here but me, and I am all too familiar with these kinds of tears. Let us mourn together for we have both lost someone dear, and our lives will never be the same."

Dr. Welch sat across the table from her and took her hands in his. The man began to cry, and Talisa released a sobbing, body-shaking keen that continued in wave after wave. Tears wet the table as steaks sizzled on the grill.

***

The last charcoal-encrusted sirloin spun through the air toward the water below the patio and joined its fellows with a splash. It sank to soften into an expensive dinner for aquatic fine diners of the underwater neighborhood surrounding the dock.

"I'm so sorry." Talisa apologized for the fourth time.

"Miss Hollenbeck, no need to apologize. A shared grief is as good as a feast. Look at me. Do you think missing a meal is anything but a service to this body? Now tell me truly, don't you feel better?"

Talisa smiled through moist eyes and nodded. "I have been trying to cry less when I should have been crying more."

"It's a common mistake. I made it myself at first. The tears hurt, but eventually, they heal. I have done a whole study of the physiological effects of tears during my own dark period. Tears release toxins that are a byproduct of grief and depression. They literally do cleanse the body. The process of crying itself is stress relieving. It releases leucine-enkephalin, an endorphin that improves mood and reduces pain. If you criticize yourself for crying. You can cancel out the benefits. God gave us tears for good. Accept them and appreciate them."

"Thank you so much," Talisa told Welch. "You've been a Godsend."

"Now that is praise I can accept. I am sure that is exactly what this evening has been. And look, we now have a breathtaking sunset to complete the Father's plan. Would you care to join me down on the dock to watch it?"

"I would love that." Talisa gathered herself off the patio chair, and together they walked to the bench at the end of the pier. They sat marveling at the changing colors. "My father and I used to do this. It's why he built this bench. We would talk for hours, and I used to swim while he sat. With Daddy, I always felt closer to God. I used to float on my back and look at the sky while the water moved me up and down. It was like God was rocking me."

After a moment, Welch slapped his hand on the wooden armrest. "Well-done construction. It's an art to make something comfortable out of hard material."

Talisa regarded Welch out of the side of her eye. "An observation or a lesson?"

"A thought for our lives, perhaps. For him who has ears to hear or a posterior to appreciate."

"Mine has been feeling a little kicked around lately. But then again, I guess my ears have been stopped up, also."

"Depression is a self-centered occupation. No offense intended. I speak from my own experience. But I know the look, and I suspect we are comrades in arms in that battle."

Talisa nodded. "Just before I joined you tonight, I was thinking about my daddy, and I couldn't remember what he looked like." The confession brought more crying, but it soon subsided.

Welch was quiet for a moment, his eyes focused on some other time. "I don't think the images we have of people are important. They are an opaque representation of the individual at best, and at worst a distortion. It is easy to make the memory into what we would want the person to be instead of celebrating the life that our Father permitted us to interact with for a time. Whatever comes to our minds is our own manufacture, and our mental constructs can never compete with God's creation."

Talisa pushed her hair behind her ears. "It feels wrong to forget details about someone you love so much. I'm glad I'm not the only one this happens to."

The man gave a deep sigh. "I have come to accept the graininess of human memory as a gift, lest I ever mistake it for the real person that I once knew." Welch shifted on the bench toward Talisa. "And, in our blessed situation, the people that we will one day know again. And then we will know them more fully than was possible in this world." He leaned in to give her a gentle elbow to the side. "Where seats are softer and posteriors more resilient."

Talisa's face softened. "Thank you."

"This has been beneficial to me as well."

Talisa nodded again. Inhaling, she shifted the topic. "I wanted to talk to you about Teddy."

"Now, my dear, don't let your gratitude lead you to violate your conscience concerning Mr. Baskins."

"Well, it is more about my sister, Janie. She and Teddy are *special* friends. I use that term because they have a common bond in that they both have special needs. Janie was diagnosed with Fragile X Syndrome, and Teddy is a Willie. He has Williams Syndrome. Since you are doing studies in these areas, I suspect you are familiar with the terms."

"I am. Both syndromes can result in various levels of developmental disabilities and medical issues. Fragile X is perhaps the more challenging of the two. Willies usually have the benefit of being happy and optimistic. They get along well with people because they are always trying to please."

"That's Teddy. He's been a blessing to our family because he brings those traits out in Janie as well."

"They are special people. That is what has drawn me to this research. Both syndromes are characterized by a heightened level of sensitivity. There is so much of the mind that we do not understand. The human brain has far more storage capacity and computing power than can be explained by simple electrical interaction. It is believed that the brain is a quantum computer. As I told you earlier, I wonder if this might be where the spirit-mind connection exists. Mind you, this is just a theory at this time, and I have yet to explore it fully. I've developed a hypothesis that when the mind doesn't have the normal abilities, perhaps God allows it to reach deeper into the quantum realm to compensate. That could sometimes enable abilities such as Teddy's gift. It would be just like the Lord to allow someone with a disability to serve a special purpose in His plan. Have you ever noticed any such abilities in your sister?"

"Not really. Nothing like what happens with Teddy."

"Excuse me. I didn't mean to bring things back to Teddy's gift. Tell me about your sister. Was there something that you thought I might be able to help with?"

"Forgive me if I ask something outside your field. I know you're not a therapist or a specialist in this area, so if this isn't something you feel comfortable answering, tell me. But I wanted to know what might cause someone with Fragile X to act unusual around a certain person. You know, unusual in a negative way."

Welch considered. "There is always the possibility that an individual's voice or mannerisms might adversely affect a person with sensory processing or sensory integration issues, such as can be present in Fragile X."

"Is it possible to change that?"

"I know studies are being conducted on mice that have been genetically altered to mimic human Fragile X syndrome. They hope to learn how certain drugs might help with hypersensitivity to sound. Currently, though, most of this is experimental. Is this a significant problem with your sister?"

"Today it was. It's been a long time since I've seen her act like that. It was embarrassing."

"It is my understanding that individuals with Fragile X are often prone to anxiety. Is there something about this person that might make Janie anxious?"

"I don't think so. He…seems nice. I thought he was very patient with Janie."

"Still, perhaps it might be best if Janie could avoid that person. Is it someone that she has to see frequently?"

"Well, no. Not at the moment."

Dr. Welch regarded Talisa. "But there is the potential this person could become a more regular part of her life?"

"I'm not sure. Janie is a part of my life, and I think I will always need to care for her now that our parents are gone. I don't think she could ever live on her own. And if this person became a bigger part of my life… You can see the problem."

Welch's unmanaged hair went up and down. "It sounds like you might be faced with a difficult decision."

"For a long time, I've known that Janie's care might someday be my responsibility. It's not like it's a burden, but I never imagined it would come so soon or force me to make such a choice."

"Might I suggest we pray about it."

"Absolutely. I would appreciate it."

Talisa started to bow her head when she noticed Welch gazing open-eyed to the horizon.

"Father," he began, "thank You for this marvelous sky You created from the interaction of a million different components reacting chemically and thermodynamically—simple beauty from complex ingredients. Lord, my friend, Talisa, has a complex problem. I pray You can give her a simple perspective. Make things clear to her in Your way and Your time. Build the answer for her as we speak. You moved heaven and earth for Your children, defying sin with grace and conquering death with resurrection. Please do it now, again, for her. In the name of Jesus, Amen."

Talisa's eyes were raining again. "Thank you. That's what I have been praying—that God makes things clear to me."

"The Bible says that God knows what you need before you ask. It is only natural that He would lead us both to pray about it."

"It's neat to see that. Well, I'd better get back and check on Janie and Teddy. I left them napping. I'll have to call Teddy's parents again and put him in the guest room. I think he spends more time at our place than he does at home."

"How do his parents feel about that?"

Talisa surveyed the area to be sure no one could overhear. "To be honest, they always act like they're glad. Like I told you, it has been quite an ordeal for them. They aren't—how shall I say it—socially experienced people. They haven't handled it too well."

"Teddy is lucky to have your support."

"He's part of the family now."

"A rare family indeed."

"That's funny. Someone else recently said something similar."

"I hope they meant it as kindly as I did."

"He seemed to. Now if I can just get my rare family to like him."

"God repeats things for a reason. So perhaps He plans to give you clarity about your rare family."

"That would be awesome. I know He got me out of a bad depression tonight, thanks to you." Talisa reached out her hand to Welch.

Shaking it, he said, "Good night, Ms. Hollenbeck."

"Please, call me Talisa," she said as she turned to go. As she made her way up the hill, she told him, "I'll try to bring Teddy down to meet you sometime."

"When you feel comfortable, Talisa. When you feel

comfortable."

Chapter 12

It was well past the end of his shift when Luke left the office. He sat in his Tahoe for a moment, thinking. Taking out his phone, he searched through his numbers and pushed *call*.

A friendly voice answered. "Pastor Cooper speaking."

"Pastor, this is Luke Sanders. Have you got a minute?"

"Of course, Sheriff. What can I do for you?"

"If you're not busy, I was wondering if you had a little time for me to stop by and talk?"

"Sure. We just finished a late dinner. Knowing you, you're probably still at work and haven't eaten yet, so if you hurry, you might get here before Maddie starts putting things away."

"Well, okay. When you hear the siren approaching, just open the front door and stand back. I know my way to the kitchen."

***

Pastor Ross Cooper sat in an armchair and watched as

Luke leaned back on the sofa and engaged in serious food digestion. "You know," he said, "I'm a preacher. Most people give me the courtesy of letting me start to talk before they fall asleep."

Luke used the fingers he had interlaced behind his head to lift it enough to look at the pastor as he spoke. "Here's an idea. If your wife cooked breakfast each Sunday, you'd never have to worry about anyone breaking the Sabbath. Cut your counseling in half also. By the end of your sermon, everyone would be relaxed and well rested."

"Hold on a minute," Pastor Cooper pretended he was scribbling on his hand. "Let me write that down. Never let my wife feed people before I preach. You know, it's amazing what they don't teach you in seminary."

Luke forced his body to sit up. "So, speaking of the mysteries of women, Pastor, I need some advice."

Pastor Cooper chuckled. "You'd better go back to sleep because you must be dreaming if you think I have the answer to that."

"Well, at least you got one to cook for you. That's a start."

"Yes," Pastor Cooper smirked at Luke, sarcasm in his voice. "One of the many benefits of marriage. You might look into it. It's kind of like having a caterer on retainer. There's a little more to it, but I'm just hitting the highlights here."

"See, I knew we were thinking along the same lines. I tell you what, I'll just give you the girl's number, and you work things out and tell me when to show up for the wedding."

"They tried that back in the dark ages, but there was a high level of female dissatisfaction."

"Figures."

The pastor settled back into his chair with a shrug of his shoulders. "I love the way we're focusing this session. Let's see, it's June. At this rate, I should still have time to prepare for next Easter's service. Let me ask this. This cook you're looking to engage, and I use that word in all its fullness, does she have a name?"

"Pastor, if you don't know the answer to that question, then you don't know me very well."

The Pastor gave a sad smile. "Talisa Hollenbeck?"

Luke grimaced. "Am I wasting my time?"

"Why do you ask that?"

Leaning back on the couch again, Luke pondered the question. "I guess she got tired of me, and I don't know if I'm fooling myself, thinking that's going to change somehow."

"What makes you think she's tired of you?"

"She started going after someone else."

The pastor thought for a second. "I don't see her with anyone. Why isn't she with that person now?"

"It wasn't any one person. She just seemed to be flirting with other guys."

"That sounds more like a person looking *for something* than a person who found *someone*."

"Maybe. But it sure wasn't me she was looking for."

"Maybe that's your problem."

Luke gave Cooper a sideways glance. "Pastor, this is starting to feel like one of my interrogations, except it's upside down. I get the feeling you have some information I need, but you're asking all the questions. And, now you're telling me things I already know."

Pastor Cooper sniffed a laugh. "That could be because you're the only one who can answer your questions."

Luke looked bewildered. "Then we're in trouble because I know less every minute."

Cooper sat up in his chair. "Let's start with one of the misconceptions people have about relationships. People are not looking *for someone*, people are looking *for something*. They are looking for something that meets their needs. They look *in* people to find that something. So, if you want to be the person that Talisa is looking for, you must possess the qualities she needs *in* a person."

"Okay, I guess I don't have that, so we're right back where we started."

"Not exactly. Once you know what the other person needs, you can develop those qualities *in* yourself. You can make yourself the person she is looking for."

"Bam," Luke said. "Back to the beginning again. How do I know what she needs?"

The pastor gave him a penetrating look. "I'm going to give you the secret. Are you listening?" He leaned forward. "Here it comes, pay attention."

Luke smiled a little. "I'm ready."

The pastor sat back in his chair and folded his arms. "Obviously not."

Luke looked at him sheepishly. "I really was listening."

The pastor's smile returned. "Then how did you miss it? I told you the secret."

Luke's face was blank.

"What was the last thing I said?"

Searching his memory, Luke finally responded with uncertainty, "Here it comes, pay attention?"

"Exactly."

"I didn't hear anything after that."

"There wasn't anything."

Another blank look from Luke.

"The secret is to— *pay attention.*"

Luke grinned and dropped his head. "You're good at these games."

"It's all for a good cause because women are like that. They will tell you what their secrets are, what they need. But you have to *pay attention* because it can be buried in a hundred other thoughts and emotions they are communicating. A woman may be complaining about your not picking up after yourself, but what she is really communicating is that she wants you to notice how hard she works around the house. You have to pay attention to learn what the real issue is. To learn her."

Frustration covered Luke's face. "You can see how good I was at that."

Pastor Cooper took in a breath and heaved it out as he said, "Like you said, it all comes back to the beginning, your original question. Are you wasting your time?"

Head sagging, Luke looked up at his counselor. "Don't suppose you could take it easy on me this time, could you?"

"Sure. Think about this. If you don't love Talisa enough to spend the time to learn these things—to learn her needs—you're wasting your time, and hers. Better move on and let her find someone who loves her that much."

Luke was digesting again. After a moment he said, "Pastor, I'm never taking you to the shooting range with me. Your aim's too good."

The other man gave Luke a twisted smile. "If it's any consolation, I shoot myself in the foot about half the time. I do have some tips for you that might help."

"I'm all ears, but I'll probably still miss 'em."

Cooper gave a calm shake of his head. "This part's easy to hear. It's the doing that's hard. Whenever you're having trouble, the first thing is to check how you're praying. Any relationship you care about, should be getting frequent prayer. And I don't mean to pray that she changes to make you happy. Pray that God helps you to be the man He wants you to be so that you can cherish her and put her before yourself. When you fail, be a man, treat it like everything else you work so hard at. Don't wallow there, get back up and get back in the fight." The pastor grinned. "But don't fight."

Luke rubbed the stubble on his cheek. "Pastor, why do you think God made relationships so hard?"

The Pastor's face softened. "I think you're blaming God for something we do to ourselves. When we start deceiving ourselves and others, we set ourselves up. Then sin comes in and gets in the way. We also let our emotions rule us.

Emotions are God given, and they are useful and wonderful if we control them and don't let them control us. If we allow ourselves to get our feelings hurt, we end up striking out at the people we love the most. That's why I don't think I would give up on Talisa just yet. You might be experiencing some of that."

Luke nodded in thought.

Pastor Cooper continued. "Talisa is suffering from grief. Don't try to make light of that. Remember the second half of Romans 12:15, *Weep with those that weep.* It takes time to heal from heartache like what Talisa has suffered. You may not always be able to understand her, and you're not going to be able to fix it. Just tell her that you love her and you're sorry she's going through so much pain. If you're sincere, that can carry you through a lot of tough times—with God's help. We're men, so we may not be able to empathize with everything that a woman feels, but we can sympathize. Often, that's enough."

Luke hung his head and shook it. "I'm not saying I'm giving up, but it's enough to make a man wonder some days if it's possible to win."

The pastor gave him a deep look. "Perhaps you need to kill yourself."

Luke could feel his own wide eyes divulge his shock. He had never told anyone what he had felt in those dark days after he walked away and joined the Marines. Could God have shown the pastor something so intimate, and if so, why now when the Lord had taken him past all that?

A smile spread on Cooper's face. "Bet I have your attention now. You won't miss this part. Ephesians 5:25 says, 'Husbands, love your wives, even as Christ also loved the Church, and gave Himself for it.' Christ died for the Church. If you want to love a woman as Christ loved the church, you have to give up your own life and invest it in her. If you keep that in mind, it makes the stings much easier to bear. Rest assured, she will be absorbing painful barbs from you also. If you've already decided to die for the other person, it makes it harder for offenses to hurt. Dead men feel no pain."

Luke smirked, "I guess I'm only half dead then."

Pastor Cooper returned the look. "It's amazing what a righteous beating God can give that old sinful man inside us and he still keeps kicking." The pastor leaned forward. "Remember how Jesus taught us to pray, 'forgive us our trespasses as we forgive those who trespass against us.' You forgive her, she forgives you and then God will forgive you both and help your relationship flourish. There are going to be times when you're not treated fairly. Guess what, there are times she won't be treated fairly either. Ask God to let you see that side of the equation—what you do that hurts her. That's the secret of surviving and improving all your relationships. In the end, you can't control what the other person does. The only real way to influence people is to control what you do. If you work on that, and give the rest to God, you'll be surprised what happens."

The two men sat in silence for a while.

Luke stood and stretched. "I appreciate it, Pastor. I'd better get home, but you've given me quite a bit to work on. Maybe after a good night's sleep, that is."

"Just don't take too long," Pastor Cooper rose with a look of mock seriousness. "We can't keep feeding you forever. You need a full-time cook."

"Hey, don't close the kitchen too soon. At this point, I'd be lucky to get a cookie."

Luke started toward the door. Then he looked back at his counselor. "You ever thought about law enforcement, Pastor? I could use another good interrogator."

The man shook his head. "If I quit pastoring, what would I do for excitement?"

Chapter 13

The gray transport van traveled the dark highway leading into Havilah from the Oklahoma Mental Health Detention Center. Trees surrounded the road, reflecting the van's headlights, causing the sensation of driving through a tunnel. Driveways flashed by giving a brief view back into the foliage where lights from an occasional structure played peek-a-boo with the van as it passed. Intermittently, the moonlight sparkled on the waters of Lake Gallant at the end of a side road before it vanished again, behind the wall of trees.

The driver reached up and wiped sweat from his forehead again. He hoped the dash lights were not enough to allow the young man in the seat beside him to see how quickly the perspiration reappeared. The man wore a uniform that matched his own. It was fortunate the kid was a well-fed Oklahoma country boy, otherwise the pants and shirt would be too small for the switch. The young man was lost in his own world, watching the trees go by.

The driver glanced in the rear-view mirror that he had adjusted when he had first climbed into the van. In the glow of the security light aimed at the rear passenger seats, he could see the occupant that inhabited that area of the van, separated from the front seats by metal mesh. The wrinkled, bald head stuck out of an orange jumpsuit like an old apple on a traffic cone. The driver swept his arm up and rubbed the back of his head in a gesture that could be seen even from the rear seats. He watched the furrowed face make a slight upward movement in acknowledgment.

"Ooooh," the old man moaned. "I'm gonna be sick." The driver saw him vanish from the mirror's view as he doubled over in the seat.

The kid turned around and looked at the man through the mesh. "What's wrong?"

The man groaned and breathed in gasps.

The driver called back to him, "Don't you throw up in my van."

"I can't help it." The old man moaned.

The side road that the driver had scouted a few days earlier was coming up. "Just hold on. I'm going to pull over."

The young man glanced at the driver in astonishment. "You think we oughta do that? We'll be at the hospital pretty soon. Let him throw up there."

"That's another ten minutes. You wanna clean up a bunch'a puke outa that back seat? 'Cause I ain't gonna do it. 'Sides what you think that redheaded nurse's gonna think of you if you bring in some old geezer that's blowin' chunks all over?"

The driver turned onto the road and drove into some wisps of fog coming off the lake. The kid scanned the dark trees as if something might be waiting there for them. The road opened to a lonely clearing with an unused firepit in the middle. From the vantage of the van seats, they could see above the overgrowth that marked the edge of the lake. Moonlight drifted on the water through breaks in the fog. The driver maneuvered the van so trees blocked them from the view of the road as he aimed the headlights at a trail through the brambles.

He grabbed a flashlight as he jumped out of the driver's seat and rounded the van to the sliding door.

The other man climbed out as well and surveyed the surroundings. "I don't know. The LT always says we ain't supposed to stop 'til we get where we're goin'." The kid was taking out his cell phone.

The driver covered the phone in the young man's hand. "That's why we ain't gonna tell him." He smiled at the kid. "What he don't know won't hurt us."

The driver opened the sliding door and climbing inside, unfastened the old man's seat belt. "Get out before you spew."

Still grabbing his stomach, the elderly inmate shuffled his hobbled feet to the door. The two gray-uniformed men grabbed him by the arms and helped him down. The younger man scanned the area again for any threats.

"Come on. Don't spoil the campsite for anyone." The driver pulled the old man toward the trail through the brush that led to the water. "You can throw up in the lake, feed the fish. You might as well be good for somethin'."

A flock of grackles perched in the dark trees above. Each bluish-black head, darker than the night itself, turned a golden eye, reflecting the vehicle lights that had invaded their quiet setting.

A gunshot scattered the birds in every direction. The sound of winged bodies flapping through leaves and branches mixed with the echo of the blast.

The noise ceased, and the night was again dominated by the humming of the van engine. After a while, a splash. Later, the two gray uniforms emerged. The driver returned to his position behind the wheel of the van, and the other man climbed in on the passenger side.

The wrinkled, bald head, now perched on the gray uniform, turned to the driver. "We never discussed anything like that."

"Did you think we were just gonna leave him tied up somewhere to tell the whole story to someone when he was found or got loose. We'll take responsibility."

"Like that's gonna make any difference now."

"No other way." The driver glanced at the old man. "We ain't leavin' any witnesses."

"Yeah, well I kinda feel like I just witnessed that."

"Relax. Not much we're gonna do without you."

"Not yet anyway. Why are you keepin' both the guns?"

"I feel safer that way. At your age, you might shoot me by accident."

The craggy face considered him with a twisted smile. "It ain't accidents you're worried about. And I don't blame ya." The old head motioned forward. "Let's get movin'. Where do we meet 'em?"

"You'll find out tomorrow."

"Tomorrow?" The old face scowled in shocked disapproval. "We need to get out of the state—tonight."

"We can't leave yet. We'll lay low tonight and meet them tomorrow. He's got to pick up something first."

"By then, this whole place is going to be crawling with cops and marshals. What could he need to pick up that's worth hangin' around for that?"

"Something very special." The driver's smile was more of a sneer.

"Why can't he get it tonight? Ain't nothing worth us all ending up back in prison."

"No one's going back to prison. But he decided this is something he can't leave without, and we're with him on it. It's just gonna take a little creative motivation to make it happen."

The old man chewed around his mouth with his government-issued dentures while he evaluated the younger man. "Just remember, you'll be on the other side of the bars this time and I know some people on that side that ain't too fond of you. Let's forget the others, and you and I light out tonight. I'll make it worth your while."

The driver peered at the old man for a moment, then shook his head. "We're sticking with the plan. Don't worry. He knows how all this works. Knowing everything the cops and the marshals are going to do will be the easy part. If there's anyone that can make this happen, it's him. If he says wait 'til tomorrow, that's what we'll do. So relax. Until then, we've got a safe place to hide out. And remember, you still owe us."

The old man faced front and settled into his seat. "Don't worry, you'll get paid." He took in a breath and adjusted his shoulders. "As long as we don't get caught."

The driver reached up and adjusted the rearview mirror. "Our chances of avoiding that are better if we stick with him. Just be patient."

The old man smiled. "Kid, you're wastin' your breath. I didn't sit this long in prison without learnin' patience. You got me curious enough now to wait 'til tomorrow just to lay my eyes on something that's worth this kind of risk. Let's get to that hideout."

***

"You could use my drag to throw out there and hook it and bring it in." Monty Iverson's hand was gently rocking his fishing boat back and forth. With a loud "smuck," he pulled one of the boots on his waders out of the ankle-deep mud where he stood a few yards from the bank. He then shifted to the other leg and repeated the process in the same way he had been doing since Luke had motioned him to shore.

On the bank, Luke stretched and rubbed at the last of the sleep in his eyes before pulling on the second leg of his own waders. He paused and gazed at the fisherman who stood in the middle of the pre-dawn glow reflecting on the water.

"Monty, this ain't some trout. One of the things we like to look for are wounds. I don't need any help inflicting any that aren't there already." Luke shook his head at the man as he pulled the suspenders over his shoulders.

"You know I'd help you." Monty shifted again with another smucking sound. "But I ain't never touched a dead body before."

"It's okay. All I need is to borrow your boat. When the coroner gets here, we'll bring it in."

"Does it have to go in my boat?"

"We'll put a tarp down and then put it in a bag. It won't touch your boat." Luke watched Monty doing his mud dance. "Right now, I want to go out and take a look for myself before he shows up."

Monty glanced back at what looked like an old rag snagged on the end of a downed tree that was lying about twenty-five feet out into the water. "But I just bought this boat. This is only the second time I've had it on the lake."

"It's a bass boat, not a show car. It slides around in slime all day. Now, look out. I'm coming out there."

"Don't the Sheriff's Department own a boat?"

"They do. And it would take me over an hour to have a deputy go get it and haul it back here. You wanna wait around here all day, or you wanna get this over with and get back to fishin'?" Luke was wading into the water as Monty's face became a scowl.

"Couldn't keep my mind on fishin' after this." Monty inched his boat away from Luke.

Luke stopped and tipped his head back. "Monty, you gonna let me borrow that boat or am I gonna have to confiscate it?"

The disgruntled fisherman pulled the craft toward Luke like a man handing over what he lost in a bet. "What's the difference?"

Chapter 14

As the Sunday sun rose, Talisa was up early, plans percolating in her mind. Pete's Peat also operated a greenhouse that he called "Grown Ups," and they were having a Memorial Day plant sale. Her plan was to do a friendly neighbor drop-in before they went to church and take Sawyer a housewarming gift of the cookies she and the kids made the night before. She made an extra-large batch, having prior experience with Teddy's other talent—making her cookies disappear.

While she was dropping off the cookies, she might happen to mention that she was going plant shopping tomorrow, and since Sawyer was helping with her garden, maybe he would like to join her. If that worked out, perhaps she could work it into them sharing the garden space and doing some planting together. They could talk, get to know each other. Talisa daydreamed of warm summer weekends spent with her hands in warm soil with Sawyer beside her, sharing her dream. Helping her work through her depression.

Then she realized that she didn't feel depressed. She'd been so excited about the day's prospects, she didn't noticed that for the first time in months, she was not battling the blues that had become such a part of her life. She slept well with no dreams. The absence of gloominess was almost foreign. It made her pause. She felt like something was missing, like she was forgetting something. *Talisa, you've been going through this for so long that you can't even enjoy feeling better.* She felt a sudden twinge of guilt. *Sorry, Lord. I should be thanking You. Forgive me.* Her conscience was talking to her again. *I suppose I should invite Sawyer to go to church with me.* She thought he had said something about attending a church out of town. *I don't want to scare him off by making him think I am trying to get him to change churches.*

She shook it off and started getting ready, spending time making sure she looked her best without making it obvious. When she was satisfied, she checked on Janie.

"Hey beautiful, better get yourself up. I've got to run over to the neighbor's. Get yourselves some cereal. I'll be back in a little bit, so be ready for church."

Janie stretched in the bed. "Okay, Tee."

"You can use my bedroom and bathroom to get ready and let Teddy use the guest bathroom." The girl crawled out, grabbed some clothes, and headed down the hall.

Talisa had decided not to tell Janie that she was going to Sawyer's. Better to take things slowly with her sister.

She knocked on the guest room door and heard a sleepy voice.

"Come in."

She peeked in on Teddy. "Time to hit the shower. We need to get the church's number-one greeter there early, so he doesn't miss anyone." Talisa laid a twenty-dollar bill on the table beside the door. "Here's some money for food. You and Janie can walk over to The Ground Up Burgers with the youth group after church. I'm going to step out for a minute. Make sure you're ready by the time I get back."

"If you're late, I can drive in with Janie."

Talisa turned and gave Teddy a stern look. "I'm proud of you for getting your license, but driving here on the back roads is one thing. It is more dangerous to drive into town, especially with someone else in the car. You remember what Luke told you. I don't want Janie in the car to distract you. Don't keep asking, okay?"

"Okay. Thanks for helping me study for the test." Teddy smiled, seemingly waiting for Talisa to return it.

She did him one better, and with her smile, she walked over and tousled his hair. "You're welcome. Make sure you're ready to go."

"Okay. I'll be ready." He accompanied the response with a big yawn.

She gave him a knowing look. "And no more cookies this morning."

Teddy gave a sheepish grin and threw the covers back over his head.

Talisa headed for the kitchen. She still wasn't sure the driver's license was a good idea, but what choice was there if Teddy's dad was going to keep sending him into town without one. That appeared to be the reason he bought the old junker for his son—to have him run errands for him. Like Luke said, it was either help get the license or start arresting Teddy. Even with the weeks that Luke spent with Teddy in the old canning plant parking lot, she was amazed when he made it through the driving test.

Teddy's father was as much of a handicap for the young man as was his Williams Syndrome. If Teddy's parents would let him go to a doctor who could diagnosis his condition, he could work at the Adult Achievement Center with Janie. But Talisa had given up on that ever happening. She was thankful the AAC manager let Teddy mow their lawn while Janie worked there on Saturdays.

Talisa stopped in the kitchen and grabbed the plastic container full of cookies that she had filled the night before.

Then she headed out the door with her gift.

As she stepped into the morning air, a rustling in the trees across the road met her ears, and she caught a glimpse of something large disappearing into the undergrowth. *Must be a deer.* All around, the birds were calling to each other as they drifted through the branches that were silhouetted by the sunlight filtering between them. Feeling lighthearted, she saw Teddy's rusted hulk in the driveway. *If he's gonna drive, the Enigma needs some better wheels. The Batmobile, that is not.*

Talisa paused on the way to Sawyer's and examined her freshly-tilled garden, savoring the smell. Sawyer's tractor was still there. She took a second look. He'd done more work. The tilled area was even bigger now. Soon she would have enough room for some corn.

Only a few bags remained on the trailer, the little white beads of fertilizer all over the ground around it. He must have forgotten that she wanted organic. *Oh, well, at least things would grow well.*

She had not heard the tractor yesterday. He must have done the work while they were at the Sheriff's Department watching Teddy's and Luke's interview. It was the sweetest thing that anyone had ever done for her.

She noticed gouges in the bank where the hillside went up past the clearing to the top of the hill. Sawyer must have needed some fill dirt to level out the garden area. He was a man who did things the right way. She liked that.

Talisa hurried down the hill but took her time up the other side. She didn't want to arrive all sweaty. Pausing at the top of the hill, she debated whether or not to go around to the front door. She took a cleansing breath. It all felt new. *Sawyer won't mind me coming to the back.*

An engine was running. The sound was coming from a storage shed. Inside, a scuba tank compressor was running, working on filling an underwater diving tank. *Just like Daddy used.* When the thought came to mind, Talisa cringed, wondering if the thought of her father would trigger the depression that had been absent from the morning. Instead, she reflected on how much in common she shared with Sawyer. He was a diver also.

This could be something special. She climbed the steps of Sawyer's beautiful deck. Each end sported an octagonal bump out with a gazebo, a round breakfast table under one end and a hot tub under the other. A porch swing sat against the house in the middle, perfect for a long talk. As she walked up to the back door, she prayed one more time. *Thank you, God, for making things clear.*

Talisa reached out and rang the bell, then she took the lid off the cookie container and held it in front of her at the perfect height to let the smell greet Sawyer when he opened the door. Footsteps approached. The door opened, and she was face-to-face with. "Luke? What are you doing here?"

Chapter 15

"I was wondering the same thing about you," Luke stared at the plastic offering she held.

Talisa couldn't move. She felt guilty like she had been caught cheating.

Luke took a cookie. "Really," he stared at the round crisp tasty like he'd found a pearl in an oyster. "Thanks."

Talisa pulled the container back. "They aren't," she faltered, "that fresh. I made them last night. I, um…came to…"

Luke grinned at her, then his expression became serious again. "It doesn't matter," he said. "Whatever it is, you'll have to come back later. We're talking to the doc right now." He rubbed his teeth across his lower lip and made a thoughtful sound with his tongue. He stepped out of the house and closed the door behind him. "We found the woman." He paused. "Don't repeat any of this, but it won't be long before it gets out. A fisherman found her body this morning, floating in the lake about a hundred yards downshore from where her car was parked."

Talisa sucked in a breath like something had grabbed her.

"Now, the doc is saying he thinks she committed suicide. He says he was counseling her for suicidal thoughts, and when he had to reject her, she must have walked to the lake and drowned herself. He says he couldn't say anything about this before because of patient-client confidentiality."

She's dead? Talisa had put the woman out of her mind, satisfied that she must have left town. Now she was dead, floating in the lake all this time, so close.

Luke let out a heavy breath.

She'd been looking right through him, stunned.

He spoke gently. "I wouldn't say this to anyone else, but I don't feel comfortable with you coming over here right now. Maybe this was an accident, or maybe this woman killed herself, but right now it's like you said, none of this fits what Teddy described."

"You think Sawyer...I can't believe that. Is there any proof?"

Luke tipped his head back, as if he was studying her. "Come here." He opened the door and motioned for her to come in. "Just go with me on this."

She followed Luke into the living room where Sawyer was talking to a deputy who was taking notes.

"Doctor Kincade, you have a visitor."

Sawyer glanced at her. "Talisa. I'm sorry, I'm in the middle of this business with that woman again. Did they tell you that she drowned herself?"

Luke spoke before she could answer. "Doc, after you had a chance to witness Teddy Baskins' abilities, I am sure that you understand what an asset he is to us in these types of cases. It's good for everyone. It clears innocent people from suspicion and allows us to focus on the real suspects." Luke paused for a few beats. "What I'd like to do here, if you're willing, is bring Teddy over and let him look over your property, put his hands on things, take your hand for a minute, see what he feels. If Teddy can get that close to where the woman was last seen, he'll be able to tell us what happened here that night. I am sure you wouldn't object to clearing your name from this mess right up front."

Sawyer stared at the sheriff. He glanced at Talisa, then his eyes lowered and contemplated the coffee table in front of him before looking back at Luke. "No, Sheriff, I don't mind, providing that it's only Mr. Baskins. This is embarrassing enough without bringing anyone else into my home."

Luke leaned back and placed his hands on his hips, he seemed to be evaluating Sawyer. He smiled. "I'm sorry, Doc, but Janie needs to come too. They're kind of a package deal. She's Teddy's support through the whole process. He wouldn't be able to do his work without her. I'm sure you don't mind." Luke swiveled to face Talisa. "Ms. Hollenbeck, could you have both Teddy and Janie step over here?"

Sawyer was on his feet. "Sheriff, I do mind. This is my house. You have no warrant, and the only reason you are here is that I have allowed it. I have been cooperative, but I'm not going to allow my home to be the site of some clairvoyant circus."

Talisa took a step back. Was this what Luke wanted her to see?

Sawyer was talking fast and continued, "I did witness the display of Mr. Baskins' art yesterday. As an expert in criminal psychiatry, I have to inform you, Sheriff Sanders, that you have been duped. This is an elaborate hoax. I work at the prison every day with the criminally insane. I know their uncanny ability to manipulate and deceive. I could produce expert testimony to debunk these type of things, not that any of this would ever be allowed in court. I, myself, have been called to give expert testimony in such cases numerous times."

He softened his expression toward Luke. "Sheriff, please don't take my comments as any slight on you. It is obvious that you are an experienced professional, which is why I cannot stand by and watch you be embarrassed by a charlatan."

Sawyer turned to Talisa. "I'm sorry. I had hoped to help you face this slowly. So much of your life has been affected by this that you'll feel like something has been torn away from you. You are an intelligent woman, Talisa. Don't think you're not. The scheme has been professionally executed. No one without training could have seen it."

He continued. "It's not Janie's fault either. She could never understand how she's being used. That is why I don't want her involved any further."

Sawyer addressed Luke again. "It's one thing for Mr. Baskins to come over here and run his hands over a few things, take my hand, and then say he can't feel anything. Isn't that how it happens, Sheriff? It's always his timing, isn't it?"

Looking at Talisa, he said, "Remember how Janie inserted herself right in the middle of our conversation, how insistent she was? Timing is everything in these games—when they know their partners are in place ready to play their part. Sheriff, you said the girls have not testified against your assailant in the past. I'm sure you will find that is the case this time as well. It's nothing for your snake-tattooed friend to have another arrest record because he knows there will never be a conviction."

Luke's face was incredulous, "What would be in it for him?"

"You're not using your imagination, Sheriff. Maybe it was just for fun. Maybe just to embarrass the sheriff. But there might be more to it. You might find this little girl has a good reputation, comes from a good family. Maybe she and her boyfriend made a mistake, and she thinks she's pregnant. How best to salvage her reputation, take the heat off her boyfriend. Your snake-tattooed friend is willing to play the bad guy—he's been doing it all his life."

Sawyer looked at Talisa like he was reluctant to make his next statement. "Maybe the young lovers are able to scrape together a little money for the service of him playing the rapist so the pregnancy could be explained, or maybe the little girl is desperate enough to give him something else. Under the right circumstance, a wealthy family might even pay or be blackmailed to avoid some type of embarrassment. Then get a quiet abortion, completely understandable under the circumstances. There would be no DNA testing, all the evidence destroyed. And, of course, the little girl is too traumatized to go through a trial. And that is just one scenario. There are a dozen different reasons why this type of service might be valuable to someone."

Talisa had to say something. "I can't believe Teddy would be dealing with some criminal. I think you've misread this situation."

Sawyer ran his hand across his chin. "I'm sorry. This is not how I wanted to tell you. What do you actually know about Teddy and his family?"

"I know…" Talisa realized how unprepared she was for the question. "I know there are rumors about his family…having problems where they lived before. But I've been around Teddy. I can't believe he's some kind of fraud."

Sawyer's kind smile seemed genuine. "I know. I'm sorry I have to be the one to tell you. My position at the prison makes it necessary for me to access information that is not even available to law enforcement." Sawyer directed a brief gaze at Luke.

Luke met it. "What kind of information?"

Shifting his attention back to Talisa he continued. "Even for my incarcerated clients, I must keep my conversations with them privileged. It is important for you to know that I would not be revealing any of this except I'm convinced you and Janie are at risk."

The words had Talisa's full attention. The tone that Sawyer used unnerved her. She opened her mouth to ask him what he meant, but he went on.

"I have counseled inmates that have information about Teddy's past."

Sawyer again addressed Luke. "Because of the risk, I am willing to work with your agency and provide records that might help if you can give me until tomorrow to access them. They are secured at the prison, but I can justify limited access in this circumstance. I will need time to redact unrelated patient information. Teddy and his family actually have an extensive history of fraud. They have managed to keep ahead of any criminal convictions, but I think this business about Teddy supposedly having powers shows that things have progressed to a new level."

He faced Talisa. "It would not be proper for me to talk about what I know at length with non-law enforcement, but trust me when I tell you there is real concern. I am even more convinced of that after seeing how your sister acted yesterday. You noticed a change in her behavior, didn't you?"

Talisa's gaze had fallen to the floor. She looked up. "I…yes…but what you're saying is that she is part of some kind of—. Are you sure about Teddy? Maybe that's just his family. I've been there when he's had visions. How could he fake that and why? He has seen things that have helped people in serious trouble. How could he do that if the visions weren't real?"

Sawyer's face conveyed sympathy. "It all hinges on belief, so you're going to start by building your reputation. That could have started innocently. Just a way for an underprivileged kid to get some recognition. Then maybe you do something big, like find a lost toddler. Kids go missing all the time. You see your chance one day when you see a kid unattended. The kid can't talk so he'll never tell. You put him in an old abandoned house or cellar or a hole in the ground."

Talisa was staring at the floor as she spoke. "A well."

"Or a well, that would be perfect. Then you use your amazing powers and he's found. Pretty soon, you're a psychic. But your powers have limits that help keep anyone from being able to confirm or deny their validity."

Sawyer shrugged. "The operation shows clever planning. It serves Mr. Baskins well to play the mentally challenged medium, but I suspect he is much like the people I deal with at the prison, teetering on the edge of genius and insanity."

When his attention returned to Talisa, his face conveyed sorrow. "And when he met Janie, he found his perfect partner. He can ask her to do bizarre things, and no one will think anything of it because of her disability. But for Janie, it's real. Teddy plays the fool while Janie protects him. Like she did against me yesterday. It's a part for which I am sure he has groomed her well. She is being used and doesn't realize it. I fear for her, Talisa. If she ever became a liability to him, or they were exposed, I'm not sure what he might do."

Talisa's imagination came alive. What if it was true? She thought the gift was too amazing to be real, but seeing it in operation had convinced her. It seemed so true. But she had seen magicians do things equally as amazing, and she knew they were tricks. Maybe Teddy was that good. Could he have fooled her into inviting him into her home and letting him be friends with—Janie! She was home alone with him. Talisa spun around to leave and stumbled, grabbing onto the wall to right herself. The accelerator on her heart jammed at full throttle. She ran to the door.

"Talisa," Luke called after her. "Talisa, come back here. I'll go with you. Let me drive you over."

Talisa couldn't wait. She had to get to Janie. Even if there was the slightest possibility...she couldn't take the chance. She couldn't lose Janie too.

Out the back door and across the deck. She leaped, touching only one of the steps on the way down. Jumping and skip-stepping she made it to the bottom of the ravine, then headed up the other side. Talisa pounded the hill like a stair-climber until her legs burned when she reached the top.

She misjudged in her panic and found herself running

across her freshly plowed garden. She stumbled in the rough earth and face planted. The dirt didn't taste as good as it smelled. She did a pushup to her knees while spitting out chunks of the pure black soil. She was up and running again. Panting she came over the rise and held her arms out to keep her balance as she plunged down the slope to her house.

Around the side and her full-throttle heart stalled. Teddy's car was not in the driveway. She glanced at her watch. It was too early for them to have left for church. And Teddy had promised— She dashed across the cement and threw open the back door.

"Janie." She called into the quiet house. Traversing the entry, she raced through the living room. "Janie." Her shout sounded hollow. She ran from room to room—kitchen empty, no one in the bathroom. Back and forth in the hall, each room a heartbreaking, agonizing, uninhabited tomb.

Chapter 16

Anger mixed with her fear. He took her. The liar. Janie was gone, and she had let it happen. They wouldn't leave without telling her...not unless it was true. She didn't want to believe it. She had hoped she was wrong, that Sawyer was wrong, but they were gone. She tried to come up with another reason, some place they might be, but there was none. After what happened yesterday, Teddy must have been waiting for his chance. Had Janie gone willingly?

Talisa struggled to get her thoughts under control. She had to do something. She had to find Janie. *Okay, they don't have much of a head start. Maybe I can catch them.* She seized her purse and fished out the keys as she hurried to her car. In moments, she was tearing down the dirt road.

Would he take her to town or someplace out in the country? What would Teddy do? Was that even possible for her to know? He wasn't the person that she thought he was.

Teddy. She had trusted him. Pastor Cooper, Luke, her daddy—they had all trusted him. He was so active in the church. He seemed so sincere. Granted, his family was a little rough, and no one in Havilah knew much about their past, but could he have fooled them so completely? His disability seemed so real. Teddy made lots of ignorant mistakes. Were they a cover for real character issues?

She reached the blacktop and decided to head away from town. That seemed logical. Why go toward more eyes that could see you?

Talisa tried to think of anything that Teddy might have displayed that she'd overlooked. Something that would fit the profile that Sawyer presented. She needed to start over and recreate his character in her mind, to figure out how he had fooled them. She ran through memories. Times she had laughed, cried, been horrified, amazed. It was still the same Teddy in her mind.

Talisa, how can you be so naïve? Don't even think like Teddy. Think like a smart kidnapper. Okay, I would know that the police would be looking. I would want to get off the main road as soon as I could. But the police were not looking. Talisa had failed to tell Luke that Teddy and Janie were missing. She needed to call him.

Talisa dug in her purse for her phone. It should be right on top. A sign flashed by—Lakeside Dr. She slammed on her brakes sending the purse to the floor. Should she take off her seatbelt to get the purse or make the turn? She cut the wheel hard and let her tire go off the pavement in order to swing onto the other road.

Lakeside Drive was just what it implied. A scenic, narrow blacktop that wound around the lake and connected with other backroads on the other side. It would be the less-traveled road. There would be more chance of leaving the area without contact. The early morning fishermen would already be on the lake, and the family-outing crowds would still be at home getting ready. She wound down to the lake and onto a straight section of road.

Talisa unbuckled her seat belt and leaned for the purse. Lean, lean, got it. Sitting up she had to jerk the wheel to avoid going off the road. She scanned the visible blacktop ahead for vehicles and saw none. Her hand fished in the purse for the phone. Where was it? An awful realization materialized. Talisa pulled into the small parking lot of a fishing area. She emptied the purse onto the seat and pawed through her belongings. The phone was not there.

What do I do now? How do I find them?

Talisa's head filled like a bathtub, thoughts pouring in like water and swirling together in her rattled mind. Where was her phone? Where would they go? Why hadn't she seen the truth about Teddy?

She threw her arms across the steering wheel and buried her face in them. The maelstrom swirled, but one thought floated to the surface and sat in the center. *Teddy is an imposter, he has Janie, and I have no way to find them. I asked You to make this clear, but please, Lord, don't do this to me. Don't let me lose her. I need Your help.*

Tap. Tap. Tap. Talisa jumped and saw someone standing outside her car. Luke's grinning face peered through the window, his large hand rapping on the glass. Talisa threw open the door.

"Where are you go—" was all Luke managed before she threw her arms around his neck and buried her head in his shoulder sobbing. She slid off the seat as Luke wrapped her in his strong embrace.

"He's got her," was all she could manage. "They're gone. We have to find them."

Luke stroked her hair. His voice was gentle. "What happened?"

Talisa sniffed and calmed her racing heart but didn't let go. She felt like she was right where she needed to be. She needed Luke's firm hold on her, on the situation. He would know what to do. And he wasn't letting go. "They weren't at the house. They're gone. He must have taken her in his car. I was trying to catch them."

His voice held sympathetic amusement as he said. "I

didn't know you could drive like that. I could barely catch up with you. You scared me to death when you leaned over and about went off the road. What were you doing?"

"Trying to get my phone to call you."

"I told you I was coming."

"I'm sorry. I thought if I hurried, I might catch them. I was trying to guess which way they might go." She hugged him tighter. "How could he have fooled us?"

"Just because Sawyer says something doesn't make it a reality." There was contempt in Luke's voice when he said Sawyer's name. "Let's not convict Teddy without a trial."

"But it all made sense, and now they're gone."

"Well, the doc made it sound good." Luke's eyes held concern. "He's right that some criminals can become experts at fooling people. I always thought I was pretty good at reading people. Maybe I've been too sure of myself. I've had reason to wonder lately." Luke closed his eyes as if he was praying. When he opened them, he appeared more determined. "Let's try to find them, then we can worry about what Teddy is or isn't. Janie doesn't have a cell phone, does she?"

"No, Daddy would never let her have one. I was going to buy her one but haven't had time."

"Okay, I know Teddy couldn't afford one." Luke pulled away from her, and she let go. He kept his firm, warming hands on her arms as he gazed at her face. His eyes and smile were tender, confident, just what she needed.

"Is there any place they might have gone?"

"We need to call the church and make sure they're not there, but they wouldn't have left until I got back."

Luke gave her his phone. The church secretary said she hadn't seen Janie or Teddy, but she agreed to call Luke's phone if they showed up.

The way Luke was looking at her, she knew worry had to be covering her face.

He took her hand again. "Let's drive back to your house

and start from there. Maybe we might find a clue to where they went. On the way, I'll get on my radio and get the other units looking for them. Dispatch can find Teddy's tag number, and we'll get out a statewide endangered-adult alert."

Talisa wiped her eyes and cheeks with her hands. She nodded, then climbed back into her vehicle.

"Hey," Luke called before she closed the door.

She glanced over her shoulder and saw his big grin.

"You follow me, so we can keep this race fair."

Chapter 17

When they parked in her driveway, Luke's face was somber as he got out.

Talisa hurried to him, feeling the panic rising again. "What is it?"

He shook his head. "Can anything else go wrong in this county? Now a prisoner's escaped."

"What?"

"I just got word. Donald Boggs is missing. He complained of being sick, and a couple of guards were taking him to the hospital in Havilah. They never made it, and neither guard is answering his phone. We have to assume he did something to the guards and he's on the loose."

"What are you going to do?" Talisa had a heart-sinking feeling that Luke would have to leave her.

He must have seen the fear in her eyes because he took her hands and assured her. "I told them I had to work on finding Janie. I assigned my undersheriff to coordinate with the prison officials on assisting with the manhunt."

"Thank you." Talisa wanted to kiss him. The thought

seemed out of place, but she had no time to think about it as she hurried inside. "Donald Boggs, don't I know that name?"

"Million Dollar Don. He's the prisoner they tell all the stories about." Luke searched the entryway landing.

Talisa remembered. "We used to hunt for his treasure when we were kids. People believed he found some lost Native-American gold back in the sixties but was put in prison before he could get it, and now he won't tell anyone where it is. Daddy told me the marina used to be called Million Dollar Marina because it was built on the site of Boggs' old house." Talisa moved into the kitchen, searching for her phone.

"That's him," Luke called from the living room. "He originally got caught with a stolen boat, but while he was doing time for that, he tried to escape and a guard got killed. Now he's serving a life sentence. Otherwise, he would have been out by now."

"Sounds dangerous."

"He's gotta be in his eighties. Makes you wonder how on earth he escaped. I doubt if he'll get very far on his own."

Talisa came into the living room and saw that Luke had a pensive look. "You think he had help?"

He looked like he was considering whether to tell her something.

"What is it?"

"That first night, when the doc told me about the Agnew woman coming to his house, I had no reason to doubt his story. Sounded like something she would do. But when she didn't turn up the next day, I started doing some checking on her. She's the granddaughter of a woman Boggs was spending time with before he was locked up. She's the source of most of the stories about Boggs. She has cashed in on the lure of that treasure more than once. She gets some treasure hunter convinced she can help him find the loot by what Boggs told her grandmother. They wine and dine her all night, and she feeds them all the stories and supposed clues. Then she sleeps it off the next day while they wear themselves out wandering through the woods and hills following all her bogus clues. The little con lives high until they get wise to her. She made a number of people mad, but no one killed her for it before."

"So you still think she was murdered, but maybe it wasn't Sawyer?"

Luke shook his head. "Maybe." He grinned. "It works better if I think the worst until I can prove otherwise. That way I don't get blindsided in my investigation. I don't know yet. But, now Boggs is missing."

"I'm sorry this thing with Janie is keeping you from your other important cases, but thank you so much for helping me." She checked to be sure she had not somehow left her phone in the guest bathroom.

Luke sounded more serious when he said, "You all mean a great deal to me, so I was going to help anyway, but now I'm not so sure the cases aren't related."

Talisa came out and headed to Janie's room.

Luke opened his mouth and ran his tongue over his upper teeth. "There's one more thing I haven't told you."

Talisa stopped.

"The doc is the psychiatrist at the prison. He has worked with Boggs." Luke waited, like he expected a fight.

She had no fight in her. "Are you saying that you think Sawyer might be involved in the woman's death and Boggs' escape?"

"Sawyer's involved in the woman's death by his own admission. We just need to figure out what kind of death that was." Luke frowned. He studied the ceiling like he had a thought, then closed his eyes and lowered his shaking head. "Unless the doc's idea about the woman killing herself after he rejected her was just ego on his part. Maybe you were right about something happening to her after she left the doc's house. Could be we are thinking about this the wrong way round. Maybe this woman used the doc to get Boggs out of prison. It wouldn't be the first time that old man used that fictitious treasure to buy himself some accomplices. Sawyer might not be as hot as he thinks. Maybe Ms. Agnew was after some information that he had, and they spent more time together that night than he's saying. If she was able to get the information, the little scene that you heard could have been an excuse to leave and meet the people and tell them what she'd found out. It's possible that once she passed on the info...she was no longer needed. Maybe she died quick and quiet right after she left Sawyer's." Luke clenched his teeth and gave a frustrated jerk of his head. "I have to admit I never liked Sawyer. I hope I didn't miss something because of that. There are so many connections that must lead somewhere. Now Teddy and Janie are missing."

Talisa brought her hand to her chest. "Could Teddy be involved with Boggs?"

Luke leaned against the wall in a defeated manner. "Who knows? If what the doc said about him is true, he might be capable of anything. It's still hard for me to believe that. If he is, what good would it do to kidnap Janie?"

Talisa froze. She looked at the floor and then back at Luke. "They wouldn't use her as a hostage to make sure they can get away, would they?"

Luke's face looked grim. "It's possible, but I think she would be more of a liability than she would be worth." His face showed regret for what he said. "I didn't mean that the way it sounded. It's just that when you're trying to make a fast getaway, you don't need to be worried about someone that's not in on the plan." Luke seemed to be choosing his next words carefully. "Is there any possibility Teddy could have convinced Janie to be a part of this?"

Talisa grabbed the door jamb to steady herself. "I didn't want to believe it, but I don't know anymore. If Teddy fooled us, who knows what he might have talked her into."

Luke crossed the room and took her arm. "I'm sorry. I'm just thinking out loud. We don't know anything, and it won't do any good speculating until we have more info. Let's get back to trying to find those two. If we can find them, at least we might get some answers to that half of the equation. Did you find your phone?"

Talisa shook her head. She steadied herself with a hand on Luke's shoulder for a moment, then pushed away. "Let me check the bedrooms." She cleared her eyes with her fingers, pushing the emotions aside like Luke suggested. But it was hard to keep out the thoughts.

Her phone wasn't in Janie's new room or her old one. Talisa stepped into the guest room and looked around. She hadn't been in the room since she woke Teddy, so she was sure she had not lost it there. Nothing on the nightstands or the desk. She glanced at the table by the door and stopped. The twenty-dollar bill was still where she had placed it. *If Teddy is a criminal, why would he leave behind twenty bucks?*

Talisa hurried to the master bedroom. Everything was too confusing. Maybe Teddy saw his opening when Talisa left the house and was in a hurry. *Boy, he must have been in a hurry.* Teddy was always broke. His job paid so little. She had never seen him turn down money. Would that make him agree to an offer from Boggs? Then a thought occurred to her. *Maybe he thought he wasn't going to have to worry about money anymore.*

When she returned, she told Luke, "It's not here. I'm sure it was in my purse. Teddy must have taken it. Call it, and I'll listen for it just to be sure."

"We don't want to do that. If Teddy took it, that's good. I can get an emergency trace on the phone's location, since Janie might be in danger. We don't want to call it and give away the fact that we know it's missing. Let them think we're not onto 'em yet."

"What can I do?"

"You don't have another phone, do you?"

"No. But I can borrow Mack's if he's home."

"Great. Do that, and while I work on the trace, call anywhere you think they might go or anyone that might have seen them. While you're at it, see if anyone around here saw them leave. See if Janie looked in distress."

"Okay." Talisa was out the door.

When she was halfway down the hill, she saw that Mack's pickup was not at his trailer. He must have gone into town.

The marina was in front of her, boats lazing in the sun. Several cars were in the parking lot with a few boat owners checking their vessels, preparing for a day's sailing.

Dr. Welch would let me use his phone. She hurried through the marina, asking everyone along the way, but no one had seen anything. She knew it had been doubtful since the house was some distance through the trees from the marina, and the driveway was on the other side.

Talisa ran to the slip where Dr. Welch's sailboat was moored. She yelled as she approached the boat. When she reached it, she pounded on the deck.

"Yes, yes," she heard from the inside, and the boat rocked with movement. She ran around the slip to the side of the craft as Dr. Welch emerged from below with a towel in his hand.

"What's wrong, child?" The man examined Talisa like he was looking for injuries.

"I think Teddy's kidnapped my sister."

"Teddy Baskins?"

"Yes. Did you see a vehicle leave my house a little while ago?"

"I've been getting ready for church in the cabin. I wouldn't have seen them. All I heard was a boat go by. Have you called the police?"

"The sheriff is at my house right now. He wanted me to ask around if anyone had seen anything. I also wanted to know if I could borrow your cell phone?"

"Certainly, but why would Mr. Baskins kidnap your

sister?"

"Let me ask you something, Dr. Welch. Do you think it's possible that abilities like Teddy has could be faked?"

"Of course. More often than not, I would say. You might recall I told you that I am a specialist and have exposed many fakers. Come here and sit down." Dr. Welch motioned toward the built-in benches on the deck of his sailboat as he disappeared below. He returned with his phone.

Talisa climbed aboard and sat across from the man.

His face held concern, "Do you think Mr. Baskins has faked his abilities?"

"I don't know. My neighbor is a psychiatrist who works with criminals, and he thinks so."

"Did he say why?"

"He saw Teddy give information that helped the sheriff stop a rape, and he said it was all a fake set up by the rapist and Teddy. After he said that, I ran home to check on my sister who was alone with Teddy. They were both gone, and Janie never goes anywhere without telling me."

"What does the sheriff think?"

"He said not to convict Teddy without a trial, but he's not sure either. He's trying to track them right now and said to wait until we find them."

"Sounds like good advice."

"I know. But what if Janie's in danger? Is there some way to tell if something like this is fake or not?"

Dr. Welch leaned back against his cushion and took in a breath. "Well, this psychiatrist has an advantage on me, having seen an actual event. But it sounds like your sheriff saw this happen as well. It has been my experience in dealing with frauds of this type that the world of psychiatry is more easily fooled in these cases than law enforcement. Granted your neighbor sounds like he has more experience than most dealing with the criminal mind, but police are a rare breed. Over time they develop an intuition about criminal behavior that education can never equal."

"Luke didn't actually see it," Talisa said. "He was on the other side of it. We told him over the phone what Teddy was saying, and he caught the rapist."

Dr. Welch nodded as if putting everything together. "So, Teddy, as you call Mr. Baskins, was able to tell you the exact location that the attack was occurring?"

"I figured it out from the things that he was seeing."

"And what was it that Teddy told you?"

"He was at the river and said the victim was thinking about getting help at Pony Park. I figured out that meant Pinto Pony Park, and I knew about a rope swing hooked up over the river near there. It's a common place for kids to hang out. We did it when we were young."

"Was Mr. Baskins familiar with this location? Did he mention seeing a rope swing?"

Talisa considered the question. "I don't think so. I went there with my high school friends. I never took Janie there, and Teddy has a phobia of water. He told us he had a bad experience when he was little."

Dr. Welch's brow bent toward his eyes. "Seems like a stretch for him to know you could put that all together. If this was part of a plan, it appears he left much to chance. He would have to know you well."

Talisa lowered her head. "I'm afraid he would." She looked up again. "That's exactly what scares me."

"There is another thing to consider. While Teddy might have faked this *gift*, didn't you tell me that he had been diagnosed with Williams Syndrome? That would be much harder to fake, impossible if it were verified through DNA testing. Who told you that Teddy had Williams?"

Talisa thought for a moment, then breathed out, "Teddy."

Dr. Welch patted her hand. "Do not despair. Why did you need to use my phone?"

"Luke, the sheriff, wants me to call around and see if anyone has seen them."

The man handed her the phone. She dialed a number, then

stood up and paced the deck as she waited.

"Pastor Cooper."

"Pastor, this is Talisa Hollenbeck. I know you're about to start church, but this is important. I was wondering if you have seen Janie or Teddy?"

There was a pause. "Not since Friday night at your house after the tribute. You sound upset. What's wrong?"

"I think Teddy might have kidnapped Janie. They're gone, and…something just came up that…I'm not sure we can trust Teddy anymore."

"What? Why would Teddy…?"

Talisa related the events to the pastor.

He was silent for a few moments. "I wonder if…now I feel terrible. I guess I should have…" His voice trailed off.

"What is it, Pastor?"

Another thoughtful pause. "Teddy came to me a while back and asked me a strange question. I had a hard time following him, but he wanted to know if it was all right to let people think you were someone special when you weren't, even if people wanted you to be special. At the time, I just wrote it off as Teddy being Teddy and feeling unworthy like we all feel sometimes. I encouraged him by saying that God gave us all different gifts and not to worry about what people thought, but just try to please God. I never thought…but he did mention something about thinking he might hurt Janie. I just thought he meant 'hurt' her like disillusion her."

Talisa collapsed on one of the boat seats and started shaking.

The pastor's voice was coming from the phone in her drooping hand, "Talisa, I'm so sorry. If I had any idea—"

After several sobs, she said, "I know, I know. It's not your fault. I just don't know what to do now."

"Have you called Luke?"

"He's working on trying to find them right now."

"How about calling Teddy's folks? They might have an idea where to look."

Talisa recovered. "Okay, that's a good idea. I'll try that. I'll let you go, Pastor."

"Okay. We'll be praying."

Talisa dialed the Baskins' home number. How should she handle the call? Even if the family were frauds like Sawyer said, she saw no advantage to confront them.

The phone picked up after two rings. "Hello." Talisa recognized Arnie Baskins' thick accent.

"Mr. Baskins, this is Talisa Hollenbeck."

The man responded with, "Miss Talisa, that boy o' mine's a man now. If he wants to stay at your place, that's up to him. Ya'll don't have to be callin' me every time. T'ain't necessary."

Talisa jumped in. "Teddy's not here, Mr. Baskins. I was wondering if you knew where he was?"

"Well, no, I don't."

"Has he been home today?"

"No, I ain't seen him."

Talisa considered how to proceed. She didn't want to accuse Teddy to his father, but she decided Janie was more important. "Mr. Baskins, Janie and Teddy are gone, and I'm worried that Teddy might have taken her."

"Well, that might be. We all know, they's like peas in a pod."

He didn't get it. Talisa was going to have to spell it out for him. She decided to act like it was only Teddy she suspected and not his family. "I'm worried Teddy might have been fooling us. I'm not sure I can trust him with Janie anymore."

There was a huff on the other end of the line. "What's that boy done?"

Talisa ran things through her mind. What could she say? Even if Arnie Baskins wasn't a criminal, he was not a man to put any credibility in the opinion of a psychiatrist. "It's just that we were going to go to church, and now they're gone."

"Well if they don't want to go to church, we can't make

'em. They's grown. Truth be told, I been talkin' to Teddy about being his own man. Maybe he decided not to go today."

Talisa didn't like the sound of that. "What do you mean, 'be his own man?'"

"I told Teddy he needed to be gettin' him a real job. You know, I been workin' a regular job since I been sixteen years old. I know he a little slow and I 'preciate you helpin' him out and all, but it's high time for him to get on with his life. He been causing this family a mess a trouble with all his shenanigans. We still get people callin' here, but none of them want to pay Teddy to study him. I just hang up. I told Teddy that power for seein' things was okay when folks was in trouble, but it ain't gonna make a livin' for him. Matter of fact, I let Teddy know that he needed to be gettin' him a place of his own soon. I can't afford to be feedin' no grown man if he ain't bringin' nothin' in. Sometimes you just gotta kick 'em outta the nest."

Talisa was shocked at the revelation. She knew the Baskins had suffered through all the people wanting to research Teddy's gift for various reasons, but she didn't expect Mr. Baskins to give up on his son. "When did you tell Teddy that?"

"Been a few weeks now. I don't think he's been looking a'tal."

"Okay. If you see Teddy or Janie, could you call the sheriff right away? I'm worried about them."

"Sheriff? The sheriff involved?"

Oh what have I done? Should she have told him Luke was involved? It could be good, scaring him into giving up some information. Or, it could be bad forcing him to do something desperate. Either way it was too late to lie now. "Yes, he's trying to find them."

The line was silent. Then Baskins said, "Miss Talisa, I know yer sister's a little simple, but if y'all are accusin' Teddy of takin' advantage of her, I gotta say the same thing about her—she's a grown woman, and that boy of mine would do anything for her. I never seen 'em doin' nothin' but holdin' hands, but if they decided to go somewhere together, well…it's like I said, they's grown."

Talisa tried to keep her anger under control. Who was he calling simple? And for him to insinuate that this was in some way Janie's fault—. "I'll let you go, Mr. Baskins."

Talisa hung up the phone. She took a couple of breaths. *Arnie Baskins is the one who's simple. How could he throw out his own disabled son? He can't expect Teddy to be able to—.* Realizing what she was doing, she changed her thinking. She no longer knew what to expect out of Teddy. A few weeks ago, his dad told him he needed to get out. Yesterday Sawyer questioned him. Maybe Teddy got desperate and thought he had to act. How would he know to go to Boggs?

You're thinking like he has special needs. What if he doesn't? What if he and the Agnew woman were working together? Luke said she was a con artist. What if they developed the persona to make his gift look real?

But what would he do? Would they go somewhere else where Teddy could fool a whole new group of people? And one nagging thought kept coming to her. How much did Janie know? It was overwhelming, but Talisa determined she had no time to be overwhelmed or depressed or emotional. She had to find her sister.

Dr. Welch stood and climbed into the cabin area of the boat as he talked. "I'm not sure I have enough information to determine if Teddy is a fraud. But I do have a suggestion." The man came back on deck, leafing through a book. "I want to read you something."

Talisa recognized the book as a Bible.

"King David had many enemies." Dr. Welch found the verse. "Some of them in his own family. He would be able to sympathize with your situation. Here is what he said at the beginning of Psalm sixty-four."

Dr. Welch read, "Hear my voice, O God, in my prayer: preserve my life from fear of the enemy. Hide me from the secret counsel of the wicked."

The man peered up at her, a sweet smile encircled by disheveled hair. "I don't know if you are facing 'the secret counsel of the wicked,' but I see you have fears about that. Let's do what David did and pray."

And they did. Dr. Welch prayed for Talisa's fears to be quieted, the truth to be revealed, and the innocent protected. Talisa prayed for Janie's and Luke's safety and for them to know one way or another about Teddy.

They prayed until Talisa heard the rattle of the metal walkway and looked up. Luke spotted Talisa and hustled toward her. He appeared frustrated. "They're doing some kind of repair on the cell tower, so it will be a little bit before they can give me a current location. The storm caused some issues last night. I came to get you because I need to check something out, and I knew you would be worried if you came back and I was gone." Luke nodded to Welch. "Good to see you again."

Talisa stood. "I forgot you met Doctor Welch the night we heard the scream. Did he tell you he is a professor at OSU and an expert on people like Teddy?"

The professor extended his hand and connected with Luke. "A better explanation might be to say that my current fascination is in the biophysics of the brain. If Mr. Baskins is a legitimate phenomenon, he might help us understand some of the more interesting abilities of the human mind."

Luke nodded. "I would like to understand all of that myself. Teddy has helped me a number of times. It would be nice to apply it when needed instead of waiting for it to happen. That is, if it's real. Maybe we can talk sometime. Right now, I need to steal this lady to help me with a missing person case."

"I understand. Talisa explained a little. God bless your search."

Luke offered his hand across the gap between the dock and Welch's boat. Talisa took it and stepped back to the floating walkway. He set off toward the steps, and Talisa hurried after him, calling over her shoulder. "Thank you, Dr. Welch. Please keep praying for us."

"I certainly shall." Welch's reply was already faint as Talisa rushed to catch up with Luke.

"Where are we going?" Talisa matched Luke's pace by taking more steps.

"The cell company gave me a location for the last few hits your phone made on the tower. One of them is nearby."

"I thought you said they were repairing the tower."

"They are right now. This happened before they started. The company doesn't keep a constant fix on your phone. The way it works is the cell company only records the phone's location when it communicates with the tower, or the tower communicates with it. If you call someone or receive a call, it logs it. Fortunately, the same goes when your phone sends or receives a text message or communicates with a WiFi. A while before the repair started, the cell company sent a message warning about the outage. The tower logged it. At that time, your phone was just down the road. Right after that, they started the repair, and everything was put on hold."

They made it back to the house, crawled into Luke's Tahoe, and took off. A few minutes down the road, Luke pulled onto an overgrown drive leading toward the lake. Talisa was familiar with the property. It had been years since anyone lived there. Trees and bushes invaded the drive and branches scraped by the sides of the SUV as they lumbered down the rutted road. The drive twisted and opened up into what was once the front yard of the lake house, now in disrepair. The condition of the vehicle sitting in the driveway would have suggested that it belonged to the house, if not for its familiarity to Talisa.

She pointed. "Teddy's car." A rush of adrenaline made her fingers shake.

Luke stopped. Talisa pulled the door handle, but Luke's hand shot out and stopped her. "Now hold on. You stay here while I find out what's going on."

The grave expression on his face—rare for him—stunned Talisa.

"Any reason for those two to come here?" he asked as he did a visual scan of the house and the trees around it.

"No," Talisa answered. "Not that I know of. We knew the family who lived here, but that was years ago."

Luke got out. Talisa examined the house. The sound of Luke's handgun exiting its holster drew her attention to him. He eased toward Teddy's car, still looking around. Nothing registered on his face as he peered in the windows of the vehicle. He made a fresh visual search of his surroundings and then went to the house.

From her position in the Tahoe, Talisa watched as Luke tried the front door without success. He walked to the edge of the structure, scanning the ground as he disappeared around the corner.

When he didn't return after a minute or so, a nervous feeling settled on Talisa. She rolled down the window and listened but heard nothing. She didn't like sitting alone not knowing what Luke was doing. Should she call out to him? No, bad idea to make noise when Luke was being so cautious.

The solemn look on his face came back to her, igniting a fuse of thought. Why would Teddy bring Janie to an abandoned house? Horrible images flashed through her mind involving Janie and a faceless attacker. She still couldn't bring herself to put Teddy in that role of evil. But Sawyer was an expert in such things, and he had said he feared for Janie's safety. Had the interaction with Sawyer signaled Teddy that he was about to be exposed? If Teddy was such a devious criminal, what was he capable of?

She shook loose from the awful thoughts.

Terror pushed out the depression. Instead of feeling

emotional paralysis, Talisa was ready to act. But the clarity also spotlighted her lack of options. She wanted to run into the woods searching for Janie. Her sister was here not long ago. It was the last connection that Talisa had with her, and she wanted to grab the thread and make it lead her to Janie. But she knew it would be foolish.

Every time she determined to get out of the vehicle and go, sense stopped her. Luke knew what he was doing. She needed to wait for him. But what was taking him so long? Could something have happened to him? It was hard to think of Luke as being vulnerable to anything, but as she entertained the idea, she had the same sinking feeling she had when she thought of losing Janie.

Please Lord, make it be okay. Keep Luke safe. Help us find them and let it all be a big mistake. I'm begging You. Don't let me lose Janie...or Luke.

Luke appeared at the side of the house. Talisa's heart lifted. He walked to Teddy's car and reached inside. He came out with the keys, which he used to open the trunk. He appeared unimpressed with its contents and closed it, putting the keys in his pocket. Still examining the area, he moved back to the SUV and crawled in.

"There's a fresh wide trail in the weeds leading down to the property's boat dock." He looked around as he talked. "From the dock, it looks like a smaller trail goes off into the woods. I didn't follow that one. It looks like someone might have left in a boat."

Talisa's mouth stood open. "Where would Teddy get a boat? You usually can't get him around the water."

"I know. I think even bathwater scares that boy. Maybe Teddy's not in control of this."

A thought came to Talisa. "Or maybe that is what he wants us to think."

Luke shifted in his seat, taking in his surroundings. "This place is hidden. The shore bends so you can't see that dock from the marina, but it's close to your house."

Talisa watched him as if she might see his thoughts. "Do you think this was part of some plan?"

"Maybe. If someone came in here with a boat, they could move up through the trees and watch your house. When they saw you leave, they could grab Janie and Teddy and bring them down here in his car. It would have had to have happened that quick because you weren't gone long. Good plan. We would be searching for Teddy's car on the roads while they got away in the boat."

"Dr. Welch said a boat went by the marina earlier this morning."

Luke nodded. "That would fit." He looked back toward the corner of the house. "At least there were no signs of a struggle or anything being dragged through the grass, so Janie and Teddy must have been well enough to walk to the boat dock."

Talisa's stomach twitched at his thoughts, too real, too unthinkable.

"There's a broken window on the back of the house. I'm going to see if I can get in and check the place. I don't see any recent foot traffic around the window, but someone could have climbed in that way at some earlier time and gone through the front door since then. It could have been locked from the inside. I want to make sure."

Talisa didn't want Luke to go—just a feeling, nothing she could voice. "Be careful."

Luke's eyes locked on hers and held for a moment. "I will." His voice was almost a whisper.

He closed the door and she watched him walk across the drive and around the corner. She was waiting again.

***

Luke holstered his gun and examined the window. It was broken at the top near the latch, which was unlocked. A jagged piece of glass lay on the ground. He picked it up.

Looking through the window, he saw pieces of glass on the floor inside.

Glass fascinated Luke. One of his evidence instructors described it as a liquid in a solid state. It would bend and stretch at imperceptible levels before it broke, causing patterns on the broken edges. Luke held the piece up to the window and identified where it had come from, like fitting a jigsaw puzzle together. He examined the pattern on the edge of the glass in his hand. It told him the window was broken from the outside.

"Go figure," he said to the window. "Who breaks out of a vacant house?" He smiled at the specimen in his hand. "Still, your secrets are mine, little buddy." Luke used the light to examine the glass for fingerprints and found none. "Hmm," he said frowning at the glass. He tossed his forensic experiment over his shoulder, pushed the window open, crawled inside, and drew his gun.

***

Talisa drummed her fingers on the dash. She tapped her foot on the floor and rocked back and forth in the seat. *What are you doing, Luke?* She leaned back in the seat and her hand wandered to a piece of metal beside her while she stared at the house.

If Teddy had a boat, where would they go? She fiddled with the metal piece, tracing her finger along the edge, keeping her eye on the house for Luke's return. *Most people were friendly to Teddy, but she never knew of him staying anywhere besides home and her house.*

Talisa's thumb encountered a small round button. She pushed it and it clicked. The sound was a pleasing distraction to her subconscious, but her thoughts went on. *If it wasn't Teddy that had taken Janie, then someone would have had to have taken both of them. Neither one of them had anything that anyone would want.* Talisa's finger found a button on the other side and pushed that with a click. The button popped out for her thumb again and she pushed it—click.

Something new came to her mind. She recalled stumbling on Janie's diary one time when she was cleaning her room. She remembered chuckling at her sister's hard-to-decipher scrawl. It had talked about the secret that she and Teddy shared. In nervousness, she began to move the button back and forth.

Click, click. Click, click.

Talisa had read a little more just to make sure the two of them were not getting physical. But Janie had referred to "the secret about Teddy's gift." At the time, Talisa remembered thinking to herself, *That's not much of a secret. Everybody knows about that.* Why hadn't Talisa remembered it until now? Janie had asked God to forgive her if she lied. All the entries had been so jammed together that she thought they were two separate subjects and Janie was asking God's forgiveness for general lies she might have told. Now, she recalled that her first impression had been that the two items were part of the same entry.

Talisa, how could you not have seen this? Just like Teddy had told the pastor. It was all a lie. Her heart broke. *They were in on it together.* Her anger boiled against Teddy. He had deceived her sister and used her to make everyone think he had a special gift.

Click, click. Click, click.

What is taking you so long, Luke?

Click, click. Click, click.

She needed to tell him about this.

Click, click. Click, click.

Talisa glanced toward the noise she was making and for a moment watched her hand flip the safety on and off on the shotgun in the rack beside her.

"Oh!" she jerked her hand back and slid over against the door. Wobbling her head around in frustration, she admonished Luke in her mind. *Would you come on!*

***

The house was bigger than it looked from the outside. Luke had cleared the main level, but some things disturbed him—a food odor in the kitchen that should have dissipated long ago and a card table in the dining room with a half-burnt candle. Someone was using the house.

The addition on the back of the house had two stories. He saw one set of stairs in the kitchen, and now he found a second staircase in the living room. He had his gun up, pointing to the landing above as he started up. There was a sound. Something from upstairs. He hurried up. No use lingering where someone at the top of the stair had all the advantage.

He hugged one wall of the stairs as the upper landing came in view. Nothing. The landing had an open railing that looked down to the great room. The opposite wall had several doors.

He crossed and turned the knob on the first door. Pushing it open, he panned the room with his gun using the door jamb for cover. Empty. The room had two doors on opposite walls. He went to the first and threw it open, addressing anything inside with his weapon. Closet clear. Another sound. Luke whirled around, gun at ready. Nothing.

He dashed to the door and scanned the outer room. Empty. Then he went back into the room. The other door led to a Jack-and-Jill bathroom open to the bedroom beyond. Time to move on through to the next room. Searching forward, ears hypersensitive. Another empty room to secure. Clear. Another closet. As he moved to it, another sound.

Luke forgot the closet. The sound came from the other side of the wall in the next room. He transitioned to the outer landing and then to the next room. Gun in one hand, he used the other to push open the door. The room went around a corner, so Luke could only see half of the space. A sleeping bag lay against the far wall by a window.

The sound again, toward the back around the corner or maybe downstairs. Luke had no choice, he had to move forward. Better make it quick. Luke rushed ahead, gun up ready to engage. He ran the wall to his right making a rapid circle around the room. A bathroom, five-gallon bucket of water by the toilet and then…the top of the staircase that went down to the kitchen. There was another sound, this time no mistaking where it came from.

***

What on earth could be taking Luke so long? The door of the house crashed open. *Finally.* A form shot out, tall, skinny. The guy's head turned and gave a start at the sight of the sheriff's vehicle. Long hair, beard. *That's not Luke.*

The long thin body took off across the drive, away from the Tahoe and headed for the woods.

Where's Luke? One thought filled Talisa's attention. *That guy knows where Janie is and he's getting away.* The concept bypassed rational cognizance and landed in the reactionary part of her brain. She jerked open the door, rounded the vehicle, and ran. The long-haired man had reached the trees, throwing his arms forward, clearing his way.

Talisa could outswim most men in the county. This guy wasn't getting away. Her toned thighs pumped full of adrenaline, and she flashed across the drive. Sucking in oxygen, she yelled, "Luke!" as she cleared branches.

Talisa propelled herself forward, hurdling logs and ducking limbs, pushing the smaller branches out of the way. The man disappeared into the undergrowth. She followed his trail by the movement of the brush ahead of her and the occasional sound of larger branches snapping. *He knows about Janie.* She willed more speed into her limbs. It was a race she couldn't lose.

Flashes of the man appeared ahead through the thick green ocean of leaves. She heard him crashing through the brambles. *You're not getting away.* Talisa barreled through the trees, ignoring the sting from the tentacles of the forest.

More of the man came into view. Less foliage was between them as Talisa closed the distance. She managed her breathing like finishing up in a freestyle swim meet. Stroking forward, squeezing every ounce of power out of her strong legs.

The man grew larger. She ducked and dodged as the branches came whipping back at her. The man's ragged shirt filled her view. She pushed forward with her legs and was on him. Within an arms length, she drove her hands forward like she was setting up for a breaststroke and smacked her palms into the man's back. He stumbled and tumbled headlong into the brush.

Talisa landed on his back and grabbed him around the neck. The man got his hands under him and was pushing up. Talisa snatched at his arms, pulling out his supports. The man's face imbedded in the undergrowth.

"Get off me," he yelled, cursing. They were both panting, heaving air in and out. He shot a fist back toward her. Even at the awkward angle, it rattled her head. Wiry hands reached back and grabbed onto her wrists with a powerful grip. Before he could get a good hold, Talisa twisted her arms back and forth and freed herself. Her self-preservation instinct kicked in and she pushed away from him. Gathering in all the wind she could, she yelled, "Luke!"

Free of her weight, the man scrambled to his hands and knees. As he started to rise, Talisa shoved him hard and he crashed back into the brush. The man shook his long hair out of his face in exasperation. His eyes went up and down her, taking in her form with a confused look.

"Luke!"

He put his hands on the ground again and tried to get up. Talisa shot behind him and pushed him down again. The man threw out his arm trying to grip her ankle, but Talisa danced out of his reach and set up for the next round.

He glared at her, "What's with you, lady?" His voice was gravelly and hard.

"Luke!"

The man kept his eye on Talisa as he rose on his hands. Behind her, something crashed through the brush.

"Talisa! Where are you?" Luke's voice echoed through the trees.

"Luke!"

The man shot up and took off. Talisa closed the distance and jumped on him, wrapping arms and legs around him, taking him off balance and down again. Talisa could feel the panic and rage shoot through the man. He twisted free from her grasp and grabbed at her. She snatched, scratched, clawed but so did he.

Then he had her. An iron grip clamped her arm and bit into her bicep, pulling sideways and toward the ground. She landed hard. A forearm went across her chest and pinned her, grinding her skin into the grass and sticks. His sweaty body scrambled on top of her. He raised himself, straddling her waist. Foul breath panted all over her as she looked into yellowed, bloodshot eyes beneath an angry brow. His arm jerked back, and a bony fist came flying toward her face.

It stopped a few inches from her nose, jerked backward as the man's body was lifted into the air. Luke towered above, holding the long-haired man like a crawfish, arms and legs flaying before he plowed him into the ground several feet from Talisa.

The stunned man struggled to rise to his hands and knees. Luke's powerful grip clamped the man's right hand and twisted it behind his back. His other arm wrapped around the man's neck, closing off his carotid arteries and jerking him to his feet. The long-haired man groaned, and his eyelids fluttered.

Talisa's eyes went wide. "Don't kill him. He knows

where Janie is."

Luke scowled at her. "I'm not going to kill him." He lifted the long-haired man up and flipped his legs out from under him, driving him face down into the weeds and saplings again. In a few seconds, Luke had him cuffed.

Luke came for Talisa. Reaching down, he scooped her up and brought her to her feet. Brushing the hair from her face he examined her. "You okay?"

Talisa was fourteen again and looking into affirming eyes. For a second, she lost herself in them, then came to her senses. She focused on the long-haired man on the ground. "Make him tell you where Janie is."

He huffed out a breath and shook his head. Turning, Luke jerked the man back on his feet and shoved him ahead of him, back the way he came. Talisa followed, brushing off her clothes and pulling sticks from her hair.

The man looked over his shoulder. "You Luke?"

"Yup."

"Who's Janie?"

Luke tilted his head toward Talisa. "Her sister."

The man scowled back, past Luke. "What's with that woman anyway?"

"She thinks you know where Janie is."

"How should I know that?"

"Well, you'd better come up with an answer before we get back to my vehicle."

"Why?"

"Because she's the one that didn't want me to kill you. Me, I'm thinking it might be less paperwork."

"What am I under arrest for?"

"Breaking and Entering, Trespassing."

"That house's been empty for a long time. I ain't got no home. Why shouldn't I live in it?"

Luke huffed. "Yeah, but you're thinking too small. I hear the White House has plenty of rooms they're not using."

The man flipped his hair over his shoulder and flashed his

rotting teeth. "Sure, if you can stand the company."

Luke raised an eyebrow. "You just have to wait awhile. I'm sure someone will come through that'll be right up your alley." Luke was looking the man over. "You're called 'Gravy,' aren't you?"

The long-haired man swiveled his head around and took a better look at Luke. "You know me?"

"Know of you. The city guys said they removed a man who was living in an old shed down by the railroad a couple of weeks ago. Description fits."

Gravy snorted. "Nobody usin' that place either. Why can't you straights give a guy a break?"

"I might be in a generous mood, depending on what you can tell me."

Gravy didn't say anything.

When they reached the Tahoe, Talisa was beside Luke, glaring into the man's face. "Make him tell you where she is."

The man countered, "I don't know your sister, lady. Never met her. Never saw her."

Luke uncuffed the man's hands and forced his back against the Tahoe.

Talisa was surprised. "You're not letting him go?"

Luke held up his hand toward her. "That depends."

Gravy gave Talisa a smug look. "Just chill, Dragon Lady. Let the man and me talk."

Luke stepped in close to him. "Listen, you irritate the lady, you irritate me, so don't press it."

Gravy shrugged and dipped his head.

Luke continued. "Like she said, all we want is to find her sister. Have you seen anyone around the house today?"

"Yeah, a bunch of people. A boat, that car, you guys. I'm gonna have to put up 'no trespassing' signs." When the man smiled, it disgusted Talisa.

"Tell me about the boat."

"Early this morning, I heard a boat come up to the dock.

A guy snuck up through the woods that way." The man indicated the direction toward Talisa's house.

"What did he look like?"

"I don't know. I could barely see him moving up through the trees."

"What color did you see?"

Gravy thought a second. "It looked black. Might have been a black t-shirt."

"How did this car get here?"

The man glanced at Teddy's vehicle. "Just pulled in and parked. I figure it's lifted 'cause why else would they leave it here, but I didn't have anything to do with it. You can print me or whatever else you want. I ain't touched the thing. I know better than to steal cars. Too easy to get caught."

Luke had a get-to-the-point look on his face. "Who was in it?"

"Don't know. I didn't want to go to the front in case they could see me, so I didn't see who got out. I heard people go by the side of the house. I don't know how many. I thought they were coming around back, and I hid up near the front door, so I could run out if I had to. Pretty soon, I heard the boat leave. I figured the first guy must have done a house job somewhere close and picked up the car to haul the stuff. Pretty slick. You guys be lookin' for a car, and they're on a boat."

"Yeah," Luke stated. "Real genius. What else do you know?"

"What else could I know? Knowing things don't help me much. If you let me go, that'd be a first."

"Well, here's your first. Clear out of the house and move on. If I come back and you're still here, you go to jail. Now we've got things to do."

Was Luke bluffing? "You can't let him go. He hasn't told us anything."

Gravy was already hurrying toward the house. "Keep her away from me."

Talisa started after him.

Luke grabbed her wrist. "He doesn't know anything."

"He's lying. Let go of me."

"That guy's been hanging around the county for months. The other cops and deputies have arrested him for trespassing a bunch of times. He's not ambitious enough to kidnap anybody. He's just homeless. You think if he had something to do with this, he'd still be here? Everything he said made sense. I want to get Janie back as much as you do, and we won't do it by wasting time with that guy. Let's get you back to the house so you can..." Luke looked Talisa up and down, still holding her arm, "clean up a little."

Talisa relented, still looking in the direction of the front door of the house into which the man called Gravy had disappeared. "You're sure?"

"I'm sure."

Luke let go of her and motioned to the passenger door, "Crawl in, Dragon Lady. Let's get back on the case."

***

When they arrived at the house, Luke climbed out and strode across to the trees closest to the lake. He moved up and down the road until he stopped at one area and examined the weeds. "Here's where he came out. I see a trail leading back into the trees like we thought. I'm sure if I followed it, I'd end up at the abandoned house we were just at."

Talisa put her hand over her mouth. "I saw him this morning."

Luke jerked his head up. "What did he look like?"

Talisa let out a defeated breath. "Like a deer."

As Luke walked back to where Talisa stood near the Tahoe, his face a mixture of his usual amusement and curiosity. "This wasn't any deer."

"I thought it was. I didn't really see him. I heard a noise and saw something disappear in those trees. I thought it was a deer. I should have checked on it."

Luke took her hands. "No, you shouldn't have. If that was the kidnapper, then all you would have done was gotten yourself hurt."

Talisa was touched by the tenderness in his voice. Then his words registered. "So, Teddy didn't kidnap Janie?"

Luke shrugged. "Maybe."

Talisa regarded him. "What do you mean, maybe? Teddy was already here. Now you're telling me that someone was hiding in the trees and came in after I left? That wasn't Teddy. You were the one that said not to convict Teddy without a trial." Talisa stopped. Her shoulders slumped. "When I was waiting on you, I remembered something I read in Janie's diary. She wrote about needing forgiveness for lying about Teddy's gift. The pastor told me that Teddy said something similar to him. The whole thing was a lie. But I still can't believe it. I mean, I have to believe it, but it feels so wrong."

Luke sighed. "I know. I don't want to believe Teddy had anything to do with this either. And especially not Janie. But I need to think realistically. One of the things I am trying to figure is what this is all about. I was hoping we would find it was a misunderstanding, that the two of them went somewhere and just didn't tell you. But now it looks like this was planned. Who would plan it? Why would someone kidnap them? There's no big money involved here to account for a kidnapping. I don't want to believe what Sawyer said, but not much else makes sense."

"Then who was the person in the trees?"

"The guy with the snake tattoo. They call him Hiss. He bonded out yesterday. It could have been him. He was wearing a black T-shirt."

"So you think Teddy might have known he was about to be caught and fled with this guy and Janie?"

"We have to consider it."

Talisa took a breath. "There's more. Teddy's dad was

kicking him out. He had no money and was soon going to be out of a place to live."

Luke eyebrows furled together. "They might have hooked up with Boggs and the Agnew woman who promised them part of the treasure." He thought further. "If they bought that story, then maybe Teddy is not that devious. Maybe just desperate and gullible."

Talisa felt fatigued. "But they still lied about Teddy's gift. I don't know what to think anymore."

Luke opened the door on the Tahoe. "I need to call dispatch and let everyone know that they are probably on a boat. This manhunt for our escapee is going to divide up our resources. The hunt for Boggs will be centered on the highways out of town. I'll see who I can pull off that search to start scouring the lake shores for where they might have come out. I'm going to be on the phone for a while to get this going." Luke looked in the direction of the marina. "Is your dad's boat fueled up and ready? I'll have a couple of deputies take the Sheriff's Department boat and start searching, but it will be a little while before they can get on the water. You and I can go out in your boat. It will be faster. It worries me taking you, but I might need someone to handle the boat. I know that's one of the many things you do well."

Talisa loved to hear his praise. She wished it was under other circumstances. Luke scrutinized her with concern. She was sure he could read everything on her face. He walked over to her, and his big arms gathered her in. "Besides, if you sit around here, all you'll do is worry, and you don't need to do that because God will help us."

Talisa snuggled into his chest. She needed to feel his strength. Why was she so hard on him? He was just a man, but a good man. "I don't know how you thought for one second you were going to leave me behind."

Luke's head bent down toward her. His warm breath was in her ear and on her neck as if he was going to tell her something. Something she wanted to hear.

Unexpectedly he drew back. With a gentle grasp, he held her at arm's length.

Wondering why, she stared into his eyes and saw a haunted longing. His large hands seemed to tremble where he touched her.

His countenance shifted, and with a half-smile, he said, "You'd better hurry and change into some boating clothes. We have work to do." He pointed her toward the house and spun toward the SUV. When she looked back at him, she saw his hand go to his face. Talisa hurried into the house before her heartache reached her own eyes.

Chapter 18

Luke slammed the door on the Tahoe harder than he meant to. Its sound joined the storm door closing behind Talisa. He took in a deep breath. He almost said it, almost told her how much he still loved her. He slammed his big foot into the floorboard. *What an idiot you are, Luke. What were you thinking? Janie is missing, Teddy might be the kidnapper, and you're thinking about whispering sweet nothings in Talisa's ear? On top of everything else, she doesn't need to have to fight off some big dumb country boy that she left behind a long time ago. At least she still trusts you. Don't ruin that. Don't misinterpret a hug for something it's not.*

And, what was he thinking asking her to come with him? He was doing it again. Was he so desperate to have her near that it was messing up his judgment? He should be asking Sawyer to help. That way he wouldn't worry what was going to happen to him so much if things got hairy. But he didn't trust him, didn't like him. Or was it just that he didn't want him to have anything to do with Talisa, didn't want her to have any reason to be grateful to him?

Lord, You know my heart. Can You please straighten me out inside? Help me to have the right motives. Please show me what to do. Janie and Talisa need me to make the right decisions, and I'll never figure this out on my own.

Luke took hold of the steering wheel and straightened himself in the seat. His thoughts cleared. *God, I know You've got this. You taught me that. I'll do the best I can and let You take care of the rest.*

Okay, Luke. There are phone calls to make and a search to coordinate. It's too late to tell Talisa she needs to stay home. She's smart, she's fit, and she knows boats and this lake. Plus, you know her. Even putting your own feelings aside, there are just too many questions about Sawyer right now to trust him. Now act like a professional and get this done.

As Luke picked up his phone, the truth burst into his mind like a sunrise. *You need to consider how this all started. Everything Teddy said the night the Agnew woman screamed was consistent with a drowning. You forgot about that with everything else that's been going on. And that was what he wanted. There's no question who lied. Teddy knew how the woman died. It was that simple all the time. How else would he have known she was drowned?*

***

Talisa emerged from the house dressed for the search, wearing a T-shirt, loose-fitting cargo pants and sneakers. A bandage here and there covered some of the worst scratches she had received during her run through the woods. She hoped she had washed away all the tear stains.

Luke was coming back up from the marina. "Here's what I found out. The cell tower is back up, and they should be calling me any minute with a longitude and latitude on your cell phone's current location. They plotted a few more past hits on the phone, and they show it was headed out across the lake a little while ago, so it looks like we are definitely going to need your boat. I don't want to head out yet in case they turned around. We just have a few minutes to wait, and then we can go find Janie." He grinned at her. "I got my gear all loaded on the boat while you were in there making yourself beautiful."

The mirth had returned to Luke's eyes. But the memory of the other look haunted her and left her wondering what had been there for a moment. She felt an overwhelming clinch in her stomach. *You can't lose it now.* Talisa managed to paste on a ready-for-business expression. She tried to assume a confident voice as she told him, "I was not making myself beautiful."

"Just comes natural then, I guess," Luke told her, never losing his grin.

Talisa was confused. One minute he was pushing her away, the next minute he was flirting with her. All of it was more than she could take. Janie, Teddy, Sawyer, Luke, her dad—who were they, what did they want? She didn't know anymore. She didn't know anybody, not even herself. "Stop it!" she screamed.

Luke stared, eyes wide, mouth open.

Talisa let it out. "Stop telling me I'm beautiful. Stop being sweet and charming. Stop praising me. That's not what you do. You laugh at me, remember? You make fun of me. This is me, remember?" Talisa pushed her face toward him and exaggerated the next words, "Frog legs."

Luke jerked like he'd been slapped. He opened his mouth to say something but seemed to change his mind.

Talisa couldn't stop the flood. "And stop telling me it's going to be all right when you don't know it's going to be all right. Sometimes it's not all right. It wasn't all right with my mama. It wasn't all right with my daddy. They're gone. And now Janie's gone, and you don't know it's going to be all right. Everybody left me." Luke stood there speechless. She pointed her finger at him. "But you were the first."

He opened his mouth again. He shut it again.

Talisa stared at him, the fury ebbing out of her. *God, what have I done?* She couldn't keep her tears back. Throwing her hands in the air, she stood there, no pride left, no self-worth, no self-respect. All she had was self-examination. "You're right. I'm a mess. I deserve to be laughed at. I'm scared. I'm depressed. I'm chasing after some guy like a school girl not because I love him, but because I'm hoping he can fix me. Is that pathetic or what? Now I can't even keep it together long enough to go find my sister. So go ahead and laugh. But just stop confusing me."

It was gone, all out of her, all empty. She wasn't even crying anymore. She stood there breathing in and out. Luke looked petrified. *What he must think of me.*

***

Luke watched Talisa breathing in and out. He absorbed it all. *You're dead.* He decided to sacrifice his life for her. If she wanted to beat the corpse a little, if that's what it took for her to heal, then he was going to keep his mouth shut and take it like a man—a dead man.

It was just what he had feared. Her mother and father were dead. She had heard the last screams of another woman who died next door. Her sister was missing, and she believed a man that she had trusted might be the kidnapper. Luke was flirting with her while she was going through things no one should have to go through. He laughed at her and teased her and tore her apart. *What she must think of me!*

But he also heard that he had left her. It wasn't true, but it didn't matter. He was listening. *Pay attention, Luke. Hear what she's really saying.* What he heard was he still meant something to her. He had also heard that she wasn't in love with Sawyer. She wasn't looking for Sawyer. She was looking for someone to help her. And he loved her enough to be that person.

He needed to say something. "I'm sorry I didn't understand my teasing hurt you so much. That's not what I wanted. I never wanted to hurt you. I love you."

She scowled. "What?"

He was trying to take the pastor's advice, and he meant every word of what he said. Now he was stuck. "Huh?" was all he managed. *God, I'm no good at this. Help me.*

Talisa looked exasperated. "What did you say?"

"Which part?"

She huffed. "The last part."

"I love you."

"Stop saying that." She glared at him.

Luke dug in. "It's true." In his mind he heard, *truth is good.*

"No, it's not, or you wouldn't make fun of me."

"Sorry. It's what I do when I get nervous. I never meant to hurt you. You were always so far above me. I never thought I measured up. All I could ever do for you was make you laugh. When it stopped working, I didn't have anything else."

Emotions moved across Talisa's face like windblown clouds, shadows of hurt and revelation shifting as her mind processed what he was saying. "You left me. If you loved me, you would have tried to work things out."

"I thought you didn't want me anymore. I hoped I would die in the Marines because I didn't think I could live without you."

Talisa looked shocked. "That's not true. Don't ever say that."

Luke was tired. It wasn't working. "What do you want me to say?"

Talisa studied his face as if she was trying to see deeper. "Say it again." She continued staring at him.

Luke squirmed. He felt like he needed to be funny to lighten the mood. "You told me not to."

Talisa narrowed her eyes and pointed her finger at him.

"Don't you grin."

He clamped his lips together.

She walked toward him, finger still impaling him from a distance. "Say it again."

Luke bit his lip, trying to suppress his natural instinct. She was so close, her beautiful eyes consumed his view when he managed to say, "I love you," hoping his face conveyed the truth of the statement. Maybe it didn't matter. The truth had set them free. The hurt that had been telling her lies had been scraped away like old paint. Underneath were the feelings that had remained through it all. Her women's intuition was seeing beyond the surface.

Talisa's eyes probed him for a long time. "I think you mean that."

"Can I grin now?"

One side of her mouth lifted. "Yes."

Just as Luke grinned, she kissed the end of her finger and planted it on his lips. The softness of the touch consumed him. In the back of his mind, he was aware of another sound, but it couldn't compete with Talisa's wonderful presence in front of him. The touch erased the years they had lost. She was with him once again. She pulled back with a lovely smile on her face. All Luke could do was stand there, grinning.

Talisa pointed to his belt. "Would you quit grinning and answer your phone."

Chapter 19

"Okay," Luke said as he pushed the button on his phone that ended the call from the cell company. "I've got your phone's current location. It's across the lake and around the leg that goes to Sunset Bridge. Should be over by the southside cliffs. No way to that area except by water. Let's get the boat going, and I'll tell you the rest on the way."

As they hurried down the metal walkway, Talisa slowed when she saw the boat again. The Oklahoma Bureau of Investigation forensics team had cleaned up the cabin as a courtesy to her, but no one had touched it since. It was just too painful. In her mind, she could still see it the way she found it when she went looking for her dad. When she saw the cruiser, all shut up on a warm day, she knew something was wrong. Now she was going out looking for Janie. She was afraid of what she might find. How could she face that again?

No! She wasn't going to lose it. Janie was the reason she didn't have time for this. *God, please help me.*

Before she had a chance to hear another negative voice,

she hurried down the walkway and leaped on board. Positioning herself at the helm, she closed her eyes. *Think of something good.* The water lapped against the hull. She could smell the fishy scent of the lake and feel the warm sun. It reminded her of younger summers, and she grabbed onto the memory. It led her to...Luke. She felt the movement of him coming aboard. He stood beside her, and his arm was around her shoulder. Again she dropped her head against him and drew in his strength. She felt him reaching forward, and she heard the engine turn over and come to life. Luke pulled her tighter and guided her hands to the wheel.

His words caressed her neck. "Full speed ahead, captain. I'm right here with you."

She tilted her head to him until his lips touched her cheek. He didn't move away. "That's where I always want you," she told him.

She felt him shiver. "You're not just teasing me, are you?"

"I'm not if you're not."

He squeezed her. "Let's go find Janie and Teddy, and we'll talk about this some more."

"Sounds good."

Letting her go, Luke went to unhitch the lines. Together they maneuvered into deeper waters.

Then Luke set up the laptop and brought up the map program that displayed the coordinates of the phone. Talisa knew where she was going. The south cliffs were the highest on the lake. There was no road to the top. There was no beach to speak of. The only way to get there was by boat.

Luke used his lapel mic to let his dispatcher know they were on the way to check out the location of the southside cliffs. Then he went back and began to take inventory of what was on the boat that they might need. He opened the hold where the underwater gear was kept.

"If Janie and Teddy are on a boat, it might be better to stop somewhere out of sight, and I can scuba up to them and catch everyone by surprise." Luke hoisted an air tank out and checked it. "This tank is wide open and empty." He pulled out all the tanks and examined them. "They're all empty."

"Are you sure? My dad would never use up every tank. He would always come up with at least a little air in each. And he wouldn't drain them off until he was back on shore but…he never made it back to shore."

"I know, but they're empty now. One of the crime scene investigators must have opened them all up not knowing any better." He grunted in frustration. "Well, we can't turn around now. The scuba idea is out." He put the tanks away. "We'll have to think of something else."

Talisa steered the boat with the clank of Luke stowing the tanks behind her. The hatch closed, and then there was silence. When she glanced back, Luke was gazing at the sky.

It was a moment before he spoke. "I wish I hadn't been out of town. I'd been so busy getting my feet under me in this sheriff's position and going to all the classes I had to take that I hadn't sat down with your dad in months. We used to talk all the time. I just keep thinking if I hadn't been so preoccupied, I would have known something was wrong. If I would have known—"

Regret covered his face. She tried to change the subject. "Do you think Teddy could have tampered with the tanks for some reason?"

Luke smiled as if he knew what she was trying to do. He leaned against the side of the boat. "I don't think he had anything to do with any of this. I was overlooking something that I finally got my head around while you were—"

"Don't say I was making myself beautiful."

"Well, actually, I was going to say, 'while you were in the house.' But since you brought it up, you might as well accept the fact that you're beautiful, especially to me. And it doesn't matter what you're wearing. But if it bothers you that much to hear me say it, then I can—"

"Who said it bothers me?"

Luke opened his mouth and raised his finger. Then he wrinkled his forehead and scowled at the digit like it had almost betrayed him. "Whoever it was, it's not pertinent to this conversation anymore."

Talisa smiled. "I like the way you think, Sheriff Sanders. But it would be better if you limit saying I'm beautiful to a few dozen times a day."

"Will you be keeping track, or should I?"

She narrowed her eyes.

"Just what I was thinking." Luke slapped on an innocent look. "Rough estimates are best. Anyway, I was starting to say that Teddy is not a fake."

Talisa didn't try to hide the confusion on her face. "Seriously? I thought we had determined that he was. Where did this change come from?"

"I started thinking about…well, I think God brought it to my mind…what we already knew from the night you heard the scream. How did the woman die?"

"She drowned, right?"

"They haven't had the autopsy yet, but everything looks that way, and the doc is sure singing that song. Right away he started saying she must have gone to the lake and drowned herself."

"And how would Sawyer know that?" Talisa was beginning to track with Luke.

"But that's not the most important part. Don't you think what Teddy described from his vision was consistent with a drowning—he said that he wanted to breathe, but there was no air, then he found air and screamed. He also said someone was holding him, and he couldn't get free or something like that. It sounds like someone who was being held under water."

"You said maybe she was having a panic attack."

"That was when we were hoping she was alive. When she turned up dead, that changed everything."

"Okay, I see what you mean."

Luke continued his speculation. "So how would Teddy have known how she died if he was a fake?"

"I hate to say this, but what if Teddy had already drowned her himself?"

Luke shook his head. "That doesn't work out because we have to consider Sawyer's statement. He said that the woman was alive at his house at the time Teddy was having his vision. And you all heard her scream."

"Maybe they're working together."

"Why would Sawyer then claim Teddy was a fake and a criminal? Why would Teddy have a vision that seemed to incriminate Sawyer in the first place? No, if anything, they are working against each other. So that leaves three possibilities. Either Teddy's lying or Sawyer's lying or they're both lying. But that brings us back to the first point. Teddy's statement, no matter how fantastic, is the only one that fits the facts. So if Teddy's not lying, then Sawyer is and that means that the woman was drowned at the time that Sawyer admits she was at his house. I suspect her body was dumped in the lake later."

"It's just hard for me to consider. He seemed so... believable. And you searched his house the next day. Where would he have hidden the body?"

"I haven't figured that out yet. I don't think he had a chance to go far with it, but I searched his entire property, twice. The pastor drove around right after you heard the scream, and later I had a deputy in the area, so it would have been risky for him to move the body that night."

"What about both Janie and Teddy talking about lying about his gift?"

The confident look faded from Luke's face. "I haven't figured that out yet." Luke sighed. "But if Teddy was the kind of criminal we thought he was, he would have no remorse and wouldn't be saying anything like that in front of the pastor. The pieces still don't fit."

"I hope you're right, Luke. But if you are, I'll feel

ashamed for doubting Teddy. I'm just glad he wasn't around to hear what I said about him. How will I ever confess it to him?"

"It won't phase Teddy. He wouldn't even know how to hold a grudge."

"You're right." Talisa tipped her head back in internal agony. "How will I live with myself?"

"Like all of our other mistakes. We'll just have to give it to God."

Talisa's face turned thoughtful. "So, who kidnapped Teddy and Janie—Sawyer?"

Luke shook his head, "He was at his house talking to me when they disappeared. And what would Sawyer want with them? The answer is I don't know. Let's go find out."

Talisa pushed the cruiser to its limit, but it took over forty minutes to reach the area of the southside cliffs. While they were some distance away, Luke started searching with the binoculars. Talisa watched the GPS map on the laptop.

Pointing at the screen, she said, "It looks like they must be behind the outlying rocks in that area."

He nodded agreement, scanning five or six rocky islands each about the size of a two-car garage with an apartment above it. They were scattered in the water in front of the cliffs that replaced the shore of the lake in that area.

It had been years since Talisa had seen the rocks, but now she recalled them. The nearest one resembled a giant derby hat floating on the water. The one behind it was larger and squarer on one side, like the half-crushed hat box the derby came in. They stuck out of the water starting about a hundred yards from their boat's current position, and the last island was approximately thirty feet from the higher rock walls at the lake's edge.

Luke frowned. "I can't see anything in the open. We have no choice but to get up close. They'll hear us before we see them, but if we keep the rocks between us, they won't know it's us until we're right on top of them."

Talisa idled the engine and eased toward the derby. Luke rotated his rifle to the ready position and unclicked the safety. Nothing like a gun coming out to drive home the seriousness of the situation.

She steered around the derby, her hands shaky on the wheel. They rounded the hat-shaped island. Nothing but empty water. Talisa headed for the hatbox. She leaned, trying to see around the large rock as they slid through the water. Nothing, Nothing.

What was that? Talisa's stomach tightened until she realized it was a large log bobbing in the water behind the hatbox. Good thing Luke had the gun. She would have shot the thing. If they were closing in on Janie, they couldn't afford mistakes. The thought scared her even more. Talisa gathered her nerves and headed toward the next rock that reminded her of a skull, complete with a dark, platter-sized hole like an eye staring at her. Beyond that was one that resembled a mushroom. She glanced at Luke again. *Please steady him, Lord.*

As she rounded the skull, the view widened to gradually reveal more of the water behind. Something red caught her attention. She clenched the wheel. The sharp point of a boat appeared. Luke adjusted his rifle, leaning forward then dropped the barrel to aim at the water. Talisa drew a sharp breath. On the bow of the boat sat Janie and Teddy.

Chapter 20

The pair sat shoulder to shoulder leaning against the windshield of a sleek speedboat, watching them cruise toward them. Janie looked like she had shut down. Her face showed a mixture of fear and relief when she recognized Luke and Talisa. They both appeared traumatized. Teddy's eyes darted back and forth, but he broke into a big grin when he saw them. Without thinking, she smiled back. He looked like the same Teddy she knew, but she didn't know what to believe.

The sun was high overhead and glinted intermittently off the vessel's windshield as it bobbed gently from the slight wake they had created. Talisa recognized the craft the pair was sitting on as Sawyer's large ski boat.

Her mind was having trouble putting the pieces together. An hour ago, she believed that Teddy had kidnapped Janie, and now here they both sat looking relieved to see Luke and her. Then Talisa noticed that they both had their hands behind their backs.

Luke signaled for her to stop. Talisa throttled the engine backward enough to stop the forward momentum and killed the engine. They were left with the silence of the lake. Talisa started to call to her sister, but Luke must have sensed it and put his hand up. It was surreal looking at the pair staring at them. Then she saw Sawyer sitting behind the duo in the driver's seat of his boat. A gun in his hand.

"You need to put your rifle down, Sheriff. I would hate to see these young people hurt in a crossfire between us. How would you feel if your bullet was the one that killed one of them?"

Luke didn't move.

"I'm quite serious. Don't make me shoot you. This does not have to end like that."

"How does it have to end?" Luke's voice was calm. "So far you have not hurt anyone. You haven't done anything that bad. If this stops now, you can come out of this okay. Let's do that. Let's just let it stop. Let Janie and Teddy come over to our boat, and we'll leave. All I want is them safe. After that, you can do what you want. But if they get hurt, there will be nothing I can do for you. You'll be running from now on. Those two never hurt anyone. I don't believe you're the type of person that would want to hurt them."

"Save it, Sheriff. I've been to at least as many hostage negotiation classes as you, and I have a far clearer view of this situation than you do. We are in much too deep for anyone to just walk away. But I did not come into this without a plan. Your showing up here was not a part of it, but that plan can still work without bloodshed. It all depends on you. Don't let your ego get you or these kids hurt, Sheriff. I don't think you're the kind of man to care more for your pride than you do for Teddy and Janie."

"You've got a problem," Luke raised his voice. "Your partner gave you away. How do you think I found you? At least there's one person that's started to get smart."

A voice came from the skull-shaped rock above them. "He's lying."

Luke glanced up at the rock as if he expected what he

saw. Talisa followed his gaze. A rifle barrel stuck out from behind a protruding portion of the rock. The man aiming at Luke was concealed behind it.

"Of course, he is." Sawyer spat the words toward the man's location, looking perturbed. "He was hoping to get you to say something, so he could know where you were at. He knew there had to be another person involved. I couldn't have taken these two because I was talking to the sheriff at my house when they disappeared. So do me a favor, Harris, and try not to let him manipulate you anymore. Here is what I want you to do. If the sheriff tries anything, shoot the beautiful woman behind the wheel."

Talisa froze as the rifle shifted in her direction.

Sawyer smiled without taking his eyes off Luke. "Oh, don't worry, Talisa. I don't want to harm you. I have complete faith in Sheriff Sanders. He will do nothing to jeopardize your life."

Luke still did not move.

"My suggestion to you, Sheriff, is that being clever at this point increases the chances of you and the woman being too much of a liability for me to keep around. You need to put your gun down now." Sawyer moved farther behind Teddy and aimed the pistol. Luke bent toward the deck with his gun.

"Don't dive in the water. I know what you're thinking, and I promise if you do, Harris will shoot Talisa. She serves no purpose in the plan. If you try to get sneaky, I will be forced to start eliminating the number of people I have to deal with. All these lives are in your hands, Sheriff, and time is running out for us to do this without someone dying."

Luke continued toward the deck with his gun.

"In the water, Sheriff."

Luke huffed, then let the weapon drop over the edge of the boat. It hit with a kerplunk and was gone.

"Now the handgun, slowly out of the holster and in the water."

Luke's Glock went over the side to rest with his rifle. He crossed his arms and stared at Sawyer.

Sawyer put on a wicked grin. "You'd like to keep it, wouldn't you? Your backup gun, Sheriff. Don't even pretend you don't have one. Get rid of it."

Luke retrieved the compact auto from its hiding place and dropped it in the lake.

"You see, Talisa, you have nothing to fear. It's obvious what you mean to the sheriff. I had hoped there could be something between you and me, but I must make sure nothing gets in the way of the plan that I mentioned. I'm not the only person that has a stake in what we're doing here, and I must act responsibly."

Talisa found her voice. "What do you mean responsibly? What on earth is going on, Sawyer?"

"Before we get into that, I need to stabilize things a little, for everyone's safety. Now, Sheriff, we could have outrun you or killed you from a distance, but you're alive because I need you to speak to your dispatch center. I need you to radio in that you are okay. Tell them that you checked out a boat in this area, but it was just a fisherman. Then tell them that you will still be here searching."

Luke did as he was told. The dispatcher acknowledged him.

"That's better. Now we should have an hour alone without interruption before they check on you. Okay, take your radio off and lay it on the deck of your boat."

While he took off the radio, Luke spoke to Sawyer. "You need to make sure your partner doesn't make any mistakes with that rifle. Your leverage will disappear if something happens to anyone here. Because then I will know I can't trust you anymore, and I'll have to do something." He laid the radio on the deck.

"Relax and stop threatening me, Sheriff. Everything will be fine as long as each of you does what you're told. But do not think for a minute that you are in control here. My position at the prison allows me to assist with all kinds of training. I know law enforcement equipment and tactics. Please don't assume you can fool me. It won't end well. Now, lie on your back on the deck with your arms straight out from your sides."

Luke glanced at the rifle trained on Talisa and continued to comply.

Sawyer stood. "Now, Talisa, please do as I tell you. I am going to throw you a rope, and I want you to pull our boats together."

Talisa caught the rope and pulled until the bumper on the front of the cruiser bounced against the front of the speedboat.

"Now tie it to one of your cleats so we can all be together."

When Talisa completed the tie off, he told her, "Now sit back down." To the man above, he said, "Harris, keep her in your sights, but as the sheriff requested, be careful. We don't want any accidents."

Sawyer took another rope that was tied to the skull-shaped rock and drew the two boats to the rock until the speedboat's bumpers were resting against it. Sawyer pointed his handgun at Talisa. "Now Harris, come down and secure the sheriff for me."

Harris scrambled down to the speedboat and climbed up on the deck.

Sawyer directed Luke to sit up at the edge of the cruiser with his back toward Harris and his hands behind him. Harris took Luke's handcuffs and secured them to his wrists behind his back.

After searching Luke, he tossed his gun belt and any potential weapon into the water. He threw Luke's cell phone to Sawyer who removed the battery and dropped it and the phone overboard. He also threw the radio to Sawyer. He stuffed it into a cargo pocket of his pants and clipped the corded microphone to his lapel.

Harris stood on the deck of the speedboat with the rifle aimed in the general direction of Talisa.

Sawyer spoke to Teddy and Janie, "Okay I need you two to get down in the boat." He helped each of the duo into the seating area where they sat side by side with their hands still tied behind their backs. "Now let's find out who did betray us."

Sawyer eyed Teddy for a second and seemed to dismiss what he was thinking and turned to Janie. He took hold of her arm. When she jerked it from his grip, Sawyer jammed the pistol in Teddy's back, forcing him forward where Janie could see it. "Stand up," he commanded her.

Janie popped up, fear on her face.

Talisa shouted, "Please, don't hurt them."

"I've told you how to prevent that." He tossed the harsh admonishment at Talisa, then to Janie said, "Hold still." Sawyer ran his hand down Janie's back, then across the front of her.

Talisa felt sick when he touched Janie. He appeared to be searching for something. At the front of her pants, Sawyer said, "Here we go." Without hesitation, he thrust his hand down the front of Janie's jeans, and before Talisa could protest, pulled out her missing cell phone.

Sawyer frowned at Harris. "Did you watch them at all?"

"She was freaking out. I threatened the boy like you said, but she must have grabbed that before I got her stopped."

"And turned the sound off at some point, so it wouldn't give her away while the sheriff tracked it right to us." Sawyer paused, then said, "Can you just tell me now if this is going to continue until we're all in jail?" He held up his hand. "Please, I have all my hopes pinned on you having enough sense not to answer that question. Just get your head around what we're trying to do here."

Sawyer pulled Talisa's phone open, took out the battery, and tossed them both into the lake.

"Everyone, relax. We have a few minutes to wait." Sawyer took out his own cell and dialed. After a few seconds, he said, "It's me. You can come on in."

Talisa called out, "Janie, are you all right?"

Janie shook her head no. Her face had lost its color.

"God will help us," she told her. Knowing Teddy was as much of a prisoner as her sister produced the shame she dreaded. "Teddy, are you okay?"

"I'm okay, Ms. Tee. I'm scared. They told me they would hurt Janie if I didn't do what they said. Please, don't let 'em hurt Janie. Do you know why they said that?"

"No, Teddy, I don't. All I know is that Dr. Kincade is a bad man. Don't trust him." Talisa glared at Sawyer.

Sawyer took her gaze and held it. "Talisa, you are giving him bad advice. He should trust me and do what I say. And you had better tell him that right now to keep him and everyone else here safe. Go ahead, tell him."

Talisa narrowed her eyes at Sawyer. "Teddy, he's right. Do what he says so he doesn't hurt anyone."

"Now that is enough talk from everyone. I want you all to be quiet until our company arrives."

The water lapped at the side of the boat. It was at least ten minutes until the sound of a boat motor approached. An older cabin cruiser pulled up and cut the engine. The pilot of the new boat wore a gray law enforcement uniform.

He studied Luke and Talisa. "Who are they?"

"Unexpected visitors who have decided to be cooperative, so no one gets hurt," Sawyer told him.

The man inspected Luke's face and uniform. "That's the sheriff." There was alarm in his voice. "I've seen him when he brought new inmates out to the prison."

"I know who it is," Sawyer said. "I have everything under control. We talked about the possibility of unexpected things happening and the need to be adaptable. This is one of those things. We will work it out."

Sawyer watched the prisoners while Harris and the pilot of the new boat lashed the new cruiser to the side of Sawyer's ski boat.

"Okay, Turner," Sawyer sported an enthusiastic smile as

he spoke to the pilot of the cruiser. "Bring up our guest."

Chapter 21

The man in the gray uniform opened the door to the boat's cabin. "Come on up."

A deep raspy voice spoke from inside, "This is a little open, ain't it?"

Sawyer answered him. "That is the reason we chose this spot. No one can get close to us on shore. We are hidden and out of binocular range. We can hear a boat coming for miles, just as we heard this one. And, thanks to the sheriff, his dispatch thinks this area has already been checked out by the sheriff himself. Come up and join us, Mr. Boggs. We should have no interruptions."

An elderly man ascended from below pulling hard on the handrails to make it. He wore the same prison guard uniform, but his pale and wrinkled skin said it did not belong to him.

Boggs scanned the group including the prisoners. "Looks like you all kinda got yourselves a mess here."

Sawyer lifted his head toward Boggs and gave a congenial smile. "We have had a complication, but we planned for the unexpected. As you see, everything is contained."

Boggs chuckled. "Unexpected, huh. It's been my experience that it's hard to plan for something you don't expect."

"That's why you craft a simple core strategy that will adapt to any event. Permit me to point out that the outcome today is that you are no longer in prison. And since rapid completion is part of the core strategy, I would like to get right to the point. You are a free man, thanks to us. We hoped you would show your gratitude by telling us where the treasure is."

Boggs smiled and leaned against the top of the cabin. "It's like I told you, boys. That's not how it's gonna work. I said if you got me out, I would pay you well and I will. But I'm not givin' you the whole thing. We need to keep it low for a while. Then I'll get the treasure and give you what I promised."

Talisa yelled at Sawyer. "That's what this is all about? You think you're going to find that crazy treasure? People have been looking for that for years. You did all this to us for that?"

Sawyer snapped a callous look at her, then softened. "I need you to be quiet now. Remember what I told you about what would happen if you became a liability."

He turned back to Boggs. The old man spoke first. "Let me tell you about liabilities. I wouldn't be too all-fired ready to get that treasure. It's cursed, you know. It's done me no good. Ever since that old Cherokee told me about it, all it's done is made me a convict. Did the same for that old Indian. That's where I met him, in jail. That's where he died. I thought he was telling me about it 'cause he liked me. Now I wonder if it wasn't just the opposite. So if I were you boys, I'd be satisfied with payment for your services. Maybe the curse won't come down to you in pieces."

Sawyer continued his pleasant look. "That is thoughtful of you, but each of us is willing to assume the risk. Perhaps if you let us have the treasure, you can rid yourself of the curse."

Boggs shook his head. "Won't work, Doc. I don't have much time left, so curses on this earth ain't what I'm worried about anymore. Had a lot a folks over the years try all kinds of things to get me to tell where it was. Everyone hoping to talk me into sharing my bounty." The old man gave a snort. "The only bounty it got me was regular visitors out at the pen."

Boggs' pensive face looked to the sky over Sawyer's head. "There was one man that I thought came to visit me and didn't want that stinkin' treasure. A chaplain who made regular visits. All he wanted was my soul. He never got that either."

Boggs returned his gaze to Sawyer. "You know what he told me? He told me that 'where my treasure was, that's where my heart would be.'" Boggs took in the scene again. "Looks like that's true enough. Never had anything to do with church, but I thought I might give a donation to his if I got the chance. He was the genuine article. Maybe the good Lord will consider that, though I don't suppose there's much hope for this old soul. And there were some other people I figured I'd help. I got a granddaughter who came and saw me regular. I know she was just trying to get the treasure, but she was a pretty thing. Reminded me of her grandmother, so why not?"

At the mention of his granddaughter, Talisa glanced at Luke who shook his head at her. Boggs didn't know that Phebe Agnew was dead. Sawyer didn't say anything. *What would Boggs do if he knew? Better not risk it.*

Luke spoke. "Boggs, it doesn't work like that. You can't buy your way into Heaven. But you can get in for free if you let Jesus turn your life around, and it's never too late. For starters, everyone needs to quit this nonsense right now, before someone gets hurt."

Boggs laughed. "Well, listen there. The sheriff's a

preacher." He rotated his head and looked at the man that Sawyer had called Turner. "I think your sermon's a little late, Sheriff. I didn't get this uniform from the prison supply room. My friend Turner here gave it to me." A wry smile added to the old man's wrinkles. "We had to clean it up a little, and I noticed it's a bit tight." Then he addressed Sawyer again. "I'll tell you what we do need to do. We need to get outta this state, or the only gold any of us is gonna see is in the warden's teeth."

Sawyer sighed. "Here's the problem with that. We have taken a substantial risk. Some of us have ended our careers for an investment in something more financially lucrative. That something is you," he said, looking at Boggs. "So, in a sense, we all own a piece of you, a piece of the treasure. If I had not done the research and found evidence that the treasure is real, I would never have considered this course of action. Now you can do whatever you want with your part, once it is recovered, but we need to recover it now for us to recoup our losses. We all have to start over."

Boggs was smiling and shaking his head. "You guys came to me, remember? You said you were okay with my terms."

"And I wish we could honor those terms, I truly do. But when we first talked about this, I realized you were an intelligent and honorable man, despite where fate had placed you. I appeal to you to be reasonable and consider these young men who have helped you. Mr. Boggs, consider your own words. You are right. You don't have much time left. I've seen your medical records. You might die at any moment and take the secret to the grave with you. That is the reason we have acted now. If we part ways without the treasure, we might never have another chance. I want to make this work for all of us."

Sawyer gave Boggs the same look of compassion that he had given Talisa. "Think about your own situation, Mr. Boggs. If we recover the treasure tonight, you might have enough time to accomplish your goals. If not, the people you plan to help will be no better off. For your revealing the location now, I can promise you that I will act as the 'executor,' so to speak, of your portion of the treasure, should you pass away. That way the years of you protecting the treasure will not be wasted. I will take a small percentage for my work because it will increase my chances of being caught. I understand that you will be taking a risk by revealing it, but if I may be blunt, your age decreases the significance of your risk. The rest of us have long lives ahead of us, and we have risked it all for this dream. Please take that into consideration."

Boggs was thoughtful. He winced and rubbed his left side. Half stumbling to one of the cruiser's benches, he sat and began to shake his head again. "Doc, I have seen you talk to guys in that pen, talkin' 'em out of things they is dead set to do and into things they never thought a' doin' in their lives." The old man looked at Sawyer. "I've got to tell you, I have never seen someone that can twist words around a fellow's heart and mind the way you do. You make this all sound so noble, like you is doin' some community service. But you made one mistake. You're trying to make me think about myself that way, too." He drilled Sawyer with his gaze. "I know what I am, Doc. We're gonna do this the way we first said. That's the only way."

"Mr. Boggs, I almost think you mean that."

"You can take it to the bank, Doc."

The soft smile on Sawyer's face transformed into a deadly scowl. "My colleagues and I have decided that we can no longer accept those terms."

Boggs chuckled. "I guess we know what you are too now, don't we?" The old man leaned back on the bench and gave Sawyer his full attention. "I've been around this a lot a' times. I ain't gullible and I don't threaten. Any way you slice it, I don't have much time left. If it's next month or today, don't matter much. Then you get nothin'." Boggs peered at the other men. "And I'm sure you boys figured you could make things unpleasant for me. Well, fellows, I been in prison for more years than you've been alive. I don't figure you can show me anything new. 'Sides, Doc, you know my condition inside. Wouldn't take much to stop this old heart. Sounds like a bad play on your part."

Sawyer's smile returned, but it held no compassion. "You haven't kept up with the times, Mr. Boggs. These days, those are not the sole alternatives. As a doctor, I have a variety of drugs available to me that make people more cooperative."

Boggs sneered, "We'll see."

"Actually," Sawyer said, "Your health increases the risk of using drugs as well, so I thought we would try something even more interesting first." Sawyer strolled toward Teddy. "Perhaps, even in prison, you have heard of one of our local celebrities. Mr. Teddy Baskins, The Enigma, he is called."

Boggs began laughing. "The psychic kid? Doc, you really are desperate. You gonna put the voodoo on me or somethin? We got lots of those kind on the inside. Made a good livin' at it 'til they got caught. Okay, let me see his trick, but you're wasting my time."

Talisa couldn't stand it. "Sawyer, I can't believe you would endanger us for this. You want to use Teddy for some treasure hunt? You're not only despicable, you're insane. Teddy's gift isn't something you can manipulate. He can't just do it on command. Teddy's been through all kinds of testing over the years. It doesn't work that way. Leave him alone. Let us all go, and you play your little games. But please don't involve Janie and Teddy."

Sawyer returned Talisa's look of contempt. "After all the time you've been around this, and you couldn't see what was right in front of you." He touched his hand to Teddy's shoulder. "Stand up, son."

Janie stood, hands still tied behind her back. "Leave 'em alone."

"Calm down, my dear." Sawyer gripped her arm, and she

tried to squirm away. "I don't want you to get hurt. And I know you don't want me to hurt Teddy." Sawyer pointed his gun at Teddy's head.

Talisa jumped up and rushed toward Sawyer. "Please."

Sawyer trained his gun at Talisa. "And, I know you don't want your sister to get hurt."

Janie sat down saying, "Okay, okay."

Teddy rose, his eyes darting from one person to the other. "What does he want me to do, Ms. Tee?"

"He's not going to be able to help you, Sawyer. Don't be mad and take it out on him when nothing happens."

"Go sit over there." Sawyer directed Teddy to the bench at the other end of the speedboat. He spoke to Talisa again. "With all this motivation, you might be surprised what we can accomplish. The beauty of you being here is that if someone calls my bluff and I do have to shoot one of you to prove I'm serious, I still have motivators left."

"They don't understand all that, Sawyer. I'm begging you as a human being. Please, don't do this."

Sawyer pulled Janie to her feet and began untying her hands. "It's you who doesn't understand." When he freed Janie's hands, he moved her to where the ski boat and Turner's cruiser were lashed together. "It's like a game of chess, Talisa. If we both got to pick the most important piece on the board, you would choose the king, but I would choose the queen."

Sawyer stepped across to the cruiser deck and pulled Janie across with him. "Janie, Mr. Boggs has some information that I need, and I want you to get it for me."

"What are you doing?" Talisa exploded. "What are you expecting her to do, Sawyer?"

Janie's lips parted, and she stared at Sawyer.

He pierced her with his own gaze. "It's all right, I know. You don't have to pretend anymore. You gave yourself away that day at your house. It was your sister, wasn't it? You knew what I was thinking somehow, or maybe you knew what she was thinking."

Janie seemed to recoil from the words.

Sawyer smiled. "That was it, wasn't it?" He called to Talisa. "You felt something for me and Janie knew it."

Talisa was full of confusion. *Janie knew?*

Janie's expression darkened. Her eyes lanced him like a dagger.

"You couldn't stand to see me getting to your sister, so you had to come up with something to get between us." Sawyer directed his accusations at Talisa again. "You have always been so caught up in what was going on that you never observed the process clinically. What I saw was Janie, searching for something, reaching out with her mind. Then she said that Teddy needed to help someone and grabbed his hand."

Thoughts poured into Talisa's mind. *Janie?*

"That's the way it has always been, hasn't it? You see something and show it to Teddy and he takes the credit." Sawyer glanced at Teddy.

Talisa and Janie did the same. He sat there, head down.

Sawyer spoke to Talisa again. "You see, here is a woman who is content to stand behind her man." He cast Talisa a look of disdain. "You can have Teddy. Janie's the talent in this act."

Janie gazed at Teddy and whispered, "Sowwy." Then she jerked her head and glared at Sawyer with disgust. "You are wong. I couldn't put things in anyone else. Teddy can take it. No one else could. He can take all the feelings and da pain. He is good, and he is stwong. He is not like you."

All her outburst brought from Sawyer was another smile. "I am glad you care so much for him because that means you will get the location of the treasure from Mr. Boggs, or I will kill Teddy."

Janie's wide, fearful eyes stared at him. Sawyer raised one eyebrow at her and pointed the gun at the boy.

"Okay, okay." The way Janie splayed her fingers against

the sides of her head spoke volumes to Talisa about her anxiety level. Janie trudged across the deck toward Boggs.

The old man straightened in his seat. "You got quite a show built up here. Am I supposed to crack in fear over this mess, or what exactly are you expectin'?" He waved Janie to him. "Come here, girly, and get it over with, so we can move onto the doc's next act because the sooner we get this over with the sooner we can get outta here. We're all gonna be back in the pen if we hang around here much longer."

Janie held out her hand, and Boggs took it. His eyes fluttered for a moment, then went blank.

Janie's look was similar but more conscious. Then she spoke, "I see it, but…I need Teddy."

Sawyer hopped into the ski boat, untied Teddy and helped him across to the other boat. Janie took his hand.

Teddy displayed the same look. "I see the water, and it feels like we're going up and down. I think it's like this—yeah, we're in a boat. There's a guy with a really leathery-looking face. He looks really old. I know his name means Doublehead, so that's what I call him. Doublehead is pointing at a rock wall, like the one next to us, but part of it sticks out. He says he knew the Warrior when he stood in the air, not in the water. Doublehead tells me that to inherit the Warrior's gold, you must go in like the breath of God."

Teddy gave a startled jerk. "Whoa! I went under water. I'm digging underwater. I'm coming up for air. I'm going back, up and back, up and back. Okay, I found it. I'm reaching back under a rock. I can feel a hole. I'm holding my breath and crawling." Teddy's brow wrinkled, he closed his eyes and clamped his lips tight in between words. "I want to turn around, but the hole's too narrow. I can't see anything. I need to breathe. I'm going to die. I need to—"

Teddy gasped, then panted, then sucked in several huge breaths. His breathing slowed. "There's air. But I bumped my head on a rock, and I'm all scraped up. It stings. It's so dark I can't see anything, but I can feel air, so I'm not underwater anymore. I'm in a narrow space with walls all around. There are rocks sticking out of the sides, poking me in the ribs and the back."

Teddy's eyes grew wider. "Okay, there's light now. I have a flashlight. It's like a narrow cave that goes up for a long way. One of the rocks is poking my ankle. I step up onto it, and it's flat on top, like a step. The one on the other side is just like it but a little higher. I have one leg on the first step and I'm stretching across and up to the next step. I'm climbing. This is neat. Still climbing. Still climbing. Okay, now I'm at another hole. It's in the side of the cave like a door. There are steps going down into another big cave. There are big funny-shaped rocks all over. No, I don't think they're—"

Sawyer leaned in.

"I'm wiping dirt off of one of the rocks, and it looks like metal. I brush a bunch of dirt off the top. There are coins inside. I found it." Teddy's eyes sparkled. Over and over he said, "I found it," until tears brimmed his eyes. Janie released Boggs' hand and grabbed Teddy in a hug, pulling his head to her chest while he sobbed.

Boggs collapsed back onto the bench.

Janie gave Sawyer a sharp look. "There, now let us go home."

Sawyer jerked erect. "That's it?" he blurted. "That doesn't tell me where it is. Do it again and get more information."

"Teddy tired." Janie shoved her face toward Sawyer. "This is a memory. It different. It's old. Sometimes it bwoken and hard to find."

"Sawyer!" Turner barked at him and pointed at Boggs.

The old man was wheezing and grasping at his left bicep.

Sawyer grabbed Janie and thrust her at the man. "Do it again, now."

"It will hurt him," Janie pleaded.

"He's dying anyway." Sawyer stood, pistol in one hand,

eyes shifting from one person to the next. He pointed the gun at Talisa with desperation in his eyes.

Janie grabbed Boggs' hand. His head rolled to look at her, face twisted in pain. Janie squeezed her eyes shut, gritted her teeth, and grabbed Teddy's hand. Teddy yelled out in agony and mirrored the man's grip of his chest and arm.

Sawyer moved close to him, "What do you see?"

"It hurts, oooohhh! It's like something big is on my chest."

"Where's the treasure?" He pointed the gun in Talisa's direction again, but neither of the pair was paying attention.

Talisa leaped across the span into the ski boat.

"Talisa!" Luke started to stand but was facing Harris' gun.

Touching the ski boat deck with one foot, she continued to the next boat where Sawyer stood, watching the drama in front of him, a loose grip on his gun. A hard shoulder slammed her onto the opposite bench. Turner held her down.

Sawyer jerked the gun toward them, but when he saw that the other man had her, he pivoted back to Teddy. Bending down into the boy's face, he screamed, "What do you see?"

Teddy opened his eyes and stared through Sawyer. "It's get'n dark and cold. All I feel is cold. It doesn't hurt anymore. It's get'n darker. It's dark like I've never seen. I can feel the dark and...yeeeooooww! It's hot, horrible hot, it's burning clear inside me, I can't stand it..." Teddy grabbed onto Sawyer's shirt and blinked his eyes, gasping for air. Sawyer scraped his hands away, and Teddy collapsed backward onto the deck.

Janie was there, holding Teddy. He looked up at her with the greatest relief a face could have. "I didn't have to stay. For a second I knew I was going to be there forever, and then something grabbed me and pulled me back, and I knew it wasn't me who had to stay."

Sawyer switched his gaze to Boggs. The old man's eyes became fixed and glassy as the hideous grimace on his face faded into a lifelessness stare. Sawyer howled like an animal. He turned on Janie. "That was our last chance." He took a step toward them, raising the gun as if possessed by a thought.

Talisa yelled. "Leave them alone, Sawyer. I can tell you where it is."

Chapter 22

Sawyer spun toward Talisa. "You can? How?"

She sneered at him. "Yes, I know it's hard for you to believe I could be worth anything, but I know the place. It's called Warrior's Head Rock. We used to swim there when we were kids. And once we're there, I can tell you how to get in. I'm sure it's not anything you'd know about." Talisa didn't hide her loathing for him. "It's from the Bible."

"Let her up."

Turner released Talisa and she twisted away.

"We'll see what you're worth. How do we get there?"

"We have to go in that direction. Around Snake Head Island."

Turner moved across to Boggs and felt for a pulse. "What do we do with him?"

Sawyer looked at Boggs and huffed out a breath. He thought for a moment, then said, "Throw him over the side. This area is remote enough it will be some time before they find him."

Turner straightened up looking displeased. "If they find

him, there goes the story that he killed me and hid my body. They'll quit looking for him and start looking for me."

Sawyer shrugged. "You want to take him with us? How are we going to get him off when we dock? We're going to look a little suspicious carrying a dead body off the boat, don't you think?" Sawyer paused and studied Turner, then Harris who was still standing on the other cruiser. He continued. "We didn't kill him. He had a heart attack. When they find him, at least he won't look like a murder victim. If you've got a better idea, let's hear it. Weight him down if it makes you feel any better. Just hurry up. He was right about one thing. The longer we hang around here, the greater our chance of being caught."

Turner took a deep breath, let it out, and lumbered toward the body.

Talisa hurried to her sister. She and Janie helped Teddy up, then Talisa enveloped them in a hug and faced them away. She heard Turner lugging Boggs' body over the side. She cringed at the splash.

"Okay," Sawyer said. "There's nothing we can do about that now." He looked at Talisa. "I hope you're not lying to me. It will be better to tell me now than lead me on some contrived stalling attempt. That would greatly upset me."

Talisa continued holding the kids as she returned his glare. "I didn't know Boggs until today, but I know the area. I'll take you to the place and tell you what I think. The rest is up to you. But you have to let Janie and Teddy go."

"You're not in a position to bargain. They have to come. Their abilities might yet be useful. They will also assure you follow through with your assistance. But if this goes well, once we have the treasure, it will not be to my advantage to harm you. It would just add fire to the efforts to find us. I will put all of you someplace where you cannot give us away. I'll make sure you are found after we get out of the area. Refuse me and I'll begin hurting the good sheriff until you decide to cooperate."

Sawyer raised his voice to his partners, "Okay, everyone comes with us."

Soon they had the boats separated again. Sawyer left Luke handcuffed but held the radio mic up to him and forced Luke to tell the dispatcher that he was still okay and would continue to check the same area.

Sawyer had them tie Teddy's hands behind his back again and left him on the cruiser. They also moved Luke to Turner's cruiser. Talisa cautioned them to be careful with Teddy around the water because he didn't know how to swim. They bound Janie also and put her in the ski boat with Sawyer. Sawyer tied Talisa's wrists in front of her and had her sit in the seat beside him, so she could direct him.

Sawyer looked around. "Everybody cozy?" His eyes came to rest on Talisa. "Lead on."

Talisa directed him across the lake and toward the land mass known as Snake Head Island. The cruiser followed along behind carrying the others. She led them around and into a different branch of the lake. The sun had moved into the afternoon by the time they arrived at a tall rock wall that rose above the lake like a fortress. Following along the wall, they came to a large outcropping that indeed resembled a squared head. More rock protruded from the main outcropping, causing the effect of a large noble nose jutting out from the head and resting on the waters.

"The Warrior's Head," Talisa announced, gesturing with her tied hands. "In school, we read the work of a Cherokee writer who made reference to the Warrior's Head rising above the valley before the valley became a lake when the dam was built. That's what the Cherokee was telling Boggs. He remembered the Warrior in the air, not in the water."

Sawyer scowled at her. "We don't have much daylight left. Where is the treasure?"

"You have to go in like the breath of God."

Sawyer huffed.

Talisa hurried with her explanation, "Many of the Cherokees converted to Christianity, so I think this is a Bible reference. God gave man life by breathing the breath of life into his nostrils. From what Teddy described, going underwater and digging and finding an entrance to a cave, combined with the Bible reference, I am guessing there is an entrance underwater at the base of the nose. The cave must go up through the nose like a nostril."

Sawyer idled the boat over to the base of the nose and surveyed it. He killed the engine and relayed the information to his partners, then told them, "I'm going to go down and take a look." He moved to the back of the boat, opened a compartment, and took out scuba gear. When he saw Talisa looking at him he said, "I told you, I have planned for this. I even have explosives in the forward compartment of the boat, if needed. We have no intention of going home empty-handed."

Taking a small device out of a cubby, Sawyer moved to the scuba tank. It was a carbon monoxide detector. Her father had used one like it to test for carbon monoxide in tanks he didn't fill himself. If someone filling the tanks was careless, it was possible for carbon monoxide to get in with the air. The deadly gas was odorless and tasteless, so to check for it, a diver had to use a detector. Sawyer had his own tank filler. Why was he paranoid? *Maybe for good reason.* Considering the type of people with whom he associated, he was likely concerned someone would try to kill him for his share. *Why couldn't that happen today?*

He strapped on the gear and soon disappeared feet first over the side of the boat. Talisa rose and started back to Janie. Turner yelled at her. "Where you going?"

"My sister's scared. I'm just going to sit by her." Talisa continued to the seat beside Janie. Turner watched her but didn't say more.

"Are you all right?"

Janie shook her head. "Tee, was I bad? Did I make that

man die?"

"No, sweetie. You couldn't have known what was going to happen. You were protecting Teddy and me. Sawyer is the reason it happened. He's bad." She raised her tied hands over Janie's head and encircled her. "I'm so proud of you. How did you know to take my cell phone?"

Janie glanced over her shoulder toward the cruiser. "Luke taught me. He told me what to do if someone tried to take me. Sowwy, you phone is gone."

Talisa squeezed her tighter. "Don't worry about that. It's not important. You did great." Talisa pulled back where she could look at Janie. "Why didn't you tell me that you were the one who could see things?"

"Sowwy." Tears started down Janie's cheeks. "Mama and Daddy told me not to."

"Mama and Daddy?"

Janie nodded. "When it first started."

Talisa gave Janie a probing look. "When did it start?"

"When Luke left." Janie looked down. "I saw him first."

"Saw him? You saw something through Luke's eyes?"

Janie's face scrunched up. "You came home and you were crying and wouldn't talk to Daddy about it. Then Luke stopped coming to our house. I didn't know what was wong. Nobody would tell me. Everybody thought I was too dumb to understan'."

"Oh, sweetie, that wasn't it."

Janie didn't stop. "No, Tee. It twue. I know I'm not smart as other people. I pwayed to God. I asked him to help me see what was wong. You my sister. Luke like my big bwother. After Luke left, I pwayed every day. I asked God over and over to help me see. One day I was on my bed pwaying and it happened. My bed was gone, and I wasn't laying down. I was sitting on a bus, and I knew in my mind that I was going to basic training for the Marines. I didn't know how I knew that, it was just in my mind. It's gone now, but I kind'a rememba."

Talisa watched as Janie's eye widened at the memory.

"I could see my hands, but they weren't my hands, but I still knew them. I had looked at Luke's hands so many times I knew they was his. I knew his clothes, the gwease stains on his pants from helping Daddy fix the boat. It fweaked me out, but the scariest part was I was hurting inside so bad I wanted to die. Then it stopped."

"What stopped?"

"All of it. I was back on my bed. I ran an' told Mama. She said that God must have given me a vision and we should pway for Luke. So we did. I was gonna tell you, but mama said you were hurting too much and it would make you hurt worse. Mama told Daddy, but they said I shouldn't tell nobody else. I kept havin' visions about Luke when he was feeling wealy bad and Mama, Daddy and me would pway hard for him. Then you left and went to college…" Janie hesitated.

"What is it?"

"I started seeing fwoo your eyes when you was hurt'n."

The shock of the statement hit Talisa's mind like a slap. For a moment she was dumbfounded. She realized her mouth was agape. "What did you see?"

"Lotsa things. I saw you when those girls lied about you. I saw when you hurt your leg."

"That's how Mama knew."

Janie gave an affirmative nod, looking at Talisa like she didn't know what to expect.

Talisa realized Janie was seeing a stunned look on her face. "I'm sorry. I just never thought about you seeing me…through me. And you knew what I was thinking?"

Janie's worried look continued as she nodded. Then she smiled a little. "I was smart when I was you. Part of me wanted to stay that way, but part of me…" The frown returned to her face. "I'm sowwy you have to worry about so many things, Tee. I'm sowwy you hurt so much."

Talisa couldn't move, couldn't speak. But she

remembered. Time after time when she should have seen. After a moment, she found her voice. "I wondered how Mama knew just when to call, seemed to know what questions to ask to get me to tell her what was wrong. I started thinking God must be telling her... I guess He was."

Janie scrutinized her face again. "Sowwy, Tee."

More memories came. "It wasn't your fault. I should have been looking beyond myself, and I would have known." She peered into her sister's eyes and wondered what it would be like to see through them and behind them. To experience the world Janie lived in every day. "You went through the hard times with me."

Tears traced tracks around the contours of Janie's face. "Jus' like you did fo' me when I was wittle. Except God knew I had to be inside your mind to understan'."

Talisa held her sister but found herself staring at the horizon. "I wish I had understood as much as you. You were praying for someone other than yourself. Maybe that's why God answered your prayer." Talisa glanced to her sister again. "How did Teddy find out?"

Janie lowered her voice and looked in Teddy's direction. "I didn't tell him. I started seein' a man yelling at me, telling me that I was good for nothin' 'cause I hadn't cleaned out a pig shed. I didn't know whose mind I was in. It felt more like my mind. I didn't understan' things any better. I saw fwoo those eyes bunches of times after that. It was always the same man yelling at me. I saw a sad-looking woman sometimes, but she never said nothin'."

"Did you know who it was?"

Janie shook her head. "Then I saw myself load'n furniture on an old twuck, and the man was telling me I wasn't doing it wight. There was a mirror I was loading on the twuck, and I saw a guy's face in it and I knew it was his eyes I was seeing fwoo. Later...it was on a weekend that you was home...we all went to church, and the guy I saw fwoo met us at the fwont door. It was Teddy."

"I remember that day. Did you tell him about what you saw?"

Another head shake from Janie. "Not the part about seeing his dad yelling at him. He don't need to rememba that. I never saw fwoo Teddy's eyes again, but one day I started seeing fwoo a little girl's eyes. She was walking home from the school acwoss town. A man took me—I mean the girl—and threw her in a car. It scared me and I gwabbed Teddy's hand, and he could see what I was see'n. Teddy wanted to help, but I told him about my pwomise. So he told Luke and just left out the part about me."

Talisa let out a breath of realization. "I was home when that happened also."

Janie cocked her head sideways. "Oh, yeah. You was. I fo'got."

"So when Teddy told Luke what he was seeing, he saw it through you. You're the one the saved the girl. That was the first time Teddy…I mean we thought Teddy saw something. But it was you."

Janie frowned and shook her head. "I couldn't do it without Teddy. I could talk to Mama about you and Luke because she knew you. It hard with other people. Teddy can talk better about what people is think'n an' feel'n. When I started see'n bad things happen'n to people, I had to stop looking so hard. It hurt too much. I just see things and don't let myself feel much. Teddy can feel the hurt but not get hurt. I couldn't do that. I think it's because Teddy been hurt all his life."

Janie tipped her head back as if she were seeing events from the past. "Mama saw that Teddy was stwong. She thought it was okay for Teddy to tell what he saw, but she made him pwomise not to tell that it was because of me. Mama said he was stwong enough to cover me. She told me it was like her and Daddy. Mama supported Daddy and kept him going, and he was stwong for her. I liked that." Janie shifted and stared at the deck. "I didn't want to lie, Tee. But I wanted to do what Mama and Daddy told me. Mama said it wasn't ly'n cuz when I say that Teddy sees things, it's twue. I just see 'em first. I wanted to tell you so bad. I talked to Teddy, and he said he would talk to Pastor Cooper, but all he told Teddy was not to worry and to please God. After that we decided to wait and see what God would do."

Talisa looked down. "I guess it was wise not to tell anyone."

Janie spoke like she knew Talisa's feelings. "When Mama got sick, Daddy was gonna tell you, but Mama said you had enough to worry about. She hoped you would go back to college. She wanted you to have your dweams."

Talisa stared across the lake in thought. "Can you see things anytime you want to?"

"No. God shows me things. Most times I don't even know it's going to happen. Sometimes I ask Him." Janie wiped her cheeks on the shoulder of her blouse. "I asked that day that Sawyer was talk'n to you. I was scared. I was hoping it would make Sawyer go away. This wouldn't a' happened if I hadn't done that."

Talisa gave her sister an encouraging look. "We needed to help that girl. God knew what he was doing. The rest wasn't your fault. It was mine. I should have seen what Sawyer was." Talisa squeezed her eyes shut.

When she opened them, Janie was staring at her. She leaned close to Talisa. "Sawyer is wong. I didn't see what you was thinking. You my sister, and I know what you feeling. Not in my mind, in my heart. I was scared because you let Sawyer touch you in you heart, and that place is only for Luke."

"What do you mean 'only for Luke?' Why?"

Janie shrugged like the question was strange. "Tee, couldn't you feel it? When I was inside your mind, I knew I was supposed to be with Luke. And when I was in Luke, I knew I was supposed to be with you."

Talisa regarded Janie and decided not to take the subject

any further. She took a deep breath. There was something else she had to know. "Did you see anything when Daddy…died?"

Janie shook her head. "Not until after."

"After what?"

"When you came home, and the police came, it was scary. You was crying and scweaming that Daddy was gone. I didn't know what to do. I went to my room. I asked God to show me Daddy. I begged Him. Then I saw Him."

Talisa gasped. "Daddy?"

Janie gave her an odd look. "No. Jesus."

"Jesus? Jesus was in your room?"

Janie looked frustrated. "No, it was Daddy. It was what he was see'n. I can't tell you what I saw. I don't got enough words. But it was betta than anything. I knew it was Jesus, 'cause Daddy knew it was Jesus. And Daddy was so happy. Then it was over."

Daddy is with Him. It rolled through Talisa like a warm wave. It was true. It had always been true. "That's what you meant every time you told me not to cry, that Daddy was with Jesus."

Janie looked sad. "Tee, you knew that. Rememba' when we was wittle and I asked you where people went when they died? You told me if they loved Jesus, they went to be with Him. You were the one that told me first."

Talisa sobbed. She held on tight to her sister and buried her head in her shoulder. They cried together. After a moment, Talisa sniffed and nodded. "Thanks for reminding me. I remember now." She lifted her bound hands from around Janie and used them to wipe her eyes. She closed them again. *Thank You, Jesus, for reminding me. Sorry I haven't been listening.*

Talisa heard a bubbling sound. She looked over the edge, and Sawyer's head popped out of the water.

He swam to the back of the boat and heaved himself up. When he removed his diving mask, he spoke to the other two men. "It's there. You can see where someone dug the sand and dirt out, but most of it has filled back in. I pulled out enough by hand to feel the hole up under the nose, but the sand keeps falling back in. I need a bucket and some help. Suit up, Harris. We'll work together. The bank falls away a little farther out. If we can dig off this part of it, we should be able to push the sand over the edge after that and create enough room to get in there. You got this, Turner? Everyone is tied up, so no one should be swimming away. If they try, shoot them."

"I got it," he said, hoisting the rifle that Harris passed off to him.

Sawyer and Harris gathered what they needed. Harris wriggled into a wetsuit and they both submerged.

Janie and Talisa held each other and prayed. Talisa began to talk of their childhood to relieve some of the stress from Janie and Teddy. Janie giggled as Talisa regaled them with the funny things that they had done. Sometimes she'd call over to Teddy with something that would have him snorting.

During a lull in the laughter, Talisa called to Luke, "Did you know about Janie's ability?"

"I knew that it took both of them, but I didn't realize why."

Talisa smiled at him. "Janie seems to think there is something special between us. What do you think?"

Luke grinned. "Known that for a long time. Just been waiting for you to figure it out."

Talisa's smile turned to a smirk. "Think you're pretty smart, huh?"

Luke lifted his shoulders. "Even a nearsighted baboon can see his own nose."

"You still need help in the romance department. Did anyone ever tell you that?"

"I've known that for a long time, too. I was kinda hoping you'd apply for the job."

Talisa shook her head. "Oh, good grief. I'll have to do it

as a public service." She paused. "So, let's say that I'm submitting my resume and waiting for an offer."

Luke's grin widened "Not needed. I've always been impressed with your qualifications. I just needed to know you were still interested in the position."

Talisa returned his smile. "That's sounding a little better. I'm interested."

Luke looked up at the man standing guard. "Hey, Turner, want to be best man?"

Turner raised his head and one corner of his mouth.

Chapter 23

When Sawyer and Harris surfaced, both men seemed to be excited. Sawyer filled Turner in on what was happening. "Okay, we've got a big enough hole under the nose that I was able to stand up in the cave. It's a little tight with a tank on, and we were getting low on air, so I didn't want to risk trying to climb yet. We've got two tanks left, so we'll go down again, and I'll try to climb up the cave. If there's air up there like Boggs said, I can turn off my tank and save it. I'll let Harris know, and he can surface and save his until I find out what's up there."

Both men switched out their tanks and went down again. After ten minutes or so, Harris resurfaced. "He was able to climb up to where there's air. The water must be a little higher than when Boggs was here."

Each mention of Boggs' name brought a twinge in the pit of Talisa's stomach.

Harris crawled into the ski boat and plopped into one of the pilot's chairs to rest. After what seemed like another hour, Sawyer surfaced. As he climbed over the side, he tossed some type of metal headpiece onto the deck of the ski boat. The surface was dirty, but a gold hue showed through where the dirt had been wiped away. Harris scooped it up, grabbed a rag out of a compartment, and rubbed hard at the metal. Various colors of stones began to appear under the rubbing.

After shedding his gear, Sawyer sat beaming from the back of the boat.

Turner asked, "How much is there?"

Sawyer inhaled deeply and his hand trembled. He didn't answer right away, then he said, "More than I ever imagined. It may take us days to get it all out. We'll have to make several trips because the boats won't hold it. All the research I did said this was the accumulation of gold captured over centuries of raids of all types. After seeing what's in there, I believe it. We need more air tanks. We also should come up with a place to cache what we take out until we decide how to sneak it out of the area."

Sawyer glanced at Talisa. "I'm a little more ambitious than your father."

Talisa narrowed her eyes at him. "What do you mean?"

"Your father is the reason I knew it was real. I've always been a treasure hunter at heart. Aren't we all—always looking for the pot of gold that will make our dreams come true? It's basic human psychology. That's my strength. I accept reality instead of imagining myself loftier than I am. That's why this treasure was worth risking everything. It's not something that you'll use up in a few years of high living. It's big enough for the big dreams.

Ever since I moved here, the treasure fascinated me. I started researching it. The county museum had a Native American Treasure Horde display all about the mysterious treasure. The display included several artifacts from an anonymous donor. They were said to represent the type of items that might be found in such a treasure. I contacted the archaeologists who had evaluated the items, and they placed some of the pieces as being from a series of renegade Indian raids of Union Army shipments during the Civil War and others as eighteenth-century Native American artwork. That fit the treasure legend."

Talisa broke into the narrative. "What does this have to do with my father?"

"I started stumbling across sales to collectors and museums from an anonymous source. I also found some historic gold sold on internet auctions. It took some digging and bribery, but I traced it back to your father. I couldn't connect him to all the items, but it seemed to fit. Your father had found the treasure and was selling just what he needed to pay your mother's medical bills. Very noble, but like I said, not very ambitious."

Talisa sneered at him. "Naturally then, it should go to you who would make much better use of it."

Sawyer raised his brow. "Your father took what he needed. The history of the treasure indicates it was a legacy to powerful and ruthless men. Eventually someone would have taken it from him."

"It was no coincidence you moving in next door was it? You have to get close to someone to stab them in the back."

The side of his lip curled. "When the house came up for sale next to his, I bought it. I thought maybe he had found the treasure somewhere on his property, maybe an old mine or cave or something. So I confess, I got a little anxious and started snooping around. That's when we had our little dispute. Too bad. I admired him. Even at his age, he was still a tough old Navy Seal. The digging down there was much more recent than Boggs' time. Your dad must have been doing this on his own to keep it as quiet as he did. I wish it had worked out with your father. He would have made a great partner, but he didn't much care for me."

Hearing Sawyer talk was making Talisa sick inside. "Daddy was a better judge of character than I've been. But I'm learning."

Sawyer dropped his eyes and smiled. "When I met you, I

was surprised that you had anything to do with me, so I knew your father must have kept the treasure and the problems we had a secret, even from his family. When I saw you trying to dig around over in that clearing and you waved at me, I thought maybe you and I could start fresh. So I decided to help you out. Forgive me if I poked around a little while I had my heavy equipment up there. A waste of time as it turned out. Your father had cleared and leveled that area before I moved in next door. I guess it really was just for fill dirt for the new boat ramp at the marina, but at the time I suspected it had something to do with the treasure."

Talisa glared at Sawyer. "Daddy thought of other things besides money. Not anything you could understand."

"I think you're judging me a little harshly. I haven't hurt you, have I? I threatened you, so I wouldn't have to hurt you. I'm glad you were more congenial than your father. But then with you, it was your boyfriend who got in the way." Sawyer indicated Luke. "And him." He motioned toward Teddy. "But it all worked out. If it hadn't been for The Enigma there, I never would have gotten to know you and Janie. And we wouldn't be here today."

"I'm not impressed with the way you show your gratitude."

"Actually, I wish I was in a position to show it more. We also would make a great team. You are a beautiful and resourceful woman. Without your and Janie's help, we never would have found the treasure. You deserve your share. We could do this together. Janie could come, too. There's not much the three of us couldn't accomplish together."

The offer caught Talisa off guard, but she didn't answer.

Sawyer took on his compassionate look. "You're in a self-imposed prison of tradition and morality, like most humans. Let's make life an adventure, make our own rules, or better yet, live without any."

She found her voice. "That works out pretty well for you, doesn't it?"

"As you see it. But you could be on the other side of this situation if you wanted."

"For how long?"

"That's the beauty of such relationships. Instead of flawed conventions, in which both parties end up suffering, the continuation of the union is based on how hard each person works to make the other one happy. Satisfaction guaranteed."

"And when the adventure ends, and I don't make you happy anymore, what then? Oh, but I guess Ms. Agnew found that out, didn't she?"

Sawyer's expression altered for a second, like one of Luke's suspects.

Talisa went on. "What was it, a disagreement in the hot tub that night? Did she get her head above the surface long enough to scream, and we heard it? Or maybe it wasn't so dramatic as a disagreement. Maybe you were just done with your research and didn't want anyone else to know about the treasure. Whatever it was, an extra-long dunk that night ended the adventure for Ms. Agnew, didn't it? Then later you took her from wherever you hid her that night and she became a suicide victim."

Suicide victim. The words connected in her mind. "Just like my father." It was like a slap to her face and it dazed her, then awakened her. She stared at Sawyer. The pieces all came together. "My father didn't kill himself. The hose on his boat engine was just for show."

The compassion was slowly evaporating from Sawyer's face, but at her last words his head came erect and a hardness took over his eyes.

In her mind, she saw Sawyer using the carbon monoxide detector. "The carbon monoxide they found in his system came from his scuba tanks." The image of the shed behind Sawyer's house. The scuba fill pump laboring away. "You stole his tanks and refilled them with enough carbon monoxide to kill him, but enough oxygen so he couldn't tell until it was too late and he was far enough under water. He never tested tanks he filled himself."

She shuddered. "You must have been watching from somewhere, and when you knew he was gone and couldn't fight you anymore...you coward...you came and... got him and set up the whole scene." Talisa's voice broke and she sobbed.

Luke took over. "You had to use the tanks because carbon monoxide can't get into the system if the body isn't breathing. But you had to get rid of the evidence, so you opened all the tanks, so the carbon monoxide would drain out. All the OBI investigators saw was that there were no signs of a struggle or injury on his body and his face had the cherry red color that comes with carbon monoxide poisoning. When the autopsy verified it, case closed, suicide."

Sawyer lifted himself to his full height, the smile gone. "Well, it looks like you have me all figured out, and I hate to disappoint people. It's a flaw of mine. I'm afraid things are getting a little complicated from here on. We'll need all our time and energy to recover the treasure. We're going to take you to the place we discussed, where we can leave you until we are far away, and then we'll let the authorities know where you are."

Talisa had no illusions about what Sawyer planned to do. No one else knew about the treasure. No one else knew about the three men's involvement. There would be speculation when Sawyer and his men disappeared but no proof, except for four inconvenient witnesses. A tremor went from the middle of Talisa's back and spread. There was no advantage for Sawyer to let them live. *No, no, no. Please, God.*

Sawyer directed his gaze at Turner. "Let's get the boats started and move them together, so we can transfer everyone onto your cruiser. I'll need to take my boat back to my house tonight, so there won't be any suspicion because tomorrow

I'll need to get the air tanks and other things that we'll need."

Turner tossed the rifle to Harris, leaving his pistol tucked in his belt. He strode to the pilot's chair on the cruiser and fired the motor up. Sawyer took the other pistol from Harris and put it in his pocket. Then he started the ski boat. They maneuvered the boats alongside each other.

Sawyer approached Janie. "I am going to untie you, and I want you to step across to the other boat. Please do as I say, so no one gets hurt."

Harris stood on the back of the ski boat while Sawyer helped Janie across.

Luke still sat in the cruiser. He had been uncharacteristically quiet.

***

Luke was thinking, working things out in his mind. Sawyer was obviously lying. He and his men were going to kill them all, and they were going to do it soon. Everything had gone wrong. Luke ached inside at his own stupidity. He should never have gone into this without another officer. Once he discovered the connection between Sawyer and Boggs, he should've put it all together. But it was so bizarre, who would have imagined it? And Janie, he had missed that too. *God, how could I have been so stupid? And now I brought Talisa with me, and he'll kill her and Janie and Teddy.*

Fear twisted at Luke's gut. It seemed like he hadn't done anything right. And all the prayers he had counted on had gone unanswered. *What could be the purpose of all this, Lord? I know I've let You down, but I'm begging You to help us out of this.* A memorized scripture floated into his mind: *My grace is sufficient for thee, for My strength is made perfect in weakness.* Luke never felt weaker, handcuffed and unarmed. They had all the advantage. He kept a handcuff key hid in his boot, but there was no way to get it without them seeing. He had already tried it several times.

Your strength is all I have, Lord. I admit that I can't do anything without You. Please show me how to save the others. I don't care about myself. Just don't let me sit here and watch them die. Luke quieted his thoughts to listen to God. In his mind, an image flashed. Take out one player. It was the best he could do, and the rest would be up to God. There was still one place that he had the advantage even with his hands handcuffed behind his back.

***

As Talisa gazed at Luke, he mouthed the words "I love you" and nodded to her.

The look in his eyes said something more—a sadness that said goodbye. Was he giving up? Somehow, she knew better. She thought he had given up on her once before, and she had been wrong. Now, to her surprise, she trusted him. Even when she didn't know it, he had always been there for her. *For her.* He was planning something for her, for them. Luke knew what she knew. They needed to do something and do it quickly, but what? She couldn't lose Luke, not now.

Talisa thought of her mother, then her father. She had lost so much. An unnatural calm filled her. Lose or gain, live or die, God was all she needed. Quiet and still, His voice was telling her, *My grace is sufficient for you.*

Talisa answered. *Please Lord. I can't fight You. I surrender. I will live or die with whatever You have planned for me today, but I'm asking for Your help.*

***

Luke watched for his opening. Harris was at the edge of the speedboat, but he wouldn't be there forever. Luke knew he might not have another chance. Sawyer and the two men were busy preparing to leave. They were distracted. Unnoticed, Luke moved his body into the right position, legs under him ready to spring. Turner moved to the front of his vessel with his back to them. Luke fastened his eyes on Harris who was standing guard on the sleek speedboat, which sat lower in the water than the cruiser. He waited for the moment…then it happened. Harris turned his head to watch something that Sawyer was doing.

Luke sprung. He landed one foot on the side of the cruiser and launched his body into the air, thrusting his legs in front of him and spreading them apart. He came at the man from above and caught him right around the chest, a leg on each side. His body hit Harris hard as he clamped his legs around his upper torso. The man expelled his air in a sound of shock and discomfort and Luke thought, *He's gonna regret that in a second.* They plummeted into the water. Luke took a long deep breath, just before they went under.

***

Sawyer had directed Talisa to the chair beside the pilot seat on the ski boat. The sound of a groan and a large splash resounded over the idle of both engines. Her eyes darted to the cruiser. Luke was gone.

Turner jumped up on the outer part of the craft, gun in hand. He yelled to Sawyer, "I think the sheriff got Harris."

Sawyer raised his palms in disbelief. "He was handcuffed."

Talisa had determined she was going to be ready no matter what Luke decided to do. But what had he done? How could he have…? Her mind grasped for some way to help him. But how could she have any impact on the situation? Her hands were still bound in front of her. She could swim that way, but she knew she wouldn't get far before she was shot. And nothing could make her leave

Teddy and Janie.

***

The water swirled around Luke as he squeezed Harris with his legs, his hands still handcuffed behind his back. They were sinking into the lake. The sun had been getting lower, so the light was dim under the surface, but Luke was close enough to Harris that he could still see. The man's panic caused him to let go of the rifle and use his arms to swim up. Luke had counted on that but regretted watching the weapon fall away into the murk. When swimming up didn't work, Harris grabbed at Luke's legs, trying to free himself. He tried to beat at his attacker with his fists, but Luke just squeezed harder and curled his head into the man's body until it pressed against the other man's chest. He was too close for the man's blows to have much effect in the water.

In one last effort, Harris again tried to swim upwards. Their downward momentum was used up, and the buoyancy of the air in Luke's lungs gave lift to Harris' efforts. The man was making headway, and Luke's squeeze was no longer working to stop it. He thought about letting go and trying to get to the handcuff key, but he knew he didn't have the time or the air. This was all Luke could do. If they made it to the surface, his advantage would be gone. He was not going to let that happen. Luke pulled his head back and looked in Harris' determined face. As he gazed into the man's eyes, Luke opened his mouth and blew out the precious air from his lungs and they both sank into the depths.

***

Sawyer jumped up with his own gun pointing at where the water still churned just off the back of the speedboat.

"Watch for him. We'll get him when he comes up." Both men scanned the water.

Talisa prepared herself. She had determined that if Sawyer started to shoot Luke. she was going to do something. Perhaps if she hit Sawyer hard enough, she could drive him over the side of the boat. But she doubted she was strong enough. Sawyer wasn't like the long-haired man named Gravy, and if it hadn't been for Luke, she would have lost that fight. Sawyer was tall and fit, significantly outweighing her.

But would Luke come back up? Was that what he had planned, to take Harris to the bottom and drown them both? *No, Luke.*

Frustration and concern filled Sawyer's face. He had no hope that Harris would prevail. Everything was going wrong for him and he was desperate. Even if Luke could make it back, Sawyer would kill him the moment he broke the surface. And Luke knew it. He had to have known there was no way to survive what he was going to do.

Talisa refused to give in to her anguish. She had to do something. Her gaze landed on Janie. Her sister's face stopped her thoughts. Janie stared at the water where Luke had gone in. She sat by Teddy, her arm wrapped around his shoulders, hanging on for dear life. Their eyes told Talisa their minds were locked onto something that was playing out beneath the surface. Their faces were terrified, but not hopeless. What were they seeing? *Luke!*

Talisa didn't have time to cry or have a meltdown. She was not going back there, not giving up. If Luke made it back, she wouldn't let him be killed. She had grown up around boats and the water all her life, so she needed to use what she knew to her advantage before it was too late. Luke had sacrificed himself to take one person out of the picture. Could she do the same? It was just Sawyer and her on the ski boat. An idea came to her, but she didn't have time to act on it.

"Throw the boy in. Give him something else to worry about." Sawyer spat the command at Turner like he was ordering him to throw out some bad bait.

"No." Talisa screamed and leapt across to help Teddy. Sawyer caught her by the hair. Pain shot through her scalp and neck as he jerked her back into the ski boat. When she scrambled up to try again, he grabbed her around the neck and held her while he searched the water for Luke. She tried to twist free, but his arm clamped tighter, and she could barely breathe.

In horror, she watched as Turner grabbed Teddy and dragged him up off the chair. Teddy's eyes blinked, looking confused, as he was pulled from Janie's embrace.

Janie's attention was still locked on the water, but her hand reached out, apparently searching for what it had lost. She found Turner's wrist instead and gripped it.

The man's fingers quivered, and he released Teddy. The spasm traveled up his arm and it locked straight. The ripple went across his shoulder and hit his face. His eyes and mouth popped wide like something awful had filled his brain. Turner's face turned red. Unlike Teddy, he had no words for the vision he was seeing. His mouth opened in silent gasping like a fish. Stumbling backward, he tore himself from Janie's grasp.

Janie jumped up, eyes fluttering. She spun toward Turner. Her hand went out like she wanted to take something back, but she knew she couldn't. On her face was a look of profound sorrow. "Sowwy about you friend."

Turner's chest heaved up and down like there wasn't enough oxygen in the air. He stared at Janie, mouth still open. Then he arched his back, grimaced, and grabbed his chest. Doubling over, he collapsed onto the deck. His body lay there jerking, twitching and drooling for a few seconds, then lay quiet. It had taken only moments for the pain and terror to take him.

Talisa realized how strong Teddy truly was.

There was a gasp for air, from the water to the right of the ski boat. *Luke.* He made it. He was alive.

Sawyer flung her aside and trained his gun on the water, searching for a target. Talisa already knew what she was going to do. Praying it was not too late, she dashed to the driver's seat of the ski boat. Even with her hands tied, she jammed the throttle wide open. The boat lurched forward sending Sawyer stumbling toward the back just as his gun went off. The force of the takeoff pushed Talisa into the driver's seat, but she still had the controls in reach.

Sawyer faced the rear of the boat, trying to get his balance against the forward inertia. Before he could recover, she pulled the throttle, cutting the boat's speed and sending the momentum the other way. Sawyer went backward, landing hard on his rump.

Talisa rammed the throttle forward again and cranked the wheel back and forth, sending Sawyer sliding across the deck into the side of the boat and then back. She swung the boat wide to put distance between Luke and the rest of them. If there were explosives in the bow of the boat as Sawyer said, she didn't want there to be any chance of the others getting hurt. Maintaining the wild maneuvers, so Sawyer couldn't regain his footing, she headed the craft directly toward the rock wall and shoved the throttle to full speed. Talisa glanced back. Sawyer had just managed to get to his hands and knees, facing her.

Does he realize what I'm doing? He was too low to see where they were headed. She spun out of the pilot's chair and stood to further block his view. She thought about diving off the side. *No, Talisa, that would give it away.* If Sawyer could get to the controls, he still had time to turn the boat and return to the cruiser. She didn't know if Luke was in any condition to protect Janie and Teddy. *I can't let this guy have another chance to hurt them. A few more seconds and there will be no turning back. You have to see this through.*

Talisa yelled over the roar of the engine and the water.

"Looks like it's you and me after all."

Sawyer raised his head at the comment. There was nothing friendly in his features. His eyes returned to the deck, searching, then stopped. At the edge, under a life jacket, Talisa saw black gun metal. Sawyer lunged on all fours toward it.

She raised her voice again. "I guess the adventure's over."

Sawyer looked at her and sneered as he slapped his palm on the weapon. Taking in hard breaths, he curled his fingers around the handgrip.

Talisa rushed him. His eyes widened in surprise. As he raised the weapon, she leaped and planted her foot in the middle of his back, driving him back to the floor. At a full run, she dove from the back of the boat. She thrust her arms forward and straightened her body sleek like an arrow as she plunged into the dark waters.

Talisa flattened out her dive and rotated to see above. A fireball erupted, so bright the light penetrated the filter of gray liquid above her. Moments later, the water quaked from a shockwave, and debris began hitting the surface.

Talisa pushed hard with her legs and used her tied hands in a side stroke, putting distance between her and the danger zone. Something hit the water above. A shadowy shape drilled toward her. Talisa twisted her body to get out of the way. Some type of metal part hit her in the leg, sending a charley horse shooting through her thigh.

Above her, fire spread out on the surface and blazed brighter when the larger burning hunks hit the water. Talisa grimaced at the pain in her leg but kept going. She tipped her head back to see what was ahead. The move flipped the watery world upside down, forcing her mind to compensate. An area appeared untouched by the blaze, and she pushed in that direction, but a burning piece of debris blocked her path.

The wreckage dipped farther into the water as the buoyant part of it burned away and the heavy part pulled it under.

Talisa didn't think she could take another hit, but she didn't have enough strength or oxygen to try a different way. The burning piece began to sink, its lower jagged part jutting down to stand between her and the only area where it was safe to surface. If she pushed hard she might be able to go under it before it dropped. But if it hit her, it would stop her progress and take her to the bottom. She didn't want to drown—anything but drowning. If the jagged edge pierced her heart, it would be better.

Dear Lord, help me. If I'm going to die, please make it quick.

A thought came clear as a voice, *Tee, God doesn't want you to die. Don't quit. Swim up. He says, swim up.*

The thoughts came pure, uninhibited by a broken voice, but Talisa knew it was her sister. Janie wants me to swim up? But she couldn't swim up. The jagged wreckage blocked her.

Then another voice, strong and gentle, and she knew who it was. *Rise. Trust my child. Rise.* Talisa's lungs ached as she angled for an ascent, heading straight for the sharp metal. She craved air. The sinking, burning part plunged deeper into the water. She was going to collide with it.

Something broke free as the fire consumed the area that held the metal. It spiraled down into the water in front of Talisa. A jagged point slipped past her head. Her path was clear to the open water beyond the flames. She gave a desperate thrust toward the opening. With her oxygen depleted, it was now or never.

Something tugged on her shirt and pulled her down. In a panic, she grabbed at it. Her hand felt twisted metal. The top edge of the piece had spun and snagged her. She wrenched at it, trying to tear her shirt free, but she had nothing left. Her mind was fading and all she wanted to do was release the useless gases in her lungs and suck in whatever was there. The clear surface was not far away, but she watched it recede. Her mind could only form one thought, *Quick, Lord.*

***

"There!" Janie screamed, pointing at a piece of burning debris toward which she was pushing the cruiser at full speed. Luke knew that Janie was seeing Talisa with something other than her eyes. Fire burned on the surface between them and the place where Janie pointed. He could see more clear water just past the burning wreckage that Janie indicated. He would have to swim under the fire to get to Talisa and carry her up to the other side.

He didn't wait for Teddy to remove the other handcuff. He jerked away from the young man and leaped to the front of the craft. Janie killed the propeller and turned the cruiser as he launched himself like a torpedo from the boat. He broke the surface just before where the fire burned about twenty feet from the fiery object and opened his eyes, searching. The force of the water stung, but he strained his eyelids, keeping them wide. *God, help me reach her.*

***

No! Janie's voice echoed in Talisa's head. She didn't realize that Talisa had no choice, it hurt too much. But the other Voice was there as well. *Your life is Mine,* she felt Him say. *And it is not your time.* She obeyed and held on past the pain.

A shadow moved in fast from the side and enveloped her. It hit her hard catching her under the arms and forcing her to spew bubbles as it lifted her to the surface. Part of the back of her shirt ripped away. She clamped her mouth shut and waited. Talisa knew whose arms were lifting her out of the water. But stronger still, she was aware of Who sent them, Who enabled them to save her.

As they broke the surface, she sucked in and filled her lungs. Luke was holding her, treading water for both of them. As her mind cleared, she tasted the acrid flavor of chemical smoke. She floated on her back as Luke pulled her through the water. She made no move to help. Janie and Teddy called out their excitement over the sound of the cruiser engine puttering through the waters. Talisa was too out of breath to answer. For the moment, she was content to rise up and down with the waves, feeling Luke holding her and God rocking her.

Chapter 24

Still wearing her Sunday dress, Talisa kicked off her good shoes and slipped on her clogs by the back door. She left the cement of her driveway and strolled into the sunshine that bathed the rise and the clearing at the top. The Kubota tractor and trailer sat waiting for her over the crest.

The earth had lost its fresh smell and changed from dark to a flat gray. It would always be like that for her. Her gaze traveled down to Sawyer's house and the hot tub on the back deck. Shivering, she folded her arms around herself. Even with Sawyer gone forever, the sun was not enough to burn away the chill of what had happened there. Tears brimmed her eyes. It would never be her garden. And she was okay with that. Mingled with the other loss in her life, it seemed small in comparison. She still had grief to process, but the debilitating depression was gone. Instead, she focused on all she had to be grateful for. *Thank you for saving my life and my loved ones.*

Loved ones. So much had changed in that regard also. She was relearning the relationship with her sister and

Teddy. And Luke. He had been so busy with writing reports and giving statements to the state investigators that this morning in church was the first time they had spent any time together.

Footsteps sounded behind her, and she glanced to see the man in question following his grin over the rise. She let out a long, relieved sigh at the sight of him.

"What are you doing up here?" He eased in beside her, and his arm encircled her. She pulled his hand tighter around her waist and leaned against his shoulder.

"Needing you," she answered.

"I like the sound of that." Luke frowned at the tractor and trailer. "I'll get this stuff out of here tomorrow, and you can start planting."

Talisa sniffed and shook her head. "I could never stand thinking of who tilled it and looking at his house. I just want to plant some trees along here and block out the sight of it."

Luke examined the house below, but Talisa looked away. He asked her, "Have you thought about what you want to do with the treasure?"

"You noticed what Pastor Cooper preached about this morning?"

"You mean the 'where your treasure is, there your heart will be also' sermon? No, I didn't notice."

Her smile deepened. "The pastor assured me that he prepared his message before he heard about what happened. Do you think God is trying to tell us something?"

Luke grinned. "After everything that's happened, I have given up trying to figure out what The Almighty might be up to. I think trusting Him is a better idea."

"I agree. Ever since talking to my dad's attorney, it's been hard enough for me to comprehend what my earthly father did. I can't believe he already owned the Warrior's Head Rock property and none of us knew it."

Luke nodded. "He was an amazing man. He must have figured out where the treasure was years ago and started working on purchasing the property, so the treasure would legally be his. That's why he put all his money in the secret trust to negotiate on the land. Your dad had enough of a reputation that if anyone realized he was trying to buy the Warrior, they would have figured it out."

Talisa glanced at the house below. "Do you think that's why Sawyer—?"

Luke spoke so Talisa would not be forced to finish the sentence. "I don't think Sawyer knew about Warrior's Head Rock before you figured it out. Since the sale went through, your dad was still keeping it a secret. He was probably trying to decide on the best way to get the treasure out. With so many people looking for the treasure, it would change your lives when they knew he had it. There would also be the difficulty of securing the rock. Your dad would want to respect the cultural value of the landmark as well."

Talisa sighed. "Facing all those issues at the same time he was going through cancer with my mom, I'm sure it was easier to take out what he needed until he had time to decide what to do. Then Sawyer tracked the artifacts back to him and moved in next door."

"Sawyer must have been watching him, and your dad knew it. He might have led Sawyer to believe the treasure was somewhere else, and that's when Sawyer arranged your dad's...or maybe he just wanted to make sure your dad didn't salvage it first. Anyway, with your dad gone, he tried to go through you to find the treasure. He was also still trying to get Boggs to tell him. But none of it was working. Then, from what Sawyer said, I'm guessing two things happened. He saw that when pressed, Janie could look into people's minds at will and that Boggs was dying. I'm sure desperation made him come up with that crazy plan."

Talisa nodded. "All for the love of money. What did Sawyer say, *enough for the big dreams?* It makes me not even want the treasure."

Luke rubbed Talisa's back. "Maybe that is why God has

given it to you. It depends on the dream and the dreamer. I have an idea for a dream that's big enough and worthy. I was talking to Doctor Welch about his studies and his idea of someday being able to start what he calls a research and exploration center to help people with special needs and special abilities. He said he would like to have Janie and Teddy help with it. That seems to fit well with your dream of working in water rehabilitation. I know a great location to start construction." He motioned toward Sawyer's house. "Should be plenty of money to put in an aquatic center that could house dolphins."

She stared at him in astonishment.

"Or, at least a couple of hen houses out back."

She punched him in the arm. "If you're not careful, I'll put you in the hen house, and I'll be with the dolphins. They probably tell better jokes."

"The money's going fast. You'd better save a little for a special occasion."

"Like what, a honeymoon? That sounds nice to me." Talisa examined the sky.

"Why, you getting married?"

She scowled at him. "I was beginning to wonder that myself since no one has asked me yet. You know how some people are—making promises in the heat of the moment and then never following through with them."

"Sounds like a louse. But maybe he's just waiting for the right time. What are you doing tomorrow night for dinner?"

"I'll check my calendar."

Luke was looking down at Sawyer's house again. "Shouldn't be too long before we can use some of your new-found wealth to buy that house down there and wipe it from the face of the earth."

"Sounds good to me. But I still don't think I could ever garden here. Besides, I was going to go organic, and he put all that fertilizer in the ground."

Luke scrutinized the white beads still on the ground

around the trailer and then the garden plot. "I don't see any fertilizer in there. You should see the beads in the garden just like you see on the ground over there."

"Then where did the fertilizer go? His trailer was piled with bags when I first saw him up here. Now there's just a few left."

Luke marched over to the trailer. He rolled back one of the white bags and pulled out a plastic tarp the same color. He opened it and examined the inside surface. Then he stood up looking grim. "Now I know where he hid the body. No wonder I couldn't find it when I searched his house the next day. There are long blond hairs in here that I am betting are going to match Ms. Agnew's. There never were any other bags. These few fertilizer bags were used to conceal this tarp and what was in it"

Talisa squeezed her eyes shut. Luke hurried across the ground and led Talisa down to her house. He stopped at the door.

"I want you and the dynamic duo to pack for at least a week. I'm going to call the OBI investigators, and they will want to go over the scene up there. I'll let them know not to bother knocking, you won't be home. You have been through enough. I'm taking you to the Family World Resort. We can be there in an hour. It has a water park, and Teddy says after everything that's happened, he's going to let Janie teach him how to swim. The resort has a great restaurant. I've got some calls to make, so go get yourself ready, and we'll drive there today."

Talisa managed a tired smile and a simple nod. Time away was just what she needed. She wished it was her honeymoon, but she loved Luke for not waiting.

As she turned to go inside, Luke said, "Hey, I know you've been a little confused about what to wear lately, so I wanted to let you know it's okay to dress up tomorrow night."

She twisted up her face at him. "After that, I'm not so

sure what my answer will be."
"I like a challenge."

Chapter 25

Luke stood as Talisa strolled across the restaurant toward him wearing the new gown. The admiration on his face dressed him as well as the tuxedo that he wore. "You know, I was going to suggest that a nice honeymoon would be to see the Seven Wonders of the World, but now you've gone and spoiled that for me."

A broad smile spread over Talisa's face and without breaking it, she asked, "Why, are you getting married?"

Luke grinned as he helped her with her chair. "I've been giving this night considerable thought."

"I see. Staying up worrying what to do with the rejection?"

"You're not going to make this easy, are you?"

Talisa's lips pressed together in a playful grin.

"So, after great consideration of all that we've been through, I decided the most appropriate thing would be to have a treasure hunt."

The grin faded. "Don't you dare."

"At one of the tables in this room is a proposal, and you have to find it."

Talisa glared at him. "I am not going around the room talking to complete strangers about... You had better get down on your knee right now and—"

"It's okay, I'll go with you." Luke took her hand and nearly pulled her chair out from under her.

Talisa wobbled a little on her heels at the rapid pace of her ascension.

"Let's try that one." Luke tugged her toward the nearest table. The elderly couple looked up at his approach. "Excuse me, this young lady is looking for a proposal."

Talisa sputtered in mortification. "I'm not looking for a—"

The woman at the table said, "I'm sorry, no proposal here. I had to propose to him thirty years ago."

The room erupted in laughter, and Talisa whirled around to see all eyes were on her. She was considering running from the room.

The woman said, "All we have is this," and pulled a large box off the chair beside her. She laid the box on the table and opened the lid. Inside was the wedding dress that Talisa had been eyeing with Janie.

Talisa's mouth was ajar as she stared at Luke.

"No proposal here. Let's try the next one." He pulled her to the next table. A middle-aged couple smiled as they came close. "Excuse me. This young lady is fishing for a proposal. Any bites?"

At the word "fishing," Talisa rolled her eyes upwards. "It's okay," she told the couple. "I think I want to throw this one back."

More laughter from the room.

"That's too bad," the man said. "We don't have a proposal, but we were hoping that someone could use this." The man opened a box on the table and revealed the most beautiful wedding bouquet Talisa had ever seen.

She started to say so, but Luke pulled her on. "Dry hole, next table."

Large hats hid the faces of the two young ladies occupying the table. As Talisa approached, they both looked up. Kaylee and another friend from church grinned at her.

"Oh, drat," Luke said. "Nothing but bridesmaids here. Let's keep going."

Luke drew her to the next table. "This poor girl is desperately seeking a proposal. Please tell me you have one." The man shook his head and handed Luke a card. "A booking for the resort wedding chapel right next door. Can you imagine that? Boy, this is sure going to be embarrassing if you don't get that proposal."

Talisa noticed other familiar faces around the room. But Luke was encouraging her onward.

They came to a table occupied by a man with the most ridiculous beard she'd ever seen. "Please tell me you have a proposal for this poor girl. She's not getting any younger, you know."

The man removed the fake beard. It was Pastor Cooper. "No, but if she gets one, I'll be ready." He patted his Bible.

Talisa shot a wicked glance at Luke and asked, "Pastor, do you do funerals?"

Everyone laughed.

Luke dragged Talisa to the middle of the room and called out to the crowd. "Does anyone have a proposal for this poor, desperate old maid?" Talisa slugged him in the chest and the room erupted.

From behind a partition came Janie and Teddy, carrying a small table and giggling. They placed the table in front of Talisa and on it was a ring box.

Luke picked it up and knelt before her. "Talisa Hollenbeck, when a man finds a woman like you and he thinks she might say yes, he'd better not take any chances of letting her get away. There is no waiting period in Oklahoma, and I happen to be in good with the county clerk, who said he can issue us a marriage license tonight." Luke pointed to a man sitting at a table nearby with documents spread out on it.

"If you will just say yes, you can make me the happiest man alive." Luke waited. Everyone waited.

Talisa took a deep breath. "I may be a widow tomorrow, but what choice do I have but to say yes tonight?"

Applause rose from the crowd. Luke took a ring from the box, and Talisa extended her finger. He then stood and offered Talisa his arm. Instead, she grabbed him by the face and kissed him long and hard. When she pulled back, Luke stood there for a moment looking dumbfounded.

His stupid grin appeared. "I guess you're going to have to change again."

Talisa gave a soft purring growl and pulled him close. She whispered in his ear. "You're lucky there are witnesses. I'm only marrying you, so I can get you alone and finally strangle you." She gave his side a clandestine pinch.

"It'll be worth it," he whispered back, wincing a little. "I'll die happy."

***

Three weeks later, Luke drove Talisa back to her house, their house. They were both exhausted and elated from the most wonderful honeymoon. As he rounded the corner, he told her to close her eyes. "I want to give you your wedding gift."

He stopped the car and got out. In a moment he was opening her door. He admonished her to keep her eyes closed. She discerned they were in her driveway and he was walking her toward the rise that would never lead to her garden.

"Okay, you can look."

She opened her eyes. Was she wrong about where they were? No, there was the house, but the hillside had been transformed. Covering the rise were tiered growing beds making their way to the top of the hill and running the full length. Beautifully done walkways accessed the beds that were filled with dark, fresh smelling earth.

"It's the most beautiful thing I've ever seen."

"Not me." Luke was looking at her. "I've seen something better. But old Pete does do good work." He twisted up his mouth. "Thanks for being willing to marry a jokester like me. I know I'll be hard to put up with."

Talisa put her arms around his neck, her eyes twinkling. "Don't worry. You don't have to change on my account."

For the Lord is our judge, our lawgiver, and our king. He will care for us and save us. The enemies' sails hang loose on broken masts with useless tackle. Their treasure will be divided by the people of God. Even the lame will take their share! Isaiah 33:22-23 (NLT)

Thank you for reading *SEEING BEYOND*. If you enjoyed the story, **we would appreciate it if you would give a review on Amazon.** Next to prayer, this is the best thing that you can do to support an author. Because of how Amazon ranks books, without reviews even good books will be lost in the Amazon jungle. Also, your like and share on social media and by word of mouth would mean a lot to us. Our writing is first and foremost a ministry and we want to reach as many people as we can.

In His service,
Kent and Rebekah Wyatt

Discussion Questions

I hope the story addressed some important topics in a way that might move you to discuss it with others. If so, here are some questions that might help get that conversation going.

1. At the beginning of the story, Talisa is suffering from depression over the loss of her parents. Take a look at John 11:32-38. What was Jesus' reaction to Mary's grief? Now read Acts 8:2, considering the words "devout men" and "great lamentation." Note that this is talking about male disciples of Jesus after His ascension when the works of Christ had been accomplished. Earlier in Stephen's story we see he obviously went to

Heaven. He even saw paradise as he died. What does this tell us about mourning for Christians? Considering Proverbs 25:20, what is the best way to deal with someone who is grieving?

2. Welch seems to embody Romans 12:15 when he cries with Talisa. Did you ever find tears to be healing? When you have been at your lowest point, what did you find helped? How can we make ourselves approachable for people that are hurting? (Proverbs 12:25)

3. Considering the various relationships in the story, how were the themes of forgiveness, openness and honesty played out? (Ephesians 4:31-32, Colossians 3:9-10, Proverbs 11:13, Hebrews 4:12)

4. Both Teddy and Janie are people with special needs. Do you know any individuals with special needs? How are they a positive influence in our world? What can you do to develop relationships with those individuals? (For another interesting perspective on this issue, go to kentwyatt.org/stories from the red and blue world and read the true story of Patrick entitled, "The Santa Claus Man.") (Exodus 4:10-13, Exodus 33:11, Numbers 12:3-8, John 1:47)

5. What are some of the things that attracted Talisa to Sawyer? What are the most important things to look for in a mate? (1 Samuel 16:7, 2 Corinthians 6:14-15, Proverbs 31:10-12&30, 1 Peter 3:3-5, Ephesians chapter 5)

6. Have you ever been deceived by a person that had ulterior motives for the relationship? What are ways to avoid being taken in? (Romans 16:17-18, Proverbs 2:6-15)

7. Pastor Cooper gave Luke some interesting things to think about during their counseling session. What did you think of his advice? (Proverbs 3:1-18, 1 Corinthians 13:4-5)

8. Sawyer was willing to do almost anything to obtain a treasure vast enough for the big dreams. What does the Bible say about earthly treasure? If Sawyer was able to get away with the treasure, what do you think the final result would have been for him? Can you think of examples where people have gained a huge amount of money? Did it benefit them or not? (Proverbs 10:2, 1 Timothy 6:17-19, Esther 5:11, Ecclesiastes 2:26, 2 Corinthians 8:14-15)

9. What are some examples of situations where we must decide between investing in this world and investing in the Kingdom of God?

(Matthew 6:19-21, Mark 12:41-44, Matthew 6:24, Luke 6:38, 1 Timothy 6:17-19, Romans 8:5, Proverbs 15:16)

10. Do you feel like you really know the people in your life? What are ways that we can go deeper and understand our loved ones better? (Ephesians 4:2-4, Colossians 3:12-15, Philippians 2:3-4, 1 Corinthians 10:24, 1 Peter 3:8, Romans 15:2-4)

11. Why did Boggs go to Hell? What were his various misconceptions about salvation? (Ephesians 2:7-9, Romans 5:14-18, Romans 3:28, Romans 4:6, Romans 3:21-24, Acts 8:18-21, 2 Samuel 12:9-14, 1 Timothy 1:12-15)

For, being ignorant of the righteousness of God, and seeking to establish their own, they did not submit to God's righteousness. For Christ is the end of the law for righteousness to everyone who believes. ...because, if you confess with your mouth that Jesus is Lord and believe in your heart that God raised him from the dead, you will be saved. For with the heart one believes and is justified, and with the mouth one confesses and is saved.
Romans 10:3-4 & 9-10, (ESV)

Acknowledgements

In everything there is a first, and in every first there are so many people that helped it happen. It seems impossible to list them all. And it is. So you find yourself grabbing at the names that come to your mind and putting them on the page. You hope for forgiveness from those who, because of space, time or faulty memory, are left out.

When time allows, my family and I remain in the theater while the end credits roll. We call out the names of the third-best boy on the New Zealand scene or the 6th graphic artist for the desert episode, lest they be unsung. People so important, yet few know what a huge part they play behind the scenes, never getting the credit they deserve.

My writing is the culmination of my life. So many people have played a part in getting me to this place. I wish them not to be unsung. Roll credits.

<u>From the early life in Kansas scene</u>: Eldon Wyatt, my cowboy farmer father, a posthumous thank you for your patience with a boy who cared more about imaginary worlds than driving a tractor and feeding cows. To Vera Wyatt, my mother (only a few years gone), who listened and laughed at my foolishness, prayed for me, and took me to church. To my older sisters, Lonesa, Linda, and Deanna, who mothered me even when I kicked at it. To my school friend, Randall Ball, who was always eager for me to finish my stories. My sixth-grade teacher Mildred Kennedy, devoted saint, who saw a light in me and helped it grow. Looking forward to thanking you in Heaven. To Ms. Peterson, teacher of high

school English and encourager of dreams. Roger Cooper, for giving my songs a listen even when it was painful. Your faith is still music to my ears. To Bob Cooper (resting in the arms of the Lord) for your example.

Appearing in the Ellis, Kansas episode: Chief Whitey Kohl and the Ellis City Council for letting a green kid become a cop. Mike DeSilverio and John Wahls, together we survived those crazy times.

To those of the Colorado Springs Police Department scene: To my Police Academy classmates, we made it through. Thanks for making it fun. John Anderson, for having faith in me even when I messed up. Remember Sherlock's admonition, "Whatever remains must be the truth." Hey, Homicide Hunter, Joe Kenda, you probably don't remember walking me through my first murder scene? Lou Schmidt (past on to eternity) for sharing his investigation mastery with me. To my FTOs, thanks for showing me the ropes. Mark Drobeck, for demonstrating what a man of God looks like. Mark Devorss and Rafael Cintron and the other members of our early morning prayer meetings when we were instructors at the Police Academy. It made such a difference. To Rose Timora and Lieutenant Tobias for sticking with me. John Taylor for your Godly leadership. To all the great cops and citizens I worked alongside, too numerous to mention, but I have not forgotten the great times and all that you helped me learn.

Technical support: Richard and Jeanette Easter (now home with the Lord). You gave me your many prayers, your help, your time, and your daughter. Forever grateful.

To the Peyton, Colorado set crew: To the Coens. The lovers of children too numerous for me to count, both birthed and adopted. What an inspiration you are. To let our family, whom you had just met, stay in your basement while our home was being built, was unbelievable. Tim, I wish I were more like you. Laura, thanks for your editing work. Love those kids of yours.

To those on location in John Day, Oregon: To the Mayor and City Council, thank you for letting me be your Chief and helping me through a hard transition. To the Smucker, Boss, and Miller families and others of the John Day Valley Mennonite church. What great friends you are. I know this is not the story we started out with, but perhaps that story will yet be told. To OSP Gordon Larson and Tom Hutchison, two honorable men that meant a lot to me. You supported me and gave me good advice. I'm grateful. Brenda Rocklin, a gift from God in a hard time. Sally and Gene Dunn, thanks for your friendship. To the Pickles. Take a bow. You deserve it.

To the Washington crew: To Dennis and Leah Munday, for housing us and supporting us. You always have so much love for your family. I am blessed to be so connected. To our nieces Murky Pond and Sand Pile, always loving and encouraging us. Roger and Connie Lund for your prayers and your booky knowledge. Travis, your editing was great. Thanks to Mary and Stewart Tucker for your prayers. Rich and Christie Easter, thanks for the input.

To the foreign stars at the Mexico location shoot: To all of our friends from GFM and CTEN, thanks for giving us the experience of a lifetime serving God in a third world country. To all the missionary training students, you were like family. To our beloved Mexican friends, we will never forget you. Dios Le Bendiga.

The Pratt, return to Kansas episode: Jeff Ward, so much you did for us. Thanks, buddy. James Shelden, Nate Humble, Danny Gimpel, Ken Wright and Jon McCarley. I will always value you as true brothers in Christ. Gary Myers, thanks for being on my side. Thanks, Ed Gimpel, for all you gave us and Jim Ferbert for the fun times. Lyda Kasselman, Becky Dreese, Joyce Broaddus, and Mike LeClair, thanks for keeping me straight in dispatch. To the rest of the PPD bunch, great working with you. To Jimmy White, thanks for all your help during some tough times. Roy Headrick, you kept me laughing, what a great attitude. Ken Van Blaricum thanks for putting my cases forward and for your service to the community. To Walt Stockwell, for your servant's heart. To the Bread of Life staff, thanks for letting me serve with you. To Peggy and Dave Ellison, for your friendship and help coming and going. Doug Enick, thanks for faithfully teaching the Word. To Helen Wray, a mighty angel in a five-foot-tall disguise. I know your prayers shake Heaven and earth. All the Clan of David Skiles, our good friends. We loved worshiping the Lord in your home. Carl and Janice Rudzitis, (saints gone on to paradise), you knew the way of the kind heart. Darrel and Sharon Brehm for letting us be a part of Brehmville. To John and Pam Ford, Mike McGovney and the rest of the Judgement House gang, what a great time acting up for God. Connie McKinzie, what a unique ministry you have. Cody and Camille Nichols, our children from other parents, thanks for being good kids and loving the Lord. To Mitch and Michelle Holmes and all the Holmeslings, so proud of your service and your hearts for God. Janice Glass, who helped Patrick and so many others (See the "Santa Claus Man" at www.kentwyatt.org).

<u>To those of the Siloam Springs Police Department scene:</u> Thank you, Chief Wilmeth, for your integrity, leadership, and devotion to the Lord. To Angie Scott for reading and, of course, liking my book. Like Twain said, I could live off compliments like that for two months. To all of the SSPD team, what a fantastic group of people. You made me feel so welcome and gave room for this passion of mine.

Fellowship Bible Church sound stage: Karen and Chuck Ellcey, friends indeed. Randy and Lynna Blackwell long in faith and wisdom. Dwight and Marilyn Jackson, facilitators for the Lord. Chris Riley, thank you for reading and being a friend. Robin Orcutt, beta reader extraordinaire. The Thompsons, Toby, Kathy, Katie, Rachel, thanks for sharing your ears for consultation, your eyes for editing and your examples for inspiration. Kathy, what great editing eyes you have. George and Doris Nuss, a true picture of Godly servants. Thanks for taking a look and giving suggestions. Linda Johnstone, thanks for putting red pen to paper to make this novel the best it could be.

To those on location at Siloam Springs Regional Hospital: To Rebecca Presley for taking me on and being a mom to an old man and his boy. To Sheri Bottoms for getting me started and encouraging me along the way. Linda Yeager, Katie Henderson, and Marti Lemke for your patience, understanding, and friendship. Karl, it is a pleasure to know you for so many reasons. Tong Xiong, thanks for listening. Your smile and laugh are always uplifting. Mike Jones, for the good talks. Bonnie Baer and Sheila Rodgers for your interest in my writing. To Chaplain Tony Thomas for being willing to read. Pam, your time to listen meant so much. Nancy, for your loving nature and encouragement. Francis, thanks for the helping with the cover. The rest of the SSRH staff and the patients, you have made my life richer.

In the sound booth with the Men Out Back: To Marshall Orcutt for listening to the Lord and knowing the way to go. Don Balla for being willing to express a different view. Thanks for reading and sharing not only your edit but your heart. John Littlejohn, I have never seen a man wear out a Bible like you. Thanks for digging deep. TJ Johnstone, for the wise use of humor to bring us back to reality. Victor

Magallon, thanks for taking your faith to the mountain, to the woods, to the desert, but really to the people. Jerry Reimer, always practical, always grounded, always sound. Wayne Pope for bringing your knowledge to the table. Rob Bailey, for insight that is always well researched. All the others that come through the cabin door. I have never been involved in such a gathering of Godly men. It has changed the way I view my life and my faith.

The Outreach Center Bible study stage: Carol Kerns, for an open home and an open heart. Ron and Debi Batchelor, you lead the way in worship to the Lord. Thanks for being willing to read my work and giving me a place to share my story. All the men and women of God from the group. To me, this is what Church should be like.

To the Siloam Springs Writers Guild episode: Gene and Carol Lindsey, the models of friendliness and a positive attitude. Ted and Jane Weathers, the foundation of the group, ever working to promote the written word. Rachel Kulp, for excellent design suggestions on the cover of the book. Rosemary Matthews, a gentle spirit devoted to the craft. Charles Yancey for renowned humor. And all the other members who have talked writing with me.

The American Christian Fiction Writers NW Arkansas scene: Robyn Hook, I thought my writing was doing okay until you showed me the next level. Thanks for taking the time. Deb Rather, what a privilege to sit in the same room with so much experience all wrapped around a kind heart. Jeanie and Rod Nance, for showing such hospitality to a bunch of writers you never met. Thank you, Bud Walker for telling your stories. Jenn Pierce, for helping with our investigating small presses. And Mona Alexander for reading and commenting on my story. To all the other members of our group. We are honored to be a part of such a talented collection of new authors and expect you all to go far.

Private production consultants: To our publisher, Cynthia Hickey, for answering questions and sending us in the right direction. Thanks for giving us a chance. Sherri Stewart and Dorothy Weber, your editing skills taught me so much and saved me on so many things. Billie Thompson, for catching my little mistakes without throwing out my dominos. What a good friend you have been to us. Tabatha Raiees-Dana, for computer training and long Rebekah talks. Paul Gilmour, for knowledge of the special needs world and for good advice on a key element of the story. Calista Holmes for graphic design assistance on the book cover. Jane Wughtal, sister ACFW member, thanks for your assistance at the conference. We were so pleased to meet you. Thank you, dear librarians, especially those in Pratt, Siloam Springs, and Bentonville, who have answered so many questions. We love our libraries and the people who work in them. Jeanette Nelson, you gave your time to search out those pesky typos in the final version of the book. You have been such a supporter of this novel and we owe you so much.

Outsourced assistance: To the prayer warriors who have listened and petitioned the Father to please make something out of this mess. To all my other cousins, playmates, classmates, churchmates, friends, teachers, mentors, and wise ones who helped me along the way. The pieces of yourselves you left in me populate my imagination and inhabit my stories.

The Premiere Showing: The great cloud of witnesses who sit in the theater of Eternity watching the epic comedy that is my life. Alive now more than they ever were on this earth, they watch our race from around the throne of God. Save me a seat. I'm counting on Christ for admission. Can't wait to kick a can with you down those golden streets.

More about Kent and Rebekah Wyatt

Kent Wyatt was born and then he died. Wait a minute, I'm getting ahead of myself. (Whew! I'm glad I put that part in because, for a second there, I thought I was dead.) Now that you know the beginning and the ending of my story, let's go a little closer to the middle...

Actually, my novels are "our" novels, produced by the team of Kent and Rebekah Wyatt. My wife, Rebekah, will always be quick to tell you she is not a writer, but she contributes greatly to the finished product of our books. Rebekah (whose official title in the Wyatt Republic is Minister of Household and Finance) is a voracious reader of Christian Fiction. In the Wyatt writing world, she serves as (among other things) editor, researcher, manager, financial planner, contributor to the story board, plot, and characterization, and of course the final word on all things romantic. So, when you see our characters behaving like ladies and gentlemen instead of blowing snot, passing gas, and belching—thank Rebekah. (Disclaimer: the second half of this sentence was not Rebekah approved.)

Kent and Rebekah's novels have been semi-finalists in the American Christian Fiction Writers Genesis contest and a Finalist for the Romance Writers of America Daphne du Maurier Award for Excellence in Mystery/Suspense. Kent serves as Vice President of the American Christian Fiction Writers NW Arkansas Chapter, and Rebekah is the treasurer.

So how did such a partnership ever get started? I mean

really, a man and a woman, together, they're so different. Whoever came up with such an idea? Oh. Sorry, God. Great idea by the way. (Disclaimer: the preceding portion of this paragraph was not Rebekah approved). Of course such an unlikely alliance could only begin in somewhere remote and mysterious—like the flatlands Northwest Kansas.

I was born there. Rebekah was dropped there, like a tornado drops a rare orchid in the middle of a wheat field. Both our early days were, like most young lives, bizzare in their own ways. Mine full of the mundane misadventures of the son of a firmly planted fourth generation farmer, and Rebekah's comprised of the exotic escapades of a traveling evangelist's daughter. When we were in our early teens, we met and fell madly in opposite directions and both skinned our knees. For the few months that her family stayed at our farm, we rode horses and performed magic shows together, but then Rebekah's family was off to the next ministry opportunity. Over the years, we both strayed from God's plan in our own ways and then were thrown together again in our late twenties. In a few months, we were married. God has rescued us from our own imprudence, grown us in our understanding of His plan, and bound us together for His purpose. We love Him greatly because He has saved us exceedingly. Our prayer is that through our stories we might introduce others to THE ONE who longs to do the same for them.

To understand how this whole writing thing began, there is one thing you need to know about Rebekah: She is a faithful helpmate to her husband and selflessly supports his dream far better than he deserves.

There are two things that you need to know about me: I was born a writer, but I became a cop.

As a child on the lonely plains of Kansas, I always enjoyed reading and telling stories to the other kids. When I was thirteen years old I read *R is for Rocket* by Ray Bradbury, and I decided I wanted to write stories like that, ones that haunted you and made you think. John Boy Walton became my hero, and I was going to change the world with my pen. Over the years, I learned that I wasn't Ray Bradbury, but God had given me a writing voice of my own and He could use that if I would let Him. The only problem was I didn't have enough life experience so...

When I was seventeen years old, a car almost ran my mother and me off the road. With my terrified mama holding onto the dash beside me, I pursued the other vehicle in my 1973 Mercury Montego and forced it to pull over. It was the town drunk doing what he did best. He came at me, and I knocked him down and picked him up by his belt and threw him in the back seat of his car to sleep it off. My mother decided that I should be a police officer. She knew that writing nonsense was never going to get me anywhere.

In 1983 she saw an ad in the paper saying a small town nearby was looking for a police officer. She convinced me to apply. But all the time I was being a cop, the bite I received from the writing bug became infected and grew septic. I fed the fever over the years with short stories, award winning poetry and a humorous newsletter that I put out for a growing email list. Another life changing event was when I read *This Present Darkness* by Frank Peretti. It helped get me back on track with my faith and introduced me to Christian Fiction. I had found the direction God wanted me to go with my writing. Foolish fans encouraged me by saying that they loved my newsletters and re-read them when they wanted a good laugh. Many even said I should write a book. With my law enforcement career and my family to raise, I could never commit to writing fulltime. So, I satisfied myself with learning the craft and producing short works. After 32 years, I ended my law enforcement career. I still have many friends walking the thin blue line, and I have a deep love for the profession. But God seems to be telling me it is time to fulfill my other destiny. Now, with God's help, maybe my writing can change the world after all. Where are my old reruns of The Waltons? Look out, Ray Bradbury, something Wyatt this way comes.

You can find Kent on the web at the following locations:

Website:
https://www.kentwyatt.org (free stories both real and imagined)
Amazon:
https://www.amazon.com/Kent-Wyatt/e/B07GSHF65Q
Facebook:
https://www.facebook.com/kentwyatt.org
Twitter:
https://twitter.com/authorkentwyatt
Pinterest:
https://www.pinterest.com/AuthorKentWyatt/
Goodreads:
https://www.goodreads.com/user/show/36911883-author-kent-wyatt
Google+:
https://plus.google.com/115005163444293298582
Linkedin:
https://www.linkedin.com/in/kent-wyatt-b162b014a/
Instagram:
https://www.instagram.com/authorkentwyatt/
Youtube:
https://www.youtube.com/channel/UCW_AzksI3It_PSJQFt4oo4w
Hashtags:
#AuthorKentWyatt, #SpecialHeroes